Matthew Arnold, Richard Garnett

Alaric at Rome

Matthew Arnold, Richard Garnett

Alaric at Rome

ISBN/EAN: 9783744722155

Printed in Europe, USA, Canada, Australia, Japan

Cover: Foto ©Andreas Hilbeck / pixelio.de

More available books at **www.hansebooks.com**

ALARIC AT ROME

AND OTHER POEMS BY MATTHEW ARNOLD

WITH AN INTRODUCTION BY

RICHARD GARNETT, C.B., LL.D

LONDON: WARD, LOCK & BOWDEN, L^{TD}.
NEW YORK AND MELBOURNE. MDCCCXCVI

CHISWICK PRESS:—CHARLES WHITTINGHAM AND CO.
TOOKS COURT, CHANCERY LANE, LONDON.

EDITORIAL NOTE.

THE PRESENT VOLUME IS COMPOSED OF THE CONTENTS OF MR. MATTHEW ARNOLD'S FIRST FOUR VOLUMES, "ALARIC," "CROMWELL," "THE STRAYED REVELLER," AND "EMPEDOCLES ON ETNA," AND THAT PORTION OF THE FIFTH WHICH HAD NOT PREVIOUSLY APPEARED IN THE EARLIER VOLUMES. TO THESE HAS BEEN ADDED THE SONNET "TO THE HUNGARIAN NATION," WHICH FIRST APPEARED IN THE "EXAMINER" FOR 1849, AND HAS NEVER HITHERTO BEEN REPRINTED. THE ORIGINAL ARRANGEMENT OF THE POEMS IN EACH VOLUME HAS BEEN OBSERVED.

INTRODUCTION.

THE incontestable importance of Matthew Arnold's place in English poetical literature arises not merely from the beauty of much of his poetry, but from his peculiar distinction as one of the few eminent English poets who are enrolled among the legislators of their art, not more by the indirect influence of their metrical compositions, than by the authority universally accorded to their critical utterances. Coleridge, the most penetrating critic Britain ever possessed, is too casual and desultory to rank among legislators, and the two poets who admit of most profitable comparison with Arnold in this respect are Dryden and Wordsworth. Each of the three had definite convictions on the subject of poetry which he exemplified in his own practice; and each, along with error and exaggerated truth, contributed elements to the formation of a poetical ideal which can never be ignored. To a certain extent Arnold's work was a corrective of that of Wordsworth, the great emancipator of English poetry. In overthrowing a merely conventional orthodoxy, Wordsworth had inevitably given somewhat of a shock to those great models and eternal principles by whose corrupt following this conventionalism had been engendered. It was Arnold's mission to restore the balance, inculcating alike by example and precept the cardinal doctrines of antiquity, that form is of equal importance with matter, and that the value of a poem consists more in the force and truth of the total impression, than in isolated fine thoughts sparkling forth in the heat of composition. This, substantially, was Matthew Arnold's critical gospel, a deliverance interesting as an episode in the eternal strife between Classic and Romantic, and valuable as a corrective of tendencies inherent in the English genius. This is not generally architectonic, it overwhelms with affluence of thought and imagery, but the shaping hand is too often absent. Arnold thought that much of the characteristic English indifference to form arose from indiscriminate admiration of Shakespeare; but the truth is that while fancy, passion, and reflection come to gifted Englishmen by nature, the sense of symmetry usually has to be engrafted upon them. We are a nation of colourists, and great colourists, except by determined efforts, rarely became good draughtsmen. Arnold's admonition, therefore, was most serviceable, it may be ranked with Wordsworth's protest against the conventionalities of his day, and was perhaps even more valuable; for while Wordsworth assailed an aberration which in course of time would have corrected itself, Arnold denounced ingrained vice and besetting sin. It was, moreover, eminently seasonable, appearing in 1853, when there did seem a real danger of English poetry becoming an assemblage of purple patches upon a core of perishable wood, the very definition of a scarecrow. This did not, however arise as Arnold thought, from a special infirmity in the age, whose imperfections he greatly exaggerated, but from the abuse of what was best in it. The infinite significance of even the humblest human life was beginning to be recognized as it had never been before, but a discovery invaluable in the social sphere had not unnaturally generated the dangerous artistic heresy that what is good enough for a novel is also good enough for a poem. 1853, the date of Arnold's memorable preface, was also the period, not indeed of the culminating, but of the too exclusive influence of Shelley and Keats, who were receiving their long withheld recompense with usury. These great poets, in their more mature productions, rather surpass than fall short of the ordinary English standard of symmetrical construction, but their architecture is obscured by the splendour of their painting, and too many had come to confound the art of poetry with the art of phrasing. To such Matthew Arnold's remonstrance came like an exorcism, and its weight was greatly enhanced by the method of its delivery; not poured as from a vase into the turbid torrent of periodical criticism, but prefixed as a confession of faith to a volume of poetry designed for and destined to endurance.

It is a great reinforcement to the weight of poetical criticism when the critic is himself a recognized poet. The Goddess of Wisdom herself is not recorded to have lectured to the Muses, and the precepts of mere prose writers, however excellent, have something of the air of instructions to Hannibal in the art of war. Even

Introduction.

Aristotle qualified for his Poetics by writing a song, and a very good one. Arnold, when he came forward in 1853 to discourse on poetry, could produce sufficient credentials as the author of two poetical volumes of great though unequal merit, "The Strayed Reveller, and other Poems" (1849); and "Empedocles on Etna and other Poems" (1852). Neither of these, however, as we shall see presently, sufficiently exemplified the particular principles which he chiefly desired to enforce. His argument would have wanted the weight which theory derives from conformity to practice, if, upon the republication in 1853 of such of these poems as he then cared to preserve, they had not been accompanied by another so completely exemplifying his views respecting the supreme necessity of perfection of form, dignity of subject, unity of action, and sobriety of treatment that it might have been written to illustrate them. Great poems, nevertheless, cannot be composed to order, and it is much more probable that the preface grew out of the poem than the reverse.

No subject could better than "Sohrab and Rustum" have enabled Arnold to exemplify his own precepts :—"Choose a fitting action, penetrate yourself with the feeling of its situations ; this done everything else will follow." This exhortation, indeed, is insufficiently limited and defined. The action must be not only abstractedly fitting for a poet to undertake, but the poet must fit the action. Coleridge, perhaps, would have made no more of "Sohrab and Rustum" than Arnold would have made of "The Ancient Mariner ;" and when at a later period Arnold

Introduction.

endeavoured to dramatize the story of Merope, the unanimous voice of criticism informed him that although the subject was undeniably fitting, and the poet adequately penetrated by it, "everything else" had not followed. But "Sohrab and Rustum" suited him to perfection, for it is an heroic action whose greatness consists not in its grandeur, but in its pathos. Pathos is the note of all his best poems, there is hardly one of them which is not more or less an appeal for compassion on account of the character of the incident described, or some human or spiritual sorrow, or some real or imaginary distress of the age. No more affecting incident than the involuntary death of a son by his father's hand can be found in history or fiction, and it especially impressed Arnold, from that strength in him of the parental instinct revealed by his recently published correspondence. What he received intimately he reproduced vividly, and the conduct of his story and the tissue of his diction are masterpieces of judgment. Nothing, he rightly perceived, can be more essential to the impressiveness of a story of profound pathos than that it should be told in the simplest language, yet unrelieved simplicity throughout a long narrative must wear an aspect of poverty, perhaps even of affectation. The general homeliness of the exposition, therefore, is occasionally interrupted by elaborate similes, little poems in themselves, and involving close and accurate word-painting. These for a moment suspend, but do not divert, the reader's attention to the main action, whose pathos goes on deepening with every line, until there is no modern poem, with perhaps the exception of Tennyson's

Introduction.

"Edward Gray," that it is so difficult to read without
tears. Arnold, nevertheless, saw that although the
impression of unrelieved tragedy, created by such
poems as "Edward Gray," may be right in a lyric, it
would be amiss in an epic, and, since the situation itself
could not be modified, he has mitigated it by the
majestic concluding passage describing the course of
the Oxus, emblematic of the greatness of Nature in
comparison with the accidents of man's brief career,
and, at its termination, of the sea in which human joys
and sorrows are finally swallowed up.

Besides "Sohrab and Rustum," the volume of 1853
contained another poem of length and importance, of
an earlier date of composition, whose unlikeness to
Sohrab adds to the probability that the writer's high
and just estimate of the latter poem had much to do with
moulding the doctrine of his memorable preface. "Tristram and Iseult" is exceedingly unlike "Sohrab" in
everything but poetical beauty, and entirely fails to produce that total impression which Arnold propounds as the
chief object of the poet. While the action of "Sohrab"
is transparently clear, that of "Tristram and Iseult" is
so confused that it would be difficult to make out the
subject of the poem if this were not already known.
The merits are entirely of detail, and these are most
conspicuous in the third part, an appendage to the
poem which would never have been missed if it had never
existed, but with which no one would now consent to
part, so many and exquisite are its beauties. The
strength of parental feeling is again visible in the
description of the children at play, to be matched only
by that of the sleeping children in Part I. The story

of Vivien's enchantment of Merlin is admirably told, but, unlike the similar episode of the river in "Sohrab and Rustum," is a mere ornament with no vital relation to the poem.

"Tristram and Iseult" had been published in 1852 along with "Empedocles on Etna," which failed to re-appear in the 1853 volume. Arnold explains its withdrawal by saying that he had come to look upon this powerful representation of the discouragement of a philosopher compelled to surrender the healthy objectivity of the early Greeks as over-morbid and monotonously painful. "Everything is to be endured, nothing is to be done." There is truth in the self criticism, but, after all, there seems no reason why a poet may not paint a dejected mood in a long soliloquy, especially when this is broken by such exquisite lyrics as the songs of Callicles, which are among the loveliest examples in our language of description blent with lyrical emotion. The poem was ultimately restored to a place in the author's works at the intercession of Robert Browning.

Arnold's poems of later date than 1853, having no place in this edition, do not, strictly speaking, concern us; but the two most important cannot well be omitted from any general review of his work, especially as the principal, "Balder Dead," has received much less praise than it deserves. It is astonishing to find so competent a critic as Mr. T. H. Ward, and one who might so easily have been forgiven for a partial judgment, apparently doubting whether "Balder Dead" "has a distinct value of its own." It seems to us impossible to allow any considerable interval between this poem and "Sohrab and Rustum;" the style is very similar, the action of each equally noble and affecting; the conduct of either story equally admirable; the interspersed similes equally happy and carefully worked out; the pathos of the respective situations much on a level, and affording almost equal scope for the tenderness which, even more than depth of thought, is Arnold's strong point as a poet. It may, indeed, be said that the manner and diction of "Balder" are even more Homeric than those of "Sohrab and Rustum," while, considering the peculiarity of the locality and the action, they might with propriety have been less so; it is also true that there are more lapses into the prosaic, and more lines deficient in metrical effect. These defects, however, are very inconsiderable in comparison with the general impression of godlike grandeur and human pathos. "Thyrsis," after "Balder" the most important of Arnold's later poems, is an elegy on his friend Arthur Clough, not, certainly, a "Lycidas" or an "Adonais," but rich in beauties both of thought and description. It is somewhat marred for the general reader by a circumstance which probably enhances its charm for Oxonians, the numerous local allusions which endear the poem to those familiar with the scenery, but simply worry when not understood. The note of personal affection is unmistakable, and it may be from over jealousy for his friend's repute and his own that Arnold's poem smells somewhat of the lamp, and hardly produces so much effect as a simpler composition, the exquisite poem on the deaths of his brother and his sister-in-law, full of rich local colouring, and not too local.

With these exceptions, and his dignified but frigid tragedy of " Merope," the chief part of Arnold's poetical work was composed by 1853, and is comprehended in three volumes, one mainly a reprint. There is nothing extraordinary in the gradual impoverishment of his poetical vein, which had never been remarkable for affluence. His criticisms and private letters betray a limited sympathy with his poetical predecessors and immediate contemporaries, which, since it assuredly was not in the slightest degree inspired by envy or unworthy jealousy, can only be interpreted as betokening an undue preponderance of the critical instinct, fatal to the enthusiasm required for continuous productiveness in poetry. The teeming soul is enthusiastic and lavish of admiration, for only so can it sufficiently respond to the innumerable impressions, physical and spiritual, through which alone it is possible to sustain incessant poetical activity. Arnold's intellectual force and intellectual interests never waned, but were diverted more and more from the sphere of creation to the sphere of criticism ; in which, however, so novel and striking were his views and so original his method of developing them, that he almost became a creator. He laid English literature, in particular, under the greatest obligation by his two golden little books, " On translating Homer," and " On the Study of Celtic Literature." His own attempts at Homeric translation, indeed, were by no means fortunate, but this in no respect detracts from the value of his criticism. His more ambitious prose writings have permeated modern English thought, and furnished it with a new and most beneficial element ; it may be added, that in effecting this they have parted with their own individuality, and will soon exist rather as a tint than as a substance. This is merely to say that they were admirably suited for their time, of which his poems are comparatively independent. We entirely agree with Mr. Frederic Harrison, that Arnold's fame will mainly rest upon his poetry, and that it will be durable, pure, and high. We have mentioned his most conspicuous productions, but those which we have not mentioned, or even a few of them, would suffice for an enviable poetical reputation. The development of his mind, nevertheless, as shown in the chronological sequence of his poems (obscured by the classified arrangement adopted in his own edition) is not in the direction of poetry. In the finest productions in his first volume ("The Strayed Reveller," "The Forsaken Merman," "Mycerinus,") the poetical impulse is dominant, the treatment is healthy and objective, spiritual strivings and questionings, though the pieces are really inspired by them, are kept in the background. The finest poems in the second volume, on the other hand ("Memorial Verses," "The Buried Life," "The Youth of Nature," "The Youth of Man," above all "A Summer Night,") come from within. They are not less admirable than their predecessors, but they indicate the waning of that joy in external things without which it is most difficult to keep the flame of poetry alight, especially when, like Arnold, one is tried by the demands of a responsible and harassing official position.

If we were called upon to indicate Arnold's place upon the roll of English poets by comparison with

Introduction.

one of accepted fame, we should seek his nearest
parallel in Gray. Both are academic poets, the
dominant note of each is a tender and appealing
pathos, each possessed a refinement of taste which in
some measure degenerated into fastidiousness, and
tended to limit a productiveness not originally exuber-
ant. If they are to be judged by their strongest
performances, the palm must indisputably be given to
Gray, for Arnold has nothing that can be equalled
with the immortal Elegy. If, on the other hand,
diversity of excellence is to be the criterion, he
infinitely surpasses his prototype: who would, however, have written much more and even better, if he
had enjoyed Arnold's unspeakable advantage of living
after the second great age of English poetry instead
of before it. It may not be unreasonable to predict
that posterity will place them nearly on a level. In
venturing this prophecy, full allowance has been made
for the inevitable deduction from Arnold's charm
when, in the general mutation of things, he shall have
ceased to represent contemporary thought and feeling.
He is perhaps the most characteristic representative
that the blended religion and scepticism of our ex-
ceptional epoch have had, and he will be invaluable
as a document for the literary and philosophical
historian of the future. But for this very reason he
must some day cease to be a vital force in the present,
and must rely upon his strictly poetical merits, independent of any reference to the spiritual conflicts of
his day. That these merits will preserve his name,
we have no doubt whatever. His first charm, to our
mind, is depth of pathos; and in the next place beauty

Introduction.

of description, exquisite but not obtrusive. An analysis
of his best poems will show that pathos is hardly ever
absent: he is almost invariably representing some
sorrow, actual or ideal, but always most tenderly felt
and deeply realized. Sohrab, Rustum, Balder, Hoder,
Iseult, Mycerinus, Empedocles, the Forsaken Merman,
the Sick King of Bokhara, the Modern Sappho—what a
gallery of pathetic figures ! The note of sorrow, whether
for himself or for mankind, rings equally from nearly all
the personal poems ; it is his unique distinction to have
been at the same time so elegiac and so manly.
His descriptive passages are delightful for their grace
and accuracy, but not brilliant, like Tennyson's glowing canvas ; or forcible, like Browning's intense etch-
ing ; their charm is rather that of delicate water-colour.
His fondness for unrhymed lyric, arising probably
from defect of musical volume in his poetical constitu-
tion, sometimes, as Froude remarks, renders his " fine
imaginative painting" merely "the poetry of well-written,
elegant prose." It is hardly necessary to add that
Arnold is before all things the poet of culture, and
that, though his pathos usually appeals to the universal
feelings of the human heart, the appeal will seldom
find an echo in uncultivated or semi-educated readers.
For example, the beautiful final stanza of that beautiful
poem " On the Rhine : "

> " Ah, Quiet, all things feel thy balm !
> Those blue hills too, this river's flow,
> Were restless once, but long ago
> Tam'd is their turbulent youthful glow :
> Their joy is in their calm,"

will be lost upon him who does not know that the

Introduction.

hills which border the Rhine were at one time volcanoes.

Of the two early prize poems, which appear for the first time in this edition, "Alaric at Rome," composed at Rugby, and "Cromwell," which obtained the Chancellor's medal at Oxford, not much need be said, except that they well deserve to be retrieved from oblivion. The Rugby poem is the more important, and is one of the very few pieces of the kind from which the writer's subsequent poetical distinction might have been predicted with some confidence. It perhaps owes something of its excellence to the interest in Roman history engendered by the writer's devotion to his illustrious father, so pleasingly manifested in his correspondence. The production of such a poem as "Cromwell" was a safe guarantee of intellectual eminence; but, although much above the usual standard, it is not more remarkable poetically than the similar compositions of many who have never become distinguished as poets.

R. GARNETT.

CHRONOLOGY OF MATTHEW ARNOLD.

Chronology of Matthew Arnold.

The story of Matthew Arnold's Life is contained in two volumes of "Letters" edited by George W. E. Russell in 1895. An admirable bibliography of Mr. Arnold's works has been compiled by Thomas Burnett Smart (J. Davy and Sons, 137, Long Acre), 1892.

The Editor is indebted to Mr. Smart for much supervision of the text of this edition.

CONTENTS.

Contents.

Contents.

ALARIC AT ROME.

BIBLIOGRAPHICAL NOTE.

Alaric at Rome. A prize poem recited in Rugby School, June 12th, 1840. Imprint: Rugby, Combe and Crossley. 1840. Twenty-five copies reprinted for private circulation by Thomas J. Wise, 1893.

B

Alaric at Rome.

" Admire, exult, despise, laugh, weep, for here
"There is such matter for all feeling."
     CHILDE HAROLD.

I.

UNWELCOME shroud of the forgotten dead,
 Oblivion's dreary fountain, where art thou :
Why speed'st thou not thy deathlike wave to shed
O'er humbled pride, and self-reproaching woe :
Or time's stern hand, why blots it not away
The saddening tale that tells of sorrow and decay ?

II.

There are, whose glory passeth not away—
Even in the grave their fragrance cannot fade :
Others there are as deathless full as they,
Who for themselves a monument have made
By their own crimes—a lesson to all eyes—
Of wonder to the fool—of warning to the wise.

Alaric at Rome.

III.

Yes, there are stories registered on high,
Yes, there are stains time's fingers cannot blot,
Deeds that shall live when they who did them, die ;
Things that may cease, but never be forgot :
Yet some there are, their very lives would give
To be remembered thus, and yet they cannot live.

IV.

But thou, imperial City ! that hast stood
In greatness once, in sackcloth now and tears,
A mighty name, for evil or for good,
Even in the loneness of thy widowed years :
Thou that hast gazed, as the world hurried by,
Upon its headlong course with sad prophetic eye.

V.

Is thine the laurel-crown that greatness wreathes
Round the wan temples of the hallowed dead—
Is it the blighting taint dishonour breathes
In fires undying o'er the guilty head,
Or the brief splendour of that meteor light
That for a moment gleams, and all again is night ?

VI.

Fain would we deem that thou hast risen so high
Thy dazzling light an eagle's gaze should tire ;
No meteor brightness to be seen and die,
No passing pageant, born but to expire,
But full and deathless as the deep dark hue
Of ocean's sleeping face, or heaven's unbroken blue.

Alaric at Rome.

VII.

Yet stains there are to blot thy brightest page,
And wither half the laurels on thy tomb ;
A glorious manhood, yet a dim old age,
And years of crime, and nothingness, and gloom :
And then that mightiest crash, that giant fall,
Ambition's boldest dream might sober and appal.

VIII.

Thou wondrous chaos, where together dwell
Present and past, the living and the dead,
Thou shattered mass, whose glorious ruins tell
The vanisht might of that discrownëd head :
Where all we see, or do, or hear, or say,
Seems strangely echoed back by tones of yesterday :

IX.

Thou solemn grave, where every step we tread
Treads on the slumbering dust of other years ;
The while there sleeps within thy precincts dread
What once had human passions, hopes, and fears ;
And memory's gushing tide swells deep and full
And makes thy very ruin fresh and beautiful.

X.

Alas, no common sepulchre art thou,
No habitation for the nameless dead,
Green turf above, and crumbling dust below,
Perchance some mute memorial at their head,
But one vast fane where all unconscious sleep
Earth's old heroic forms in peaceful slumbers deep.

Alaric at Rome.

XI.

Thy dead are kings, thy dust are palaces,
Relics of nations thy memorial-stones :
And the dim glories of departed days
Fold like a shroud around thy withered bones :
And o'er thy towers the wind's half uttered sigh
Whispers, in mournful tones, thy silent elegy.

XII.

Yes, in such eloquent silence didst thou lie
When the Goth stooped upon his stricken prey,
And the deep hues of an Italian sky
Flasht on the rude barbarian's wild array :
While full and ceaseless as the ocean roll,
Horde after horde streamed up thy frowning Capitol.

XIII.

Twice, ere that day of shame, the embattled foe
Had gazed in wonder on that glorious sight ;
Twice had the eternal city bowed her low
In sullen homage to the invader's might :
Twice had the pageant of that vast array
Swept, from thy walls, O Rome, on its triumphant way.

XIV.

Twice, from without thy bulwarks, hath the din
Of Gothic clarion smote thy startled ear ;
Anger, and strife, and sickness are within,
Famine and sorrow are no strangers here :
Twice hath the cloud hung o'er thee, twice been
      stayed
Even in the act to burst, twice threatened, twice delayed.

Alaric at Rome.

XV.

Yet once again, stern Chief, yet once again,
Pour forth the foaming vials of thy wrath :
There lies thy goal, to miss or to attain,
Gird thee, and on upon thy fateful path,
The world hath bowed to Rome, oh ! cold were he
Who would not burst his bonds, and in his turn be free.

XVI.

Therefore arise and arm thee ! lo, the world
Looks on in fear ! and when the seal is set,
The doom pronounced, the battle-flag unfurled,
Scourge of the nations, wouldest thou linger yet ?
Arise and arm thee ! spread thy banners forth,
Pour from a thousand hills thy warriors of the north !

XVII.

Hast thou not marked on a wild autumn day
When the wind slumbereth in a sudden lull,
What deathlike stillness o'er the landscape lay,
How calmly sad, how sadly beautiful ;
How each bright tint of tree, and flower, and heath
Were mingling with the sere and withered hues of death.

XVIII.

And thus, beneath the clear, calm, vault of heaven
In mournful loveliness that city lay,
And thus, amid the glorious hues of even
That city told of languor and decay :
Till what at morning's hour lookt warm and bright
Was cold and sad beneath that breathless, voiceless
     night.

Alaric at Rome.

XIX.

Soon was that stillness broken: like the cry
Of the hoarse onset of the surging wave,
Or louder rush of whirlwinds sweeping by
Was the wild shout those Gothic myriads gave,
As towered on high, above their moonlit road,
Scenes where a Cæsar triumpht, or a Scipio trod.

XX.

Think ye it strikes too slow, the sword of fate,
Think ye the avenger loiters on his way,
That your own hands must open wide the gate,
And your own voice guide him to his prey;
Alas, it needs not; is it hard to know
Fate's threat'nings are not vain, the spoiler comes not
     slow.

XXI.

And were there none, to stand and weep alone,
And as the pageant swept before their eyes
To hear a dim and long forgotten tone
Tell of old times, and holiest memories,
Till fanciful regret and dreamy woe
Peopled night's voiceless shades with forms of long Ago.

XXII.

Oh yes ! if fancy feels, beyond to-day,
Thoughts of the past and of the future time,
How should that mightiest city pass away
And not bethink her of her glorious prime,
Whilst every chord that thrills at thoughts of home
Jarr'd with the bursting shout, " they come, the Goth,
     they come ! "

Alaric at Rome.

XXIII.

The trumpet swells yet louder : they are here !
Yea, on your fathers' bones the avengers tread,
Not this the time to weep upon the bier
That holds the ashes of your hero-dead,
If wreaths may twine for you, or laurels wave,
They shall not deck your life, but sanctify your grave.

XXIV.

Alas ! no wreaths are here.   Despair may teach
Cowards to conquer and the weak to die ;
Nor tongue of man, nor fear, nor shame can preach
So stern a lesson as necessity,
Yet here it speaks not.   Yea, though all around
Unhallowed feet are trampling on this haunted ground,

XXV.

Though every holiest feeling, every tie
That binds the heart of man with mightiest power,
All natural love, all human sympathy
Be crusht, and outraged in this bitter hour,
Here is no echo to the sound of home,
No shame that suns should rise to light a conquer'd
Rome.

XXVI.

That troublous night is over : on the brow
Of thy stern hill, thou mighty Capitol,
One form stands gazing : silently below
The morning mists from tower and temple roll,
And lo ! the eternal city, as they rise,
Bursts, in majestic beauty, on her conqueror's eyes.

Alaric at Rome.

XXVII.

Yes, there he stood, upon that silent hill,
And there beneath his feet his conquest lay :
Unlike that ocean-city, gazing still
Smilingly forth upon her sunny bay,
But o'er her vanisht might and humbled pride
Mourning, as widowed Venice o'er her Adrian tide.

XXVIII.

Breathe there not spirits on the peopled air ?
Float there not voices on the murmuring wind ?
Oh ! sound there not some strains of sadness there,
To touch with sorrow even a victor's mind,
And wrest one tear from joy ! Oh ! who shall pen
The thoughts that toucht thy breast, thou lonely
        conqueror, then ?

XXIX.

Perchance his wandering heart was far away,
Lost in dim memories of his early home,
And his young dreams of conquest ; how to-day
Beheld him master of Imperial Rome,
Crowning his wildest hopes : perchance his eyes
As they looked sternly on, beheld new victories,

XXX.

New dreams of wide dominion, mightier, higher,
Come floating up from the abyss of years ;
Perchance that solemn sight might quench the fire
Even of that ardent spirit ; hopes and fears
Might well be mingling at that murmured sigh,
Whispering from all around, " All earthly things must
        die."

Alaric at Rome.

XXXI.

Perchance that wondrous city was to him
But as one voiceless blank ; a place of graves,
And recollections indistinct and dim,
Whose sons were conquerors once, and now were
    slaves :
It may be in that desolate sight his eye
Saw but another step to climb to victory !

XXXII.

Alas ! that fiery spirit little knew
The change of life, the nothingness of power,
How both were hastening, as they flowered and grew,
Nearer and nearer to their closing hour :
How every birth of time's miraculous womb
Swept off the withered leaves that hide the naked tomb.

XXXIII.

One little year ; that restless soul shall rest,
That frame of vigour shall be crumbling clay,
And tranquilly, above that troubled breast,
The sunny waters hold their joyous way :
And gently shall the murmuring ripples flow,
Nor wake the weary soul that slumbers on below.

XXXIV.

Alas ! far other thoughts might well be ours
And dash our holiest raptures while we gaze :
Energies wasted, unimproved hours,
The saddening visions of departed days :
And while they rise here might we stand alone,
And mingle with thy ruins somewhat of our own.

Alaric at Rome.

XXXV.

Beautiful city ! If departed things
Ever again put earthly likeness on,
Here should a thousand forms on fancy's wings
Float up to tell of ages that are gone :
Yea though hand touch thee not, nor eye should see,
Still should the spirit hold communion, Rome, with
      thee !

XXXVI.

Oh ! it is bitter, that each fairest dream
Should fleet before us but to melt away ;
That wildest visions still should loveliest seem
And soonest fade in the broad glare of day :
That while we feel the world is dull and low,
Gazing on thee, we wake to find it is not so.

XXXVII.

A little while, alas ! a little while,
And the same world has tongue, and ear, and eye,
The careless glance, the cold unmeaning smile,
The thoughtless word, the lack of sympathy !
Who would not turn him from the barren sea
And rest his weary eyes on the green land and thee !

XXXVIII.

So pass we on.   But oh ! to harp aright
The vanisht glories of thine early day,
There needs a minstrel of diviner might,
A holier incense than this feeble lay ;
To chant thy requiem with more passionate breath,
And twine with bolder hand thy last memorial wreath !

CROMWELL.

BIBLIOGRAPHICAL NOTE.

Cromwell. A prize poem recited in the Theatre, Oxford, June 28th, 1843, by Matthew Arnold, Balliol College. Printed and published by J. Vincent, Oxford, 1843. Second Edition published by T. and G. Shrimpton, 1863. Third Edition, A. T. Shrimpton and Son, 1891. Also printed in "Oxford Prize Poems," 1846.

SYNOPSIS.

Cromwell.

Schrecklich ist, es, deiner Wahrheit
Sterbliches Gefäss zu seyn.
SCHILLER.

HIGH fate is theirs, ye sleepless waves, whose ear
    Learns Freedom's lesson from your voice of fear;
Whose spell-bound sense from childhood's hour hath
    known
Familiar meanings in your mystic tone:
Sounds of deep import—voices that beguile
Age of its tears and childhood of its smile,
To yearn with speechless impulse to the free
And gladsome greetings of the buoyant sea!
High fate is theirs, who where the silent sky
Stoops to the soaring mountains, live and die;
Who scale the cloud-capt height, or sink to rest
In the deep stillness of its shelt'ring breast;—
Around whose feet the exulting waves have sung,
The eternal hills their giant shadows flung.

No wonders nurs'd thy childhood; not for thee
Did the waves chant their song of liberty!
Thine was no mountain home, where Freedom's form
Abides enthron'd amid the mist and storm,
And whispers to the listening winds, that swell

Cromwell.

With solemn cadence round her citadel!
These had no sound for thee: that cold calm eye
Lit with no rapture as the storm swept by,
To mark with shiver'd crest the reeling wave
Hide his torn head beneath his sunless cave;
Or hear 'mid circling crags, the impatient cry
Of the pent winds, that scream in agony!
Yet all high sounds that mountain children hear
Flash'd from thy soul upon thine inward ear;
All Freedom's mystic language—storms that roar
By hill or wave, the mountain or the shore,—
All these had stirr'd thy spirit, and thine eye
In common sights read secret sympathy;
Till all bright thoughts that hills or waves can yield
Deck'd the dull waste, and the familiar field;
Or wondrous sounds from tranquil skies were borne
Far o'er the glistening sheets of windy corn:
Skies—that, unbound by clasp of mountain chain,
Slope stately down, and melt into the plain;
Sounds—such as erst the lone wayfaring man
Caught, as he journeyed, from the lips of Pan;
Or that mysterious cry, that smote with fear,
Like sounds from other worlds, the Spartan's ear,
While o'er the dusty plain, the murmurous throng
Of Heaven's embattled myriads swept along.

Say not such dreams are idle: for the man
Still toils to perfect what the child began;
And thoughts, that were but outlines, time engraves
Deep on his life; and childhood's baby waves,
Made rough with care, become the changeful sea,
Stemm'd by the strength of manhood fearlessly;

Cromwell.

And fleeting thoughts, that on the lonely wild
Swept o'er the fancy of that heedless child,
Perchance had quicken'd with a living truth
The cold dull soil of his unfruitful youth;
Till with his daily life, a life that threw
Its shadows o'er the future flower'd and grew,
With common cares unmingling, and apart,
Haunting the shrouded chambers of his heart;
Till life unstirr'd by action, life became
Threaded and lighten'd by a track of flame;
An inward light, that, with its streaming ray
On the dark current of his changeless day,
Bound all his being with a silver chain—
Like a swift river through a silent plain!

High thoughts were his, when by the gleaming flood,
With heart new strung, and stern resolve, he stood;
Where rode the tall dark ships, whose loosen'd sail
All idly flutter'd in the eastern gale;
High thoughts were his; but Memory's glance the while
Fell on the cherish'd past with tearful smile;
And peaceful joys and gentler thoughts swept by,
Like summer lightnings o'er a darken'd sky.
The peace of childhood, and the thoughts that roam,
Like loving shadows, round that childhood's home;
Joys that had come and vanish'd, half unknown,
Then slowly brighten'd, as the days had flown;
Years that were sweet or sad, becalm'd or toss'd
On life's wild waves—the living and the lost.
Youth stain'd with follies: and the thoughts of ill
Crush'd, as they rose, by manhood's sterner will.

Cromwell.

Repentant prayers, that had been strong to save;
And the first sorrow, which is childhood's grave!
All shapes that haunt remembrance—soft and fair,
Like a green land at sunset, all were there!
Eyes that he knew, old faces unforgot,
Gaz'd sadly down on his unrestful lot,
And Memory's calm clear voice, and mournful eye,
Chill'd every buoyant hope that floated by;
Like frozen winds on southern vales that blow
From a far land—the children of the snow—
O'er flowering plain and blossom'd meadow fling
The cold dull shadow of their icy wing.

Then Fancy's roving visions, bold and free,
A moment dispossess'd reality.
All airy hopes that idle hearts can frame,
Like dreams between two sorrows, went and came:
Fond hearts that fain would clothe the unwelcome truth
Of toilsome manhood in the dreams of youth,
To bend in rapture at some idle throne,
Some lifeless soulless phantom of their own;
Some shadowy vision of a tranquil life,
Of joys unclouded, years unstirr'd by strife;
Of sleep unshadow'd by a dream of woe;
Of many a lawny hill, and streams with silver flow;
Of giant mountains by the western main,
The sunless forest, and the sealike plain;
Those lingering hopes of coward hearts, that still
Would play the traitor to the steadfast will,
One moment's space, perchance, might charm his eye
From the stern future, and the years gone by.
One moment's space might waft him far away

Cromwell.

To western shores—the death-place of the day!
Might paint the calm, sweet peace—the rest of home,
Far o'er the pathless waste of labouring foam—
Peace, that recall'd his childish hours anew,
More calm, more deep, than childhood ever knew!
Green happy places, like a flowery lea
Between the barren mountains and the stormy sea.

O pleasant rest, if once the race were run!
O happy slumber, if the day were done!
Dreams that were sweet at eve, at morn were sin;
With cares to conquer, and a goal to win!
His were no tranquil years—no languid sleep—
No life of dreams—no home beyond the deep—
No softening ray—no visions false and wild—
No glittering hopes on life's grey distance smiled—
Like isles of sunlight on a mountain's brow,
Lit by a wandering gleam, we know not how,
Far on the dim horizon, when the sky
With glooming clouds broods dark and heavily.

Then his eye slumber'd, and the chain was broke
That bound his spirit, and his heart awoke;
Then, like a kingly river swift and strong,
The future roll'd its gathering tides along!
The shout of onset and the shriek of fear
Smote, like the rush of waters, on his ear;
And his eye kindled with the kindling fray,
The surging battle and the mail'd array!
All wondrous deeds the coming days should see,
And the long Vision of the years to be.
Pale phantom hosts, like shadows, faint and far,

Cromwell.

Councils, and armies, and the pomp of war!
And one sway'd all, who wore a kingly crown,
Until another rose and smote him down:
A form that tower'd above his brother men;
A form he knew—but it was shrouded then!
With stern, slow steps, unseen yet still the same,
By leaguer'd tower and tented field it came;
By Naseby's hill, o'er Marston's heathy waste,
By Worcester's field, the warrior-vision pass'd!
From their deep base, thy beetling cliffs, Dunbar,
Rang, as he trode them, with the voice of war!
The soldier kindled at his words of fire;
The statesman quail'd before his glance of ire!
Worn was his brow with cares no thought could scan
His step was loftier than the steps of man;
And the winds told his glory, and the wave
Sonorous witness to his empire gave!

What forms are these, that with complaining sound,
And slow reluctant steps are gathering round?
Forms that with him shall tread life's changing stage,
Cross his lone path, or share his pilgrimage.
There, as he gazed, a wond'rous band—they came
Pym's look of hate, and Strafford's glance of flame:
There Laud, with noiseless steps and glittering eye,
In priestly garb, a frail old man, went by;
His drooping head bowed meekly on his breast;
His hands were folded, like a saint at rest!
There Hampden bent him o'er his saddle bow,
And death's cold dews bedimm'd his earnest brow;
Still turn'd to watch the battle—still forgot
Himself, his sufferings, in his country's lot!

Cromwell.

There Falkland eyed the strife that would not cease,
Shook back his tangled locks, and murmur'd "Peace!"
With feet that spurn'd the ground, lo! Milton there
Stood like a statue; and his face was fair—
Fair beyond human beauty; and his eye,
That knew not earth, soar'd upwards to the sky!

He, too, was there—it was the princely boy,
The child-companion of his childish joy!
But oh! how chang'd! those deathlike features wore
Childhood's bright glance and sunny smile no more!
That brow so sad, so pale, so full of care—
What trace of careless childhood linger'd there?
What spring of youth in that majestic mien,
So sadly calm, so kingly, so serene?
No—all was chang'd! the monarch wept alone,
Between a ruin'd church and shatter'd throne!
Friendless and hopeless—like a lonely tree,
On some bare headland straining mournfully,
That all night long its weary moan doth make
To the vex'd waters of a mountain lake!
Still, as he gaz'd, the phantom's mournful glance
Shook the deep slumber of his deathlike trance;
Like some forgotten strain that haunts us still,
That calm eye follow'd, turn him where he will;
Till the pale monarch, and the long array,
Pass'd like a morning mist, in tears away!

Then all his dream was troubled, and his soul
Thrill'd with a dread no slumber could control;
On that dark form his eyes had gaz'd before,
Nor known it then;—but it was veil'd no more!

Cromwell.

In broad clear light the ghastly vision shone,—
That form was his,—those features were his own!
The night of terrors, and the day of care,
The years of toil—all, all were written there!
Sad faces watch'd around him, and his breath
Came faint and feeble in the embrace of death.
The gathering tempest, with its voice of fear,
His latest loftiest music, smote his ear!
That day of boundless hope and promise high,
That day that hail'd his triumphs, saw him die!
Then from those whitening lips, as death drew near,
The imprisoning chains fell off, and all was clear!
Like lowering clouds, that at the close of day,
Bath'd in a blaze of sunset, melt away;
And with its clear calm tones, that dying prayer
Cheer'd all the failing hearts that sorrow'd there!

A life—whose ways no human thought could scan;
A life—that was not as the life of man;
A life—that wrote its purpose with a sword,
Moulding itself into action, not in word!
Rent with tumultuous thoughts, whose conflict rung
Deep through his soul, and chok'd his faltering tongue;
A heart that reck'd not of the countless dead,
That strew'd the blood-stain'd path where Empire led;
A daring hand, that shrunk not to fulfil
The thought that spurr'd it; and a dauntless will,
Bold action's parent; and a piercing ken
Through the dark chambers of the hearts of men,
To read each thought, and teach that master-mind
The fears and hopes and passions of mankind;

Cromwell.

All these were thine—oh thought of fear !—and thou,
Stretch'd on that bed of death, art nothing now.

———

Then all his vision faded, and his soul
Sprang from its sleep ! and lo ! the waters roll
Once more beneath him ; and the fluttering sail,
Where the dark ships rode proudly, woo'd the gale ;
And the wind murmur'd round him, and he stood
Once more alone beside the gleaming flood.

THE

STRAYED REVELLER

AND

OTHER POEMS.

By A.

BIBLIOGRAPHICAL NOTE.

*The Strayed Reveller and other Poems. By A. London:
B. Fellowes, Ludgate Street, 1849. "The Hayswater Boat" is the
only poem in this volume which has not been reprinted.*

Ἀ μάκαρ, ὅστις ἔην κεῖνον χρόνον ἴδρις ἀοιδῆς
Μουσάων θεράπων, ὅτ' ἀκείρατος ἦν ἔτι λειμών·
νῦν δ', ὅτε πάντα δέδασται, ἔχουσι δὲ πείρατα τέχναι,
ὕστατοι ὥστε δρόμου καταλειπόμεθ'—

Ἀ μάκαρ, ὅστις ἔην κεῖνον χρόνον ἴδρις ἀοιδῆς
Μουσάων θεράπων, ὅτ' ἀκείρατος ἦν ἔτι λειμών·
νῦν δ', ὅτε πάντα δέδασται, ἔχουσι δὲ πείρατα τέχναι,
ὕστατοι ὥστε δρόμου καταλειπόμεθ'—

CONTENTS.

Contents.

SONNET.

TWO lessons, Nature, let me learn of thee—
    Two lessons that in every wind are blown;
Two blending duties, harmonis'd in one,
Though the loud world proclaim their enmity;
    Of toil unsever'd from tranquillity:
Of labour, that in one short hour outgrows
Man's noisy schemes, accomplish'd in repose,
Too great for haste, too high for rivalry.
Yes, while on earth a thousand discords ring,
Man's weak complainings mingling with his toil,
Still do thy sleepless ministers move on,
Their glorious course in silence perfecting;
Still working, chiding still our vain turmoil,
Labourers that shall not fail, when man is gone.

The Strayed Reveller

MYCERINUS.[1]

"Not by the justice that my father spurn'd,
Not for the thousands whom my father slew,
Altars unfed and temples overturn'd,
Cold hearts and thankless tongues, where thanks were
      due;
Fell this late voice from lips that cannot lie,
Stern sentence of the Powers of Destiny.

I will unfold my sentence and my crime.
My crime, that, rapt in reverential awe,
I sate obedient, in the fiery prime
Of youth, self-govern'd, at the feet of Law;
Ennobling this dull pomp, the life of kings,
By contemplation of diviner things.

My father lov'd injustice, and liv'd long;
Crown'd with grey hairs he died, and full of sway.
I lov'd the good he scorn'd, and hated wrong:
The Gods declare my recompense to-day.
I look'd for life more lasting, rule more high;
And when six years are measur'd, lo, I die!

Yet surely, o my people, did I deem
Man's justice from the all-just Gods was given:
A light that from some upper fount did beam,
Some better archetype, whose seat was heaven;
A light that, shining from the blest abodes,
Did shadow somewhat of the life of Gods.

[1] Herodotus II. 133.

30

and Other Poems.

Mere phantoms of man's self-tormenting heart,
Which on the sweets that woo it dares not feed:
Vain dreams, that quench our pleasures, then depart,
When the dup'd soul, self-master'd, claims its meed:
When, on the strenuous just man, Heaven bestows,
Crown of his struggling life, an unjust close.

Seems it so light a thing then, austere Powers,
To spurn man's common lure, life's pleasant things?
Seems there no joy in dances crown'd with flowers,
Love, free to range, and regal banquettings?
Bend ye on these, indeed, an unmov'd eye,
Not Gods but ghosts, in frozen apathy?

Or is it that some Power, too wise, too strong,
Even for yourselves to conquer or beguile,
Whirls earth, and heaven, and men, and gods along,
Like the broad rushing of the column'd Nile?
And the great powers we serve, themselves may be
Slaves of a tyrannous Necessity?

Or in mid-heaven, perhaps, your golden cars,
Where earthly voice climbs never, wing their flight,
And in wild hunt, through mazy tracts of stars,
Sweep in the sounding stillness of the night?
Or in deaf ease, on thrones of dazzling sheen,
Drinking deep draughts of joy, ye dwell serene?

Oh wherefore cheat our youth, if thus it be,
Of one short joy, one lust, one pleasant dream?
Stringing vain words of powers we cannot see,
Blind divinations of a will supreme;

The Strayed Reveller

Lost labour: when the circumambient gloom
But hides, if Gods, Gods careless of our doom?

The rest I give to joy.   Even while I speak
My sand runs short; and as yon star-shot ray,
Hemm'd by two banks of cloud, peers pale and weak,
Now, as the barrier closes, dies away;
Even so do past and future intertwine,
Blotting this six years' space, which yet is mine.

Six years—six little years—six drops of time—
Yet suns shall rise, and many moons shall wane,
And old men die, and young men pass their prime,
And languid Pleasure fade and flower again;
And the dull Gods behold, ere these are flown,
Revels more deep, joy keener than their own.

Into the silence of the groves and woods
I will go forth; but something would I say—
Something—yet what I know not: for the Gods
The doom they pass revoke not, nor delay;
And prayers, and gifts, and tears, are fruitless all,
And the night waxes, and the shadows fall.

Ye men of Egypt, ye have heard your king.
I go, and I return not.   But the will
Of the great Gods is plain; and ye must bring
Ill deeds, ill passions, zealous to fulfil
Their pleasure, to their feet; and reap their praise,
The praise of Gods, rich boon! and length of days."

—So spake he, half in anger, half in scorn;
And one loud cry of grief and of amaze
Broke from his sorrowing people: so he spake;
And turning, left them there; and with brief pause,
Girt with a throng of revellers, bent his way
To the cool region of the groves he lov'd.

There by the river banks he wander'd on,
From palm-grove on to palm-grove, happy trees,
Their smooth tops shining sunwards, and beneath
Burying their unsunn'd stems in grass and flowers:
Where in one dream the feverish time of Youth
Might fade in slumber, and the feet of Joy
Might wander all day long and never tire:
Here came the king, holding high feast, at morn
Rose-crown'd; and ever, when the sun went down,
A hundred lamps beam'd in the tranquil gloom,
From tree to tree, all through the twinkling grove,
Revealing all the tumult of the feast,
Flush'd guests, and golden goblets, foam'd with wine;
While the deep-burnish'd foliage overhead
Splinter'd the silver arrows of the moon.
  It may be that sometimes his wondering soul
From the loud joyful laughter of his lips
Might shrink half startled, like a guilty man
Who wrestles with his dream; as some pale Shape,
Gliding half hidden through the dusky stems,
Would thrust a hand before the lifted bowl,
Whispering, "A little space, and thou art mine."
It may be on that joyless feast his eye
Dwelt with mere outward seeming; he, within,
Took measure of his soul, and knew its strength,

The Strayed Reveller

And by that silent knowledge, day by day,
Was calm'd, ennobled, comforted, sustain'd.
It may be; but not less his brow was smooth,
And his clear laugh fled ringing through the gloom,
And his mirth quail'd not at the mild reproof
Sigh'd out by Winter's sad tranquillity;
Nor, pall'd with its own fulness, ebb'd and died
In the rich languor of long summer days;
Nor wither'd, when the palm-tree plumes that roof'd
With their mild dark his grassy banquet-hall,
Bent to the cold winds of the showerless Spring;
No, nor grew dark when Autumn brought the clouds.

  So six long years he revell'd, night and day;
And when the mirth wax'd loudest, with dull sound
Sometimes from the grove's centre echoes came,
To tell his wondering people of their king;
In the still night, across the streaming flats,
Mix'd with the murmur of the moving Nile.

TO A FRIEND.

WHO prop, thou ask'st, in these bad days, my mind?
He much, the old man, who, clearest-soul'd of men,
Saw The Wide Prospect,[1] and the Asian Fen,
And Tmolus' hill, and Smyrna's bay, though blind.
Much he, whose friendship I not long since won,
That halting slave, who in Nicopolis
Taught Arrian, when Vespasian's brutal son
Clear'd Rome of what most sham'd him.   But be his

[1] Εὐρώπη.

My special thanks, whose even-balanc'd soul,
From first youth tested up to extreme old age,
Business could not make dull, nor Passion wild:
Who saw life steadily, and saw it whole:
The mellow glory of the Attic stage;
Singer of sweet Colonus, and its child.

THE STRAYED REVELLER.

A YOUTH. CIRCE.

THE YOUTH.

FASTER, faster,
O Circe, Goddess,
Let the wild, thronging train,
The bright procession
Of eddying forms,
Sweep through my soul.

Thou standest, smiling
Down on me; thy right arm
Lean'd up against the column there,
Props thy soft cheek;
Thy left holds, hanging loosely,
The deep cup, ivy-cinctur'd,
I held but now.

Is it then evening
So soon? I see, the night dews,
Cluster'd in thick beads, dim

The Strayed Reveller

The agate brooch-stones
On thy white shoulder.
The cool night-wind, too,
Blows through the portico,
    Stirs thy hair, Goddess,
      Waves thy white robe.

CIRCE.

Whence art thou, sleeper?

THE YOUTH.

When the white dawn first
Through the rough fir-planks
Of my hut, by the chestnuts,
Up at the valley-head,
Came breaking, Goddess,
I sprang up, I threw round me
    My dappled fawn-skin:
Passing out, from the wet turf,
Where they lay, by the hut door,
I snatch'd up my vine-crown, my fir-staff
    All drench'd in dew:
Came swift down to join
The rout early gather'd
In the town, round the temple,
    Iacchus' white fane
      On yonder hill.

Quick I pass'd, following
The wood-cutters' cart-track
Down the dark valley;—I saw
On my left, through the beeches,

and Other Poems.

Thy palace, Goddess,
Smokeless, empty :
Trembling, I enter'd ; beheld
The court all silent,
The lions sleeping ;
On the altar, this bowl.
I drank, Goddess—
And sunk down here, sleeping,
On the steps of thy portico.

CIRCE.

Foolish boy ! Why tremblest thou ?
Thou lovest it, then, my wine ?
Wouldst more of it ? See, how glows,
Through the delicate flush'd marble,
The red creaming liquor,
Strown with dark seeds !
Drink, then ! I chide thee not,
Deny thee not my bowl.
Come, stretch forth thy hand, then—so,—
Drink, drink again !

THE YOUTH.

Thanks, gracious One !
Ah, the sweet fumes again !
More soft, ah me !
More subtle-winding
Than Pan's flute-music.
Faint—faint ! Ah me !
Again the sweet sleep.

The Strayed Reveller

Circe.

Hist ! Thou—within there !
  Come forth, Ulysses !
Art tired with hunting ?
While we range the woodland,
  See what the day brings.

Ulysses.

  Ever new magic !
Hast thou then lur'd hither,
  Wonderful Goddess, by thy art,
  The young, languid-ey'd Ampelus,
  Iacchus' darling—
Or some youth belov'd of Pan,
  Of Pan and the Nymphs ?
That he sits, bending downward
His white, delicate neck
To the ivy-wreath'd marge
Of thy cup :—the bright, glancing vine-leaves
  That crown his hair,
Falling forwards, mingling
With the dark ivy-plants ;
His fawn-skin, half untied,
Smear'd with red wine-stains ? Who is he,
  That he sits, overweigh'd
  By fumes of wine and sleep,
  So late, in thy portico ?
What youth, Goddess,—what guest
  Of Gods or mortals ?

Circe.

Hist ! he wakes !

I lur'd him not hither, Ulysses.
  Nay, ask him !

THE YOUTH.

Who speaks ? Ah ! Who comes forth
To thy side, Goddess, from within ?
  How shall I name him ?
This spare, dark-featur'd,
  Quick-ey'd stranger ?
Ah ! and I see too
His sailor's bonnet,
His short coat, travel-tarnish'd,
  With one arm bare.—
Art thou not he, whom fame
  This long time rumours
The favour'd guest of Circe, brought by the waves ?
  Art thou he, stranger ?
  The wise Ulysses,
  Laertes' son ?

ULYSSES.

I am Ulysses.
And thou, too, sleeper ?
  Thy voice is sweet.
It may be thou hast follow'd
Through the islands some divine bard,
  By age taught many things,
  Age and the Muses ;
  And heard him delighting
  The chiefs and people
In the banquet, and learn'd his songs,
  Of Gods and Heroes,

The Strayed Reveller

Of war and arts,
And peopled cities
Inland, or built
By the grey sea.—If so, then hail !
I honour and welcome thee.

THE YOUTH.
The Gods are happy.
They turn on all sides
Their shining eyes :
And see, below them,
The Earth, and men.

They see Tiresias
Sitting, staff in hand,
On the warm, grassy
Asopus' bank :
His robe drawn over
His old, sightless head :
Revolving inly
The doom of Thebes.

They see the Centaurs
In the upper glens
Of Pelion, in the streams,
Where red-berried ashes fringe
The clear-brown shallow pools ;
With streaming flanks, and heads
Rear'd proudly, snuffing
The mountain wind.

They see the Indian
Drifting, knife in hand,
His frail boat moor'd to
A floating isle thick matted
With large-leav'd, low-creeping melon-plants,
And the dark cucumber.
He reaps, and stows them,
Drifting—drifting :—round him,
Round his green harvest-plot,
Flow the cool lake-waves :
The mountains ring them.

They see the Scythian
On the wide Stepp, unharnessing
His wheel'd house at noon.
He tethers his beast down, and makes his meal,
Mares' milk, and bread
Bak'd on the embers :—all around
The boundless waving grass-plains stretch, thick-starr'd
With saffron and the yellow hollyhock
And flag-leav'd iris flowers.
Sitting in his cart
He makes his meal : before him, for long miles,
Alive with bright green lizards,
And the springing bustard fowl,
The track, a straight black line,
Furrows the rich soil : here and there
Clusters of lonely mounds
Topp'd with rough-hewn
Grey, rain-blear'd statues, overpeer
The sunny Waste.

The Strayed Reveller

They see the Ferry
On the broad, clay-laden
Lone Chorasmian stream : thereon
With snort and strain,
Two horses, strongly swimming, tow
The ferry boat, with woven ropes
To either bow
Firm-harness'd by the mane :—a chief,
With shout and shaken spear
Stands at the prow, and guides them : but astern,
The cowering Merchants, in long robes,
Sit pale beside their wealth
Of silk-bales and of balsam-drops,
Of gold and ivory,
Of turquoise-earth and amethyst,
Jasper and chalcedony,
And milk-barr'd onyx stones.
The loaded boat swings groaning
In the yellow eddies.
The Gods behold them.

They see the Heroes
Sitting in the dark ship
On the foamless, long-heaving,
Violet sea :
At sunset nearing
The Happy Islands.
These things, Ulysses,
The wise Bards also
Behold and sing.
But oh, what labour !
O Prince, what pain !

and Other Poems.

They too can see
Tiresias :—but the Gods,
Who give them vision,
Added this law :
That they should bear too
    His groping blindness,
    His dark foreboding,
    His scorn'd white hairs.
    Bear Hera's anger
    Through a life lengthen'd
    To seven ages.

    They see the Centaurs
    On Pelion :—then they feel,
    They too, the maddening wine
Swell their large veins to bursting : in wild pain
    They feel the biting spears
Of the grim Lapithæ, and Theseus, drive,
Drive crashing through their bones : they feel
High on a jutting rock in the red stream
    Alcmena's dreadful son
    Ply his bow :—such a price
        The Gods exact for song ;
    To become what we sing.

    They see the Indian
On his mountain lake :—but squalls
Make their skiff reel, and worms
I' the unkind spring have gnaw'd
Their melon-harvest to the heart : They see
    The Scythian :—but long frosts
Parch them in winter-time on the bare Stepp,

The Strayed Reveller

Till they too fade like grass: they crawl
Like shadows forth in spring.
They see the Merchants
On the Oxus' stream :—but care
Must visit first them too, and make them pale.
Whether, through whirling sand,
A cloud of desert robber-horse has burst
Upon their caravan : or greedy kings,
In the wall'd cities the way passes through,
Crush'd them with tolls : or fever-airs,
On some great river's marge,
Mown them down, far from home.

They see the Heroes
Near harbour :—but they share
Their lives, and former violent toil, in Thebes,
Seven-gated Thebes, or Troy :
Or where the echoing oars
Of Argo, first,
Startled the unknown Sea.

The old Silenus
Came, lolling in the sunshine,
From the dewy forest coverts,
This way, at noon.
Sitting by me, while his Fauns
Down at the water side
Sprinkled and smooth'd
His drooping garland,
He told me these things.

But I, Ulysses,
Sitting on the warm steps,
Looking over the valley,
All day long, have seen,
Without pain, without labour,
Sometimes a wild-hair'd Mænad;
Sometimes a Faun with torches;
And sometimes, for a moment,
Passing through the dark stems
Flowing-rob'd—the belov'd,
The desir'd, the divine,
  Belov'd Iacchus.

Ah cool night-wind, tremulous stars!
  Ah glimmering water—
  Fitful earth-murmur—
    Dreaming woods!
Ah golden-hair'd, strangely-smiling Goddess,
  And thou, prov'd much enduring,
    Wave-toss'd Wanderer!
    Who can stand still?
Ye fade, ye swim, ye waver before me.
    The cup again!

    Faster, faster,
    O Circe, Goddess,
  Let the wild thronging train,
    The bright procession
    Of eddying forms,
  Sweep through my soul!

The Strayed Reveller

FRAGMENT OF AN "ANTIGONE."

THE CHORUS.

WELL hath he done who hath seiz'd happiness.
For little do the all-containing Hours,
    Though opulent, freely give.
    Who, weighing that life well
    Fortune presents unpray'd,
Declines her ministry, and carves his own :
    And, justice not infring'd,
Makes his own welfare his unswerv'd-from law.

He does well too, who keeps that clue the mild
Birth-Goddess and the austere Fates first gave.
    For from the day when these
    Bring him, a weeping child,
    First to the light, and mark
A country for him, kinsfolk, and a home,
    Unguided he remains,
Till the Fates come again, alone, with death.

    In little companies,
    And, our own place once left,
    Ignorant where to stand, or whom to avoid,
By city and household group'd, we live : and many shocks
    Our order heaven-ordain'd
    Must every day endure.
    Voyages, exiles, hates, dissensions, wars.
    Besides what waste He makes,
    The all-hated, order-breaking,
    Without friend, city, or home,
    Death, who dissevers all.

Him then I praise, who dares
To self-selected good
Prefer obedience to the primal law,
Which consecrates the ties of blood: for these, indeed,
Are to the Gods a care:
That touches but himself.
For every day man may be link'd and loos'd
With strangers: but the bond
Original, deep-inwound,
Of blood, can he not bind:
Nor, if Fate binds, not bear.

But hush! Hæmon, whom Antigone,
Robbing herself of life in burying,
Against Creon's law, Polynices,
Robs of a lov'd bride; pale, imploring,
Waiting her passage,
Forth from the palace hitherward comes.

HÆMON.
No, no, old men, Creon I curse not.
I weep, Thebans,
One than Creon crueller far.
For he, he, at least, by slaying her,
August laws doth mightily vindicate:
But thou, too-bold, headstrong, pitiless,
Ah me!—honourest more than thy lover,
O Antigone,
A dead, ignorant, thankless corpse.

THE CHORUS.
Nor was the love untrue
Which the Dawn-Goddess bore

The Strayed Reveller

To that fair youth she erst
Leaving the salt sea-beds
And coming flush'd over the stormy frith
Of loud Euripus, saw :
Saw and snatch'd, wild with love,
From the pine-dotted spurs
Of Parnes, where thy waves,
Asopus, gleam rock-hemm'd ;
The Hunter of the Tanagræan Field.
But him, in his sweet prime,
By severance immature,
By Artemis' soft shafts,
She, though a Goddess born,
Saw in the rocky isle of Delos die.
Such end o'ertook that love.
For she desir'd to make
Immortal mortal man,
And blend his happy life,
Far from the Gods, with hers :
To him postponing an eternal law.

HÆMON.

But, like me, she, wroth, complaining,
Succumb'd to the envy of unkind Gods :
And, her beautiful arms unclasping,
Her fair Youth unwillingly gave.

THE CHORUS.

Nor, though enthron'd too high
To fear assault of envious Gods,
His belov'd Argive Seer would Zeus retain
From his appointed end
In this our Thebes : but when

His flying steeds came near
To cross the steep Ismenian glen,
The broad Earth open'd and whelm'd them and him
And through the void air sang
At large his enemy's spear.

And fain would Zeus have sav'd his tired son
Beholding him where the Two Pillars stand
  O'er the sun-redden'd Western Straits :
Or at his work in that dim lower world.
  Fain would he have recall'd
  The fraudulent oath which bound
To a much feebler wight the heroic man :

But he preferr'd Fate to his strong desire.
Nor did there need less than the burning pile
  Under the towering Trachis crags,
And the Spercheius' vale, shaken with groans,
  And the rous'd Maliac gulph,
  And scar'd Œtæan snows,
To achieve his son's deliverance, O my child.

THE SICK KING IN BOKHARA.

HUSSEIN.

O MOST just Vizier, send away
The cloth-merchants, and let them be,
Them and their dues, this day: the King
Is ill at ease, and calls for thee.

The Strayed Reveller

THE VIZIER.

O merchants, tarry yet a day
Here in Bokhara : but at noon
To-morrow, come, and ye shall pay
Each fortieth web of cloth to me,
As the law is, and go your way.

O Hussein, lead me to the King.
Thou teller of sweet tales, thine own,
Ferdusi's, and the others', lead.
How is it with my lord?

HUSSEIN.

Alone

Ever since prayer-time, he doth wait,
O Vizier, without lying down,
In the great window of the gate,
Looking into the Registàn :
Where through the sellers' booths the slaves
Are this way bringing the dead man.
O Vizier, here is the King's door.

THE KING.

O Vizier, I may bury him?

THE VIZIER.

O King, thou know'st, I have been sick
These many days, and heard no thing,
(For Allah shut my ears and mind)
Not even what thou dost, o King.
Wherefore, that I may counsel thee,
Let Hussein, if thou wilt, make haste
To speak in order what hath chanc'd.

THE KING.
O Vizier, be it as thou say'st.

HUSSEIN.
Three days since, at the time of prayer,
A certain Moollah, with his robe
All rent, and dust upon his hair,
Watch'd my lord's coming forth, and push'd
The golden mace-bearers aside,
And fell at the King's feet, and cried,

" Justice, o King, and on myself !
On this great sinner, who hath broke
The law, and by the law must die !
Vengeance, o King !"
                              But the King spoke :

" What fool is this, that hurts our ears
With folly? or what drunken slave?
My guards, what, prick him with your spears !
Prick me the fellow from the path !"
As the King said, so was it done,
And to the mosque my lord pass'd on.

But on the morrow, when the King
Went forth again, the holy book
Carried before him, as is right,
And through the square his path he took ;

My man comes running, fleck'd with blood
From yesterday, and falling down
Cries out most earnestly ; " O King,
My lord, o King, do right, I pray !

The Strayed Reveller

" How canst thou, ere thou hear, discern
If I speak folly? but a king,
Whether a thing be great or small,
Like Allah, hears and judges all.

" Wherefore hear thou ! Thou know'st, how fierce
In these last days the sun hath burn'd :
That the green water in the tanks
Is to a putrid puddle turn'd :
And the canal, that from the stream
Of Samarcand is brought this way
Wastes, and runs thinner every day.

" Now I at nightfall had gone forth
Alone, and in a darksome place
Under some mulberry trees I found
A little pool : and in brief space
With all the water that was there
I fill'd my pitcher, and stole home
Unseen : and having drink to spare,
I hid the can behind the door,
And went up on the roof to sleep.

" But in the night, which was with wind
And burning dust, again I creep
Down, having fever, for a drink.

" Now meanwhile had my brethren found
The water-pitcher, where it stood
Behind the door upon the ground,
And call'd my mother : and they all,
As they were thirsty, and the night

Most sultry, drain'd the pitcher there ;
That they sate with it, in my sight,
Their lips still wet, when I came down.

"Now mark ! I, being fever'd, sick,
(Most unblest also) at that sight
Brake forth and curs'd them—dost thou hear ?—
One was my mother——Now, do right !"

But my lord mus'd a space, and said :
"Send him away, Sirs, and make on.
It is some madman," the King said :
As the King said, so was it done.

The morrow at the self-same hour
In the King's path, behold, the man,
Not kneeling, sternly fix'd : he stood
Right opposite, and thus began,
Frowning grim down :—"Thou wicked King,
Most deaf where thou shouldst most give ear !
What, must I howl in the next world,
Because thou wilt not listen here ?

"What, wilt thou pray, and get thee grace,
And all grace shall to me be grudg'd ?
Nay but, I swear, from this thy path
I will not stir till I be judg'd."

Then they who stood about the King
Drew close together and conferr'd :
Till that the King stood forth and said,
"Before the priests thou shalt be heard."

The Strayed Reveller

But when the Ulema were met
And the thing heard, they doubted not ;
But sentenc'd him, as the law is,
To die by stoning on the spot.

Now the King charg'd us secretly :
"Ston'd must he be, the law stands so :
Yet, if he seek to fly, give way :
Forbid him not, but let him go."

So saying, the King took a stone,
And cast it softly : but the man,
With a great joy upon his face,
Kneel'd down, and cried not, neither ran.

So they, whose lot it was, cast stones ;
That they flew thick, and bruis'd him sore :
But he prais'd Allah with loud voice,
And remain'd kneeling as before.

My lord had covered up his face :
But when one told him, " He is dead,"
Turning him quickly to go in,
" Bring thou to me his corpse," he said.

And truly, while I speak, o King,
I hear the bearers on the stair.
Wilt thou they straightway bring him in ?
—Ho ! enter ye who tarry there !

and Other Poems.

The Vizier.

O King, in this I praise thee not.
Now must I call thy grief not wise.
Is he thy friend, or of thy blood,
To find such favour in thine eyes?

Nay, were he thine own mother's son,
Still, thou art king, and the Law stands.
It were not meet, the balance swerv'd,
The sword were broken in thy hands.

But being nothing, as he is,
Why for no cause make sad thy face?
Lo, I am old: three kings, ere thee,
Have I seen reigning in this place.

But who, through all this length of time,
Could bear the burden of his years,
If he for strangers pain'd his heart
Not less than those who merit tears?

Fathers we *must* have, wife and child;
And grievous is the grief for these:
This pain alone, which *must* be borne,
Makes the head white, and bows the knees.

But other loads than this his own
One man is not well made to bear.
Besides, to each are his own friends,
To mourn with him, and shew him care.

The Strayed Reveller

Look, this is but one single place,
Though it be great : all the earth round,
If a man bear to have it so,
Things which might vex him shall be found.

Upon the northern frontier, where
The watchers of two armies stand
Near one another, many a man,
Seeking a prey unto his hand,

Hath snatch'd a little fair-hair'd slave :
They snatch also, towards Mervè,
The Shiah dogs, who pasture sheep,
And up from thence to Urghendjè.

And these all, labouring for a lord,
Eat not the fruit of their own hands :
Which is the heaviest of all plagues,
To that man's mind, who understands.

The kaffirs also (whom God curse !)
Vex one another, night and day :
There are the lepers, and all sick :
There are the poor, who faint alway.

All these have sorrow, and keep still,
Whilst other men make cheer, and sing.
Wilt thou have pity on all these ?
No, nor on this dead dog, o King !

and Other Poems.

THE KING.

O Vizier, thou art old, I young.
Clear in these things I cannot see.
My head is burning ; and a heat
Is in my skin, which angers me.

But hear ye this, ye sons of men !
They that bear rule, and are obey'd,
Unto a rule more strong than theirs
Are in their turn obedient made.

In vain therefore, with wistful eyes
Gazing up hither, the poor man,
Who loiters by the high-heap'd booths,
Below there, in the Registàn,

Says, " Happy he, who lodges there !
With silken raiment, store of rice,
And for this drought, all kinds of fruits,
Grape syrup, squares of colour'd ice,

" With cherries serv'd in drifts of snow."
In vain hath a king power to build
Houses, arcades, enamell'd mosques ;
And to make orchard closes, fill'd

With curious fruit trees, bought from far ;
With cisterns for the winter rain ;
And in the desert, spacious inns
In divers places ;—if that pain

Is not more lighten'd, which he feels,
If his will be not satisfied :

The Strayed Reveller

And that it be not, from all time
The Law is planted, to abide.

Thou wert a sinner, thou poor man !
Thou wert athirst; and didst not see,
That, though we snatch what we desire,
We must not snatch it eagerly.

And I have meat and drink at will,
And rooms of treasures, not a few.
But I am sick, nor heed I these :
And what I would, I cannot do.

Even the great honour which I have,
When I am dead, will soon grow still.
So have I neither joy, nor fame.
But what I can do, that I will.

I have a fretted brick-work tomb
Upon a hill on the right hand,
Hard by a close of apricots,
Upon the road of Samarcand.

Thither, o Vizier, will I bear
This man my pity could not save :
And, tearing up the marble flags,
There lay his body in my grave.

Bring water, nard, and linen rolls.
Wash off all blood, set smooth each limb.
Then say; " He was not wholly vile,
Because a king shall bury him."

and Other Poems.

SHAKSPEARE.

OTHERS abide our question.   Thou art free.
We ask and ask : Thou smilest and art still,
Out-topping knowledge.   For the loftiest hill
That to the stars uncrowns his majesty,
Planting his stedfast footsteps in the sea,
Making the Heaven of Heavens his dwelling-place,
Spares but the cloudy border of his base
To the foil'd searching of mortality :
And thou, who didst the stars and sunbeams know,
Self-school'd, self-scann'd, self-honour'd, self-secure,
Didst walk on Earth unguess'd at.   Better so !
All pains the immortal spirit must endure,
All weakness that impairs, all griefs that bow,
Find their sole voice in that victorious brow.

TO THE DUKE OF WELLINGTON.

ON HEARING HIM MISPRAISED.

BECAUSE thou hast believ'd, the wheels of life
Stand never idle, but go always round :
Not by their hands, who vex the patient ground,
Mov'd only ; but by genius, in the strife
Of all its chafing torrents after thaw,
Urg'd ; and to feed whose movement, spinning sand,
The feeble sons of pleasure set their hand :
And, in this vision of the general law,

The Strayed Reveller

Hast labour'd with the foremost, hast become
Laborious, persevering, serious, firm ;
For this, thy track, across the fretful foam
Of vehement actions without scope or term,
Call'd History, keeps a splendour : due to wit,
Which saw *one* clue to life, and follow'd it.

WRITTEN IN BUTLER'S SERMONS.

AFFECTIONS, Instincts, Principles, and Powers,
Impulse and Reason, Freedom and Control—
So men, unravelling God's harmonious whole,
Rend in a thousand shreds this life of ours.
Vain labour ! Deep and broad, where none may see,
Spring the foundations of the shadowy throne
Where man's one Nature, queen-like, sits alone,
Centred in a majestic unity.
And rays her powers, like sister islands, seen
Linking their coral arms under the sea :
Or cluster'd peaks, with plunging gulfs between
Spann'd by aërial arches, all of gold ;
Whereo'er the chariot wheels of Life are roll'd
In cloudy circles, to eternity.

WRITTEN IN EMERSON'S ESSAYS.

" O MONSTROUS, dead, unprofitable world,
That thou canst hear, and hearing, hold thy way.
A voice oracular hath peal'd to-day,
To-day a hero's banner is unfurl'd.

Hast thou no lip for welcome?" So I said.
Man after man, the world smil'd and pass'd by:
A smile of wistful incredulity
As though one spake of noise unto the dead:
Scornful, and strange, and sorrowful; and full
Of bitter knowledge.   Yet the will is free:
Strong is the Soul, and wise, and beautiful:
The seeds of godlike power are in us still:
Gods are we, Bards, Saints, Heroes, if we will.—
    Dumb judges, answer, truth or mockery?

TO AN INDEPENDENT PREACHER.

WHO PREACHED THAT WE SHOULD BE "IN HARMONY WITH NATURE."

"IN harmony with Nature?" Restless fool,
Who with such heat dost preach what were to thee,
When true, the last impossibility;
To be like Nature strong, like Nature cool:—
Know, man hath all which Nature hath, but more,
And in that *more* lie all his hopes of good.
Nature is cruel; man is sick of blood:
Nature is stubborn; man would fain adore:
Nature is fickle; man hath need of rest:
Nature forgives no debt, and fears no grave:
Man would be mild, and with safe conscience blest.
Man must begin, know this, where Nature ends;
Nature and man can never be fast friends.
Fool, if thou canst not pass her, rest her slave!

The Strayed Reveller

TO GEORGE CRUIKSHANK, ESQ.

ON SEEING FOR THE FIRST TIME HIS PICTURE OF "THE BOTTLE," IN THE COUNTRY.

ARTIST, whose hand, with horror wing'd, hath torn
From the rank life of towns this leaf: and flung
The prodigy of full-blown crime among
Valleys and men to middle fortune born,
Not innocent, indeed, yet not forlorn:
Say, what shall calm us, when such guests intrude,
Like comets on the heavenly solitude?
Shall breathless glades, cheer'd by shy Dian's horn,
Cold-bubbling springs, or caves? Not so! The Soul
Breasts her own griefs: and, urg'd too fiercely, says:
"Why tremble? True, the nobleness of man
May be by man effac'd: man can controul
To pain, to death, the bent of his own days.
Know thou the worst. So much, not more, he *can*."

TO A REPUBLICAN FRIEND.

GOD knows it, I am with you. If to prize
Those virtues, priz'd and practis'd by too few,
But priz'd, but lov'd, but eminent in you,
Man's fundamental life: if to despise
The barren optimistic sophistries
Of comfortable moles, whom what they do
Teaches the limit of the just and true—
And for such doing have no need of eyes:

and Other Poems.

If sadness at the long heart-wasting show
Wherein earth's great ones are disquieted :
If thoughts, not idle, while before me flow
The armies of the homeless and unfed :—
    If these are yours, if this is what you are,
    Then am I yours, and what you feel, I share.

CONTINUED.

YET, when I muse on what life is, I seem
Rather to patience prompted, than that proud
Prospect of hope which France proclaims so loud,
France, fam'd in all great arts, in none supreme.
Seeing this Vale, this Earth, whereon we dream,
Is on all sides o'ershadow'd by the high
Uno'erleap'd Mountains of Necessity,
Sparing us narrower margin than we deem.
Nor will that day dawn at a human nod,
When, bursting through the network superpos'd
By selfish occupation—plot and plan,
Lust, avarice, envy—liberated man,
All difference with his fellow man compos'd,
Shall be left standing face to face with God.

RELIGIOUS ISOLATION.

TO THE SAME.

CHILDREN (as such forgive them) have I known,
Ever in their own eager pastime bent
To make the incurious bystander, intent

The Strayed Reveller

On his own swarming thoughts, an interest own;
Too fearful or too fond to play alone.
Do thou, whom light in thine own inmost soul
(Not less thy boast) illuminates, controul
Wishes unworthy of a man full-grown.
What though the holy secret which moulds thee
Moulds not the solid Earth? though never Winds
Have whisper'd it to the complaining Sea,
Nature's great law, and law of all men's minds?
  To its own impulse every creature stirs:
  Live by thy light, and Earth will live by hers.

TO MY FRIENDS,

WHO RIDICULED A TENDER LEAVE-TAKING.

LAUGH, my Friends, and without blame
Lightly quit what lightly came:
Rich to-morrow as to-day
Spend as madly as you may.
I, with little land to stir,
Am the exacter labourer.
    Ere the parting kiss be dry,
    Quick, thy tablets, Memory!

But my Youth reminds me—"Thou
Hast liv'd light as these live now:
As these are, thou too wert such:
Much hast had, hast squander'd much."

Fortune's now less frequent heir,
Ah! I husband what's grown rare.
  Ere the parting kiss be dry,
  Quick, thy tablets, Memory!

Young, I said: "A face is gone
If too hotly mus'd upon:
And our best impressions are
Those that do themselves repair."
Many a face I then let by,
Ah! is faded utterly.
  Ere the parting kiss be dry,
  Quick, thy tablets, Memory!

Marguerite says: "As last year went,
So the coming year 'll be spent:
Some day next year, I shall be,
Entering heedless, kiss'd by thee."
Ah! I hope—yet, once away,
What may chain us, who can say?
  Ere the parting kiss be dry,
  Quick, thy tablets, Memory!

Paint that lilac kerchief, bound
Her soft face, her hair around:
Tied under the archest chin
Mockery ever ambush'd in.
Let the fluttering fringes streak
All her pale, sweet-rounded cheek.
  Ere the parting kiss be dry,
  Quick, thy tablets, Memory!

The Strayed Reveller

Paint that figure's pliant grace
As she towards me lean'd her face,
Half-refus'd and half resign'd,
Murmuring, "Art thou still unkind?"
Many a broken promise then
Was new made—to break again.
   Ere the parting kiss be dry,
   Quick, thy tablets, Memory!

Paint those eyes, so blue, so kind,
Eager tell-tales of her mind:
Paint, with their impetuous stress
Of enquiring tenderness,
Those frank eyes, where deep doth lie
An angelic gravity.
   Ere the parting kiss be dry,
   Quick, thy tablets, Memory!

What, my Friends, these feeble lines
Shew, you say, my love declines
To paint ill as I have done,
Proves forgetfulness begun?
Time's gay minions, pleas'd you see,
Time, your master, governs me.
   Pleas'd, you mock the fruitless cry
   " Quick, thy tablets, Memory!

Ah! too true.   Time's current strong
Leaves us true to nothing long.
Yet, if little stays with man,
Ah! retain we all we can!

and Other Poems.

If the clear impression dies,
Ah! the dim remembrance prize!
Ere the parting kiss be dry,
Quick, thy tablets, Memory!

A MODERN SAPPHO.

THEY are gone: all is still: Foolish heart, dost thou
    quiver?
Nothing moves on the lawn but the quick lilac shade.
Far up gleams the house, and beneath flows the river.
Here lean, my head, on this cool balustrade.

Ere he come: ere the boat, by the shining-branch'd
    border
Of dark elms come round, dropping down the proud
    stream;
Let me pause, let me strive, in myself find some order,
Ere their boat-music sound, ere their broider'd flags
    gleam.

Is it hope makes me linger? the dim thought, that sorrow
Means parting? that only in absence lies pain?
It was well with me once if I saw him: to-morrow
May bring one of the old happy moments again.

Last night we stood earnestly talking together—
She enter'd—that moment his eyes turn'd from me.
Fasten'd on her dark hair and her wreath of white
    heather—
As yesterday was, so to-morrow will be.

The Strayed Reveller

Their love, let me know, must grow strong and yet
    stronger,
Their passion burn more, ere it ceases to burn :
They must love—while they must : But the hearts that
    love longer
Are rare : ah ! most loves but flow once, and return.

I shall suffer ; but they will outlive their affection :
I shall weep ; but their love will be cooling : and he,
As he drifts to fatigue, discontent, and dejection,
Will be brought, thou poor heart ! how much nearer
    to thee !

For cold is his eye to mere beauty, who, breaking
The strong band which beauty around him hath
    furl'd,
Disenchanted by habit, and newly awaking,
Looks languidly round on a gloom-buried world.

Through that gloom he will see but a shadow appearing,
Perceive but a voice as I come to his side :
But deeper their voice grows, and nobler their bearing,
Whose youth in the fires of anguish hath died.

Then—to wait. But what notes down the wind, hark !
    are driving ?
'Tis he ! 'tis the boat, shooting round by the trees !
Let my turn, if it will come, be swift in arriving !
Ah ! hope cannot long lighten torments like these.

Hast thou yet dealt him, O Life, thy full measure ?
World, have thy children yet bow'd at his knee ?
Hast thou with myrtle-leaf crown'd him, O Pleasure ?
Crown, crown him quickly, and leave him for me.

THE NEW SIRENS.

A PALINODE.

In the cedar shadow sleeping,
Where cool grass and fragrant glooms
Oft at noon have lur'd me, creeping
From your darken'd palace rooms :
I, who in your train at morning
Stroll'd and sang with joyful mind,
Heard, at evening, sounds of warning ;
Heard the hoarse boughs labour in the wind.

Who are they, o pensive Graces,
—For I dream'd they wore your forms—
Who on shores and sea-wash'd places
Scoop the shelves and fret the storms ?
Who, when ships are that way tending,
Troop across the flushing sands,
To all reefs and narrows wending,
With blown tresses, and with beckoning hands ?

Yet I see, the howling levels
Of the deep are not your lair ;
And your tragic-vaunted revels
Are less lonely than they were.

The Strayed Reveller

In a Tyrian galley steering
From the golden springs of dawn,
Troops, like Eastern kings, appearing,
Stream all day through your enchanted lawn

And we too, from upland valleys,
Where some Muse, with half-curv'd frown,
Leans her ear to your mad sallies
Which the charm'd winds never drown ;
By faint music guided, ranging
The scar'd glens, we wander'd on :
Left our awful laurels hanging,
And came heap'd with myrtles to your throne.

From the dragon-warder'd fountains
Where the springs of knowledge are :
From the watchers on the mountains,
And the bright and morning star :
We are exiles, we are falling,
We have lost them at your call.
O ye false ones, at your calling
Seeking ceiled chambers and a palace hall.

Are the accents of your luring
More melodious than of yore ?
Are those frail forms more enduring
Than the charms Ulysses bore ?
That we sought you with rejoicings
Till at evening we descry
At a pause of Siren voicings
These vext branches and this howling sky ?

Oh ! your pardon.   The uncouthness
Of that primal age is gone :
And the skin of dazzling smoothness
Screens not now a heart of stone.
Love has flush'd those cruel faces ;
And your slacken'd arms forego
The delight of fierce embraces :
And those whitening bone-mounds do not grow.

"Come," you say ; "the large appearance
Of man's labour is but vain :
And we plead as firm adherence
Due to pleasure as to pain."
Pointing to some world-worn creatures,
"Come," you murmur with a sigh :
"Ah ! we own diviner features,
Loftier bearing, and a prouder eye.

"Come," you say, "the hours are dreary :
Life is long, and will not fade :
Time is lame, and we grow weary
In this slumbrous cedarn shade.
Round our hearts, with long caresses,
With low sighs hath Silence stole ;
And her load of steaming tresses
Weighs, like Ossa, on the aery soul.

"Come," you say, "the Soul is fainting
Till she search, and learn her own :
And the wisdom of man's painting
Leaves her riddle half unknown.

The Strayed Reveller

Come," you say, "the brain is seeking,
When the princely heart is dead:
Yet this glean'd, when Gods were speaking,
Rarer secrets than the toiling head.

"Come," you say, "opinion trembles,
Judgment shifts, convictions go:
Life dries up, the heart dissembles:
Only, what we feel, we know.
Hath your wisdom known emotions?
Will it weep our burning tears?
Hath it drunk of our love-potions
Crowning moments with the weight of years?

I am dumb.   Alas! too soon, all
Man's grave reasons disappear:
Yet, I think, at God's tribunal
Some large answer you shall hear.
But for me, my thoughts are straying
Where at sunrise, through the vines,
On these lawns I saw you playing,
Hanging garlands on the odorous pines.

When your showering locks enwound you,
And your heavenly eyes shone through:
When the pine-boughs yielded round you,
And your brows were starr'd with dew.
And immortal forms to meet you
Down the statued alleys came:
And through golden horns, to greet you,
Blew such music as a God may frame.

and Other Poems.

Yes—I muse :—And, if the dawning
Into daylight never grew—
If the glistering wings of morning
On the dry noon shook their dew—
If the fits of joy were longer—
Or the day were sooner done—
Or, perhaps, if Hope were stronger—
No weak nursling of an earthly sun . . .
  Pluck, pluck cypress, o pale maidens,
  Dusk the hall with yew !

But a bound was set to meetings,
And the sombre day dragg'd on :
And the burst of joyful greetings,
And the joyful dawn, were gone :
For the eye was fill'd with gazing,
And on raptures follow calms :—
And those warm locks men were praising
Droop'd, unbraided, on your listless arms.

Storms unsmooth'd your folded valleys,
And made all your cedars frown.
Leaves are whirling in the alleys
Which your lovers wander'd down.
—Sitting cheerless in your bowers,
The hands propping the sunk head,
Do they gall you, the long hours ?
And the hungry thought, that must be fed ?

Is the pleasure that is tasted
Patient of a long review ?
Will the fire joy hath wasted,
Mus'd on, warm the heart anew ?

The Strayed Reveller

—Or, are those old thoughts returning,
Guests the dull sense never knew,
Stars, set deep, yet inly burning,
Germs, your untrimm'd Passion overgrew?

Once, like me, you took your station
Watchers for a purer fire:
But you droop'd in expectation,
And you wearied in desire.
When the first rose flush was steeping
All the frore peak's awful crown,
Shepherds say, they found you sleeping
In a windless valley, further down.

Then you wept, and slowly raising
Your doz'd eyelids, sought again,
Half in doubt, they say, and gazing
Sadly back, the seats of men.
Snatch'd an earthly inspiration
From some transient human Sun,
And proclaim'd your vain ovation
For the mimic raptures you had won.
    Pluck, pluck cypress, o pale maidens,
        Dusk the hall with yew!

———

With a sad, majestic motion—
With a stately, slow surprise—
From their earthward-bound devotion
Lifting up your languid eyes:
Would you freeze my louder boldness
Dumbly smiling as you go?
One faint frown of distant coldness
Flitting fast across each marble brow?

Do I brighten at your sorrow
O sweet Pleaders? doth my lot
Find assurance in to-morrow
Of one joy, which you have not?
O speak once! and let my sadness,
And this sobbing Phrygian strain,
Sham'd and baffled by your gladness,
Blame the music of your feasts in vain.

Scent, and song, and light, and flowers—
Gust on gust, the hoarse winds blow.
Come, bind up those ringlet showers!
Roses for that dreaming brow!
Come, once more that ancient lightness,
Glancing feet, and eager eyes!
Let your broad lamps flash the brightness
Which the sorrow-stricken day denies!

Through black depths of serried shadows,
Up cold aisles of buried glade;
In the mist of river meadows
Where the looming kine are laid;
From your dazzled windows streaming,
From the humming festal room,
Deep and far, a broken gleaming
Reels and shivers on the ruffled gloom.

———

Where I stand, the grass is glowing:
Doubtless, you are passing fair:
But I hear the north wind blowing;
And I feel the cold night-air.

The Strayed Reveller

Can I look on your sweet faces,
And your proud heads backward thrown,
From this dusk of leaf-strewn places
With the dumb woods and the night alone?

But, indeed, this flux of guesses—
Mad delight, and frozen calms—
Mirth to-day and vine-bound tresses,
And to-morrow—folded palms—
Is this all? this balanc'd measure?
Could life run no easier way?
Happy at the noon of pleasure,
Passive, at the midnight of dismay?

But, indeed, this proud possession—
This far-reaching magic chain,
Linking in a mad succession
Fits of joy and fits of pain:
Have you seen it at the closing?
Have you track'd its clouded ways?
Can your eyes, while fools are dozing,
Drop, with mine, adown life's latter days?

When a dreary light is wading
Through this waste of sunless greens—
When the flashing lights are fading
On the peerless cheek of queens—
When the mean shall no more sorrow,
And the proudest no more smile—
While the dawning of the morrow
Widens slowly westward all that while?

Then, when change itself is over,
When the slow tide sets one way,
Shall you find the radiant lover,
Even by moments, of to-day?
The eye wanders, faith is failing:
O, loose hands, and let it be!
Proudly, like a king bewailing,
O, let fall one tear, and set us free!

All true speech and large avowal
Which the jealous soul concedes:
All man's heart—which brooks bestowal:
All frank faith—which passion breeds:
These we had, and we gave truly:
Doubt not, what we had, we gave:
False we were not, nor unruly:
Lodgers in the forest and the cave.

Long we wander'd with you, feeding
Our sad souls on your replies:
In a wistful silence reading
All the meaning of your eyes:
By moss-border'd statues sitting,
By well-heads, in summer days.
But we turn, our eyes are flitting.
See, the white east, and the morning rays!

And you too, o weeping graces,
Sylvan Gods of this fair shade!
Is there doubt on divine faces?
Are the happy Gods dismay'd?

The Strayed Reveller

Can men worship the wan features,
The sunk eyes, the wailing tone,
Of unspher'd discrowned creatures,
Souls as little godlike as their own?

Come, loose hands! The winged fleetness
Of immortal feet is gone.
And your scents have shed their sweetness,
And your flowers are overblown.
And your jewell'd gauds surrender
Half their glories to the day:
Freely did they flash their splendour,
Freely gave it—but it dies away.

In the pines the thrush is waking—
Lo, yon orient hill in flames:
Scores of true love knots are breaking
At divorce which it proclaims.
When the lamps are pal'd at morning,
Heart quits heart, and hand quits hand.
—Cold in that unlovely dawning,
Loveless, rayless, joyless you shall stand.

Strew no more red roses, maidens,
Leave the lilies in their dew:
Pluck, pluck cypress, o pale maidens!
Dusk, o dusk the hall with yew!
—Shall I seek, that I may scorn her,
Her I lov'd at eventide?
Shall I ask, what faded mourner
Stands, at daybreak, weeping by my side?
Pluck, pluck cypress, o pale maidens!
Dusk the hall with yew!

THE VOICE.

As the kindling glances,
Queen-like and clear,
Which the bright moon lances
From her tranquil sphere
At the sleepless waters
Of a lonely mere,
On the wild whirling waves, mournfully, mournfully,
Shiver and die.

As the tears of sorrow
Mothers have shed—
Prayers that to-morrow
Shall in vain be sped
When the flower they flow for
Lies frozen and dead—
Fall on the throbbing brow, fall on the burning breast,
Bringing no rest.

Like bright waves that fall
With a lifelike motion
On the lifeless margin of the sparkling Ocean.
A wild rose climbing up a mould'ring wall—
A gush of sunbeams through a ruin'd hall—
Strains of glad music at a funeral :—
So sad, and with so wild a start
To this long sober'd heart,
So anxiously and painfully,
So drearily and doubtfully,

The Strayed Reveller

And, oh, with such intolerable change
  Of thought, such contrast strange,
O unforgotten Voice, thy whispers come,
Like wanderers from the world's extremity,
  Unto their ancient home.

In vain, all, all in vain,
They beat upon mine ear again,
Those melancholy tones so sweet and still.
Those lute-like tones which in long distant years
  Did steal into mine ears:
Blew such a thrilling summons to my will;
  Yet could not shake it.
Drain'd all the life my full heart had to spill;
  Yet could not break it.

TO FAUSTA.

Joy comes and goes: hope ebbs and flows,
  Like the wave.
Change doth unknit the tranquil strength of men.
  Love lends life a little grace,
  A few sad smiles: and then,
  Both are laid in one cold place,
  In the grave.

Dreams dawn and fly: friends smile and die,
  Like spring flowers.
Our vaunted life is one long funeral.

Men dig graves, with bitter tears,
For their dead hopes ; and all,
Maz'd with doubts, and sick with fears,
Count the hours.

We count the hours : these dreams of ours,
False and hollow,
Shall we go hence and find they are not dead ?
Joys we dimly apprehend
Faces that smil'd and fled,
Hopes born here, and born to end,
Shall we follow ?

STAGYRUS.

Thou, who dost dwell alone—
Thou, who dost know thine own—
Thou, to whom all are known
From the cradle to the grave—
Save, oh, save.
From the world's temptations,
From tribulations ;
From that fierce anguish
Wherein we languish ;
From that torpor deep
Wherein we lie asleep,
Heavy as death, cold as the grave ;
Save, oh, save.

When the Soul, growing clearer,
Sees God no nearer :

The Strayed Reveller

When the Soul, mounting higher.
  To God comes no nigher:
But the arch-fiend Pride
Mounts at her side,
Foiling her high emprize,
Sealing her eagle eyes,
And, when she fain would soar,
Makes idols to adore;
Changing the pure emotion
Of her high devotion,
To a skin-deep sense
Of her own eloquence:
Strong to deceive, strong to enslave—
  Save, oh, save.

From the ingrain'd fashion
Of this earthly nature
That mars thy creature.
From grief, that is but passion;
From mirth, that is but feigning;
From tears, that bring no healing;
From wild and weak complaining;
  Thine old strength revealing,
    Save, oh, save.
From doubt, where all is double:
Where wise men are not strong:
Where comfort turns to trouble:
Where just men suffer wrong.
Where sorrow treads on joy:
Where sweet things soonest cloy:
Where faiths are built on dust:
Where Love is half mistrust,

and Other Poems.

Hungry, and barren, and sharp as the sea;
  Oh, set us free.
O let the false dream fly
Where our sick souls do lie
  Tossing continually.
O where thy voice doth come
  Let all doubts be dumb:
  Let all words be mild:
  All strifes be reconcil'd:
  All pains beguil'd.
Light bring no blindness;
Love no unkindness;
Knowledge no ruin!
Fear no undoing.
From the cradle to the grave,
  Save, oh, save.

TO A GIPSY CHILD BY THE SEA-SHORE.

DOUGLAS, ISLE OF MAN.

Who taught this pleading to unpractis'd eyes?
Who hid such import in an infant's gloom?
Who lent thee, child, this meditative guise?
Who mass'd, round that slight brow, these clouds of doom?

Lo! sails that gleam a moment and are gone;
The swinging waters, and the cluster'd pier.
Not idly Earth and Ocean labour on,
Nor idly do these sea-birds hover near.

The Strayed Reveller

But thou, whom superfluity of joy
Wafts not from thine own thoughts, nor longings vain,
Nor weariness, the full-fed soul's annoy ;
Remaining in thy hunger and thy pain :

Thou, drugging pain by patience ; half averse
From thine own mother's breast that knows not thee ;
With eyes that sought thine eyes thou didst converse,
And that soul-searching vision fell on me.

Glooms that go deep as thine I have not known :
Moods of fantastic sadness, nothing worth.
Thy sorrow and thy calmness are thine own :
Glooms that enhance and glorify this earth.

What mood wears like complexion to thy woe ?
His, who in mountain glens, at noon of day,
Sits rapt, and hears the battle break below ?
  Ah ! thine was not the shelter, but the fray,

What exile's, changing bitter thoughts with glad ?
What seraph's, in some alien planet born ?
  No exile's dream was ever half so sad,
Nor any angel's sorrow so forlorn.

Is the calm thine of stoic souls, who weigh
Life well, and find it wanting, nor deplore :
But in disdainful silence turn away,
Stand mute, self-centred, stern, and dream no more ?

Or do I wait, to hear some grey-hair'd king
Unravel all his many-colour'd lore :
Whose mind hath known all arts of governing,
Mus'd much, lov'd life a little, loath'd it more ?

Down the pale cheek long lines of shadow slope,
Which years, and curious thought, and suffering give——
  Thou hast foreknown the vanity of hope,
Foreseen thy harvest—yet proceed'st to live.

O meek anticipant of that sure pain
Whose sureness grey-hair'd scholars hardly learn !
What wonder shall time breed, to swell thy strain ?
What heavens, what earth, what suns shalt thou
      discern ?

Ere the long night, whose stillness brooks no star,
Match that funereal aspect with her pall,
I think, thou wilt have fathom'd life too far,
Have known too much——or else forgotten all.

The Guide of our dark steps a triple veil
Betwixt our senses and our sorrow keeps :
Hath sown, with cloudless passages, the tale
Of grief, and eas'd us with a thousand sleeps.

Ah ! not the nectarous poppy lovers use,
Not daily labour's dull, Lethæan spring,
Oblivion in lost angels can infuse
Of the soil'd glory, and the trailing wing.

And though thou glean, what strenuous gleaners may,
In the throng'd fields where winning comes by
 strife;
And though the just sun gild, as all men pray,
Some reaches of thy storm-vext stream of life:

Though that blank sunshine blind thee: though the
 cloud
That sever'd the world's march and thine, is gone:
Though ease dulls grace, and Wisdom be too proud
To halve a lodging that was all her own:

Once, ere the day decline, thou shalt discern,
Oh once, ere night, in thy success, thy chain.
Ere the long evening close, thou shalt return,
And wear this majesty of grief again.

THE HAYSWATER BOAT.

A REGION desolate and wild.
Black, chafing water: and afloat,
And lonely as a truant child
In a waste wood, a single boat:
No mast, no sails are set thereon;
It moves, but never moveth on:
And welters like a human thing
Amid the wild waves weltering.

Behind, a buried vale doth sleep,
Far down the torrent cleaves its way:
In front the dumb rock rises steep,
A fretted wall of blue and grey;

Of shooting cliff and crumbled stone
With many a wild weed overgrown :
All else, black water : and afloat,
One rood from shore, that single boat.

Last night the wind was up and strong ;
The grey-streak'd waters labour still :
The strong blast brought a pigmy throng
From that mild hollow in the hill ;
From those twin brooks, that beached strand
So featly strewn with drifted sand ;
From those weird domes of mounded green
That spot the solitary scene.

This boat they found against the shore :
The glossy rushes nodded by.
One rood from land they push'd, no more ;
Then rested, listening silently.
The loud rains lash'd the mountain's crown,
The grating shingle straggled down :
All night they sate ; then stole away,
And left it rocking in the bay.

Last night ?—I look'd, the sky was clear.
The boat was old, a batter'd boat.
In sooth, it seems a hundred year
Since that strange crew did ride afloat.
The boat hath drifted in the bay—
The oars have moulder'd as they lay—
The rudder swings—yet none doth steer.
    What living hand hath brought it here ?

THE FORSAKEN MERMAN.

Come, dear children, let us away;
    Down and away below.
Now my brothers call from the bay;
Now the great winds shorewards blow;
Now the salt tides seawards flow;
Now the wild white horses play,
Champ and chafe and toss in the spray.
    Children dear, let us away.
        This way, this way.

    Call her once before you go.
        Call once yet.
    In a voice that she will know:
        " Margaret ! Margaret ! "
Children's voices should be dear
(Call once more) to a mother's ear:
Children's voices, wild with pain.
        Surely she will come again.
Call her once and come away.
        This way, this way.
" Mother dear, we cannot stay."
The wild white horses foam and fret.
        Margaret !   Margaret !

Come, dear children, come away down.
        Call no more.
One last look at the white-wall'd town,
And the little grey church on the windy shore.
        Then come down.

She will not come though you call all day.
　　Come away, come away.

Children dear, was it yesterday
We heard the sweet bells over the bay?
　　In the caverns where we lay,
　　Through the surf and through the swell
The far-off sound of a silver bell?
Sand-strewn caverns, cool and deep,
Where the winds are all asleep;
Where the spent lights quiver and gleam;
Where the salt weed sways in the stream;
Where the sea-beasts rang'd all round
Feed in the ooze of their pasture-ground;
Where the sea-snakes coil and twine,
Dry their mail and bask in the brine;
Where great whales come sailing by,
Sail and sail, with unshut eye,
Round the world for ever and aye?
　　When did music come this way?
　　Children dear, was it yesterday?

　　Children dear, was it yesterday
　　(Call yet once) that she went away?
　　Once she sate with you and me,
　　On a red gold throne in the heart of the sea,
　　And the youngest sate on her knee.
She comb'd its bright hair, and she tended it well,
When down swung the sound of the far-off bell.
She sigh'd, she look'd up through the clear green sea.
She said; " I must go, for my kinsfolk pray
In the little grey church on the shore to-day.

The Strayed Reveller

'Twill be Easter-time in the world—ah me !
And I lose my poor soul, Merman, here with thee."
I said ; "Go up, dear heart, through the waves.
Say thy prayer, and come back to the kind sea-caves."
　　She smil'd, she went up through the surf in the bay.
　　　Children dear, was it yesterday ?

　　　Children dear, were we long alone ?
" The sea grows stormy, the little ones moan.
Long prayers," I said, " in the world they say.
Come," I said, and we rose through the surf in the bay.
We went up the beach, by the sandy down
Where the sea-stocks bloom, to the white-wall'd town.
Through the narrow pav'd streets, where all was still,
To the little grey church on the windy hill.
From the church came a murmur of folk at their prayers,
But we stood without in the cold blowing airs.
We climb'd on the graves, on the stones, worn with rains,
And we gaz'd up the aisle through the small leaded panes.
　　She sate by the pillar ; we saw her clear :
　　" Margaret, hist ! come quick, we are here.
　　Dear heart," I said, " we are long alone.
　　The sea grows stormy, the little ones moan."
But, ah, she gave me never a look,
For her eyes were seal'd to the holy book.
　　" Loud prays the priest ; shut stands the door."
Come away, children, call no more.
Come away, come down, call no more.

　　　Down, down, down.
　　　Down to the depths of the sea.
She sits at her wheel in the humming town,

Singing most joyfully.
Hark, what she sings ; "O joy, o joy,
For the humming street, and the child with its toy.
For the priest, and the bell, and the holy well.
For the wheel where I spun,
And the blessed light of the sun."
And so she sings her fill,
Singing most joyfully,
Till the shuttle falls from her hand,
And the whizzing wheel stands still.
She steals to the window, and looks at the sand ;
And over the sand at the sea ;
And her eyes are set in a stare ;
And anon there breaks a sigh,
And anon there drops a tear,
From a sorrow-clouded eye,
And a heart sorrow-laden,
A long, long sigh.
For the cold strange eyes of a little Mermaiden,
And the gleam of her golden hair.

Come away, away children.
Come children, come down.
The salt tide rolls seaward.
Lights shine in the town.
She will start from her slumber
When gusts shake the door ;
She will hear the winds howling,
Will hear the waves roar.
We shall see, while above us
The waves roar and whirl,
A ceiling of amber,

The Strayed Reveller

A pavement of pearl.
Singing, " Here came a mortal,
But faithless was she.
And alone dwell for ever
The kings of the sea."

But, children, at midnight,
When soft the winds blow;
When clear falls the moonlight;
When spring-tides are low:
When sweet airs come seaward
From heaths starr'd with broom;
And high rocks throw mildly
On the blanch'd sands a gloom:
Up the still, glistening beaches,
Up the creeks we will hie;
Over banks of bright seaweed
The ebb-tide leaves dry.
We will gaze, from the sand-hills,
At the white, sleeping town;
At the church on the hill-side—
    And then come back down.
Singing, " There dwells a lov'd one,
But cruel is she.
She left lonely for ever
The kings of the sea."

THE WORLD AND THE QUIETIST.

TO CRITIAS.

" Why, when the world's great mind
Hath finally inclin'd,
Why," you say, Critias, " be debating still?
    Why, with these mournful rhymes
    Learn'd in more languid climes,
Blame our activity,
Who, with such passionate will,
Are, what we mean to be?"

Critias, long since, I know,
    (For Fate decreed it so,)
Long since the World hath set its heart to live.
    Long since, with credulous zeal
        It turns Life's mighty wheel.
Still doth for labourers send.
    Who still their labour give.
And still expects an end.

        Yet, as the wheel flies round,
        With no ungrateful sound
Do adverse voices fall on the World's ear.
        Deafen'd by his own stir
        The rugged Labourer
        Caught not till then a sense
        So glowing and so near
            Of his omnipotence.

The Strayed Reveller

So, when the feast grew loud
In Susa's palace proud,
A white-rob'd slave stole to the Monarch's side.
He spoke: the Monarch heard:
Felt the slow-rolling word
Swell his attentive soul.
Breath'd deeply as it died,
And drain'd his mighty bowl.

IN UTRUMQUE PARATUS.

IF, in the silent mind of One all-pure
    At first imagin'd lay
The sacred world; and by procession sure
From those still deeps, in form and colour drest,
Seasons alternating, and night and day,
The long-mus'd thought to north south east and west
    Took then its all-seen way:

O waking on a world which thus-wise springs!
    Whether it needs thee count
Betwixt thy waking and the birth of things
Ages or hours: o waking on Life's stream!
By lonely pureness to the all-pure Fount
(Only by this thou canst) the colour'd dream
    Of Life remount.

Thin, thin the pleasant human noises grow;
    And faint the city gleams;
Rare the lone pastoral huts: marvel not thou!
The solemn peaks but to the stars are known,
But to the stars, and the cold lunar beams:
Alone the sun arises, and alone
    Spring the great streams.

But, if the wild unfather'd mass no birth
    In divine seats hath known:
In the blank, echoing solitude, if Earth,
Rocking her obscure body to and fro,
Ceases not from all time to heave and groan,
Unfruitful oft, and, at her happiest throe,
    Forms, what she forms, alone:

O seeming sole to awake, thy sun-bath'd head
    Piercing the solemn cloud
Round thy still dreaming brother-world outspread!
O man, whom Earth, thy long-vext mother, bare
Not without joy; so radiant, so endow'd—
(Such happy issue crown'd her painful care)
    Be not too proud!

O when most self-exalted most alone,
    Chief dreamer, own thy dream!
Thy brother-world stirs at thy feet unknown;
Who hath a monarch's hath no brother's part;
Yet doth thine inmost soul with yearning teem.
O what a spasm shakes the dreamer's heart——
    "I too but seem!"

RESIGNATION.

TO FAUSTA.

"To die be given us, or attain!
Fierce work it were, to do again."
So pilgrims, bound for Mecca, pray'd
At burning noon: so warriors said,
Scarf'd with the cross, who watch'd the miles
Of dust that wreath'd their struggling files
Down Lydian mountains: so, when snows
Round Alpine summits eddying rose,
The Goth, bound Rome-wards: so the Hun,
Crouch'd on his saddle, when the sun
Went lurid down o'er flooded plains
Through which the groaning Danube strains
To the drear Euxine: so pray all,
Whom labours, self-ordain'd, enthrall;
Because they to themselves propose
On this side the all-common close
A goal which, gain'd, may give repose.
So pray they: and to stand again
Where they stood once, to them were pain;
Pain to thread back and to renew
Past straits, and currents long steer'd through.

But milder natures, and more free;
Whom an unblam'd serenity
Hath freed from passions, and the state
Of struggle these necessitate;
Whom schooling of the stubborn mind
Hath made, or birth hath found, resign'd;

These mourn not, that their goings pay
Obedience to the passing day.
These claim not every laughing Hour
For handmaid to their striding power;
Each in her turn, with torch uprear'd,
To await their march; and when appear'd,
Through the cold gloom, with measur'd race,
To usher for a destin'd space,
(Her own sweet errands all foregone)
The too imperious Traveller on.
These, Fausta, ask not this: nor thou,
Time's chafing prisoner, ask it now.

We left, just ten years since, you say,
That wayside inn we left to-day:
Our jovial host, as forth we fare,
Shouts greeting from his easy chair;
High on a bank our leader stands,
Reviews and ranks his motley bands;
Makes clear our goal to every eye,
The valley's western boundary.
A gate swings to: our tide hath flow'd
Already from the silent road.
The valley pastures, one by one,
Are threaded, quiet in the sun:
And now beyond the rude stone bridge
Slopes gracious up the western ridge.
Its woody border, and the last
Of its dark upland farms is past:
Lone farms, with open-lying stores,
Under their burnish'd sycamores.

The Strayed Reveller

All past : and through the trees we glide
Emerging on the green hill-side.
There climbing hangs, a far-seen sign,
Our wavering, many-colour'd line ;
There winds, upstreaming slowly still
Over the summit of the hill.
And now, in front, behold outspread
Those upper regions we must tread ;
Mild hollows, and clear heathy swells,
The cheerful silence of the fells.
Some two hours' march, with serious air,
Through the deep noontide heats we fare :
The red-grouse, springing at our sound,
Skims, now and then, the shining ground ;
No life, save his and ours, intrudes
Upon these breathless solitudes.
O joy ! again the farms appear ;
Cool shade is there, and rustic cheer :
There springs the brook will guide us down,
Bright comrade, to the noisy town.
Lingering, we follow down : we gain
The town, the highway, and the plain.
And many a mile of dusty way,
Parch'd and road-worn, we made that day ;
But, Fausta, I remember well
That, as the balmy darkness fell,
We bath'd our hands, with speechless glee,
That night, in the wide-glimmering Sea.

Once more we tread this self-same road,
Fausta, which ten years since we trod :

and Other Poems.

Alone we tread it, you and I ;
Ghosts of that boisterous company.
Here, where the brook shines, near its head,
In its clear, shallow, turf-fring'd bed ;
Here, whence the eye first sees, far down,
Capp'd with faint smoke, the noisy town ;
Here sit we, and again unroll,
Though slowly, the familiar whole.
The solemn wastes of heathy hill
Sleep in the July sunshine still :
The self-same shadows now, as then,
Play through this grassy upland glen :
The loose dark stones on the green way
Lie strewn, it seems, where then they lay :
On this mild bank above the stream,
(You crush them) the blue gentians gleam.
Still this wild brook, the rushes cool,
The sailing foam, the shining pool.—
These are not chang'd : and we, you say,
Are scarce more chang'd, in truth, than they.

The Gipsies, whom we met below,
They too have long roam'd to and fro.
They ramble, leaving, where they pass,
Their fragments on the cumber'd grass.
And often to some kindly place,
Chance guides the migratory race
Where, though long wanderings intervene,
They recognise a former scene.
The dingy tents are pitch'd : the fires
Give to the wind their wavering spires ;

The Strayed Reveller

In dark knots crouch round the wild flame
Their children, as when first they came ;
They see their shackled beasts again
Move, browsing, up the grey-wall'd lane.
Signs are not wanting, which might raise
The ghosts in them of former days :
Signs are not wanting, if they would ;
Suggestions to disquietude.
For them, for all, Time's busy touch,
While it mends little, troubles much :
Their joints grow stiffer ; but the year
Runs his old round of dubious cheer :
Chilly they grow ; yet winds in March,
Still, sharp as ever, freeze and parch :
They must live still ; and yet, God knows,
Crowded and keen the country grows .
It seems as if, in their decay,
The Law grew stronger every day.
So might they reason ; so compare,
Fausta, times past with times that are.
But no :—they rubb'd through yesterday
In their hereditary way ;
And they will rub through, if they can,
To-morrow on the self-same plan ;
Till death arrives to supersede,
For them, vicissitude and need.

The Poet, to whose mighty heart
Heaven doth a quicker pulse impart,
Subdues that energy to scan
Not his own course, but that of Man.

Though he move mountains ; though his day
Be pass'd on the proud heights of sway ;
Though he hath loos'd a thousand chains ;
Though he hath borne immortal pains ;
Action and suffering though he know ;
—He hath not liv'd, if he lives so.
He sees, in some great-historied land,
A ruler of the people stand ;
Sees his strong thought in fiery flood
Roll through the heaving multitude ;
Exults : yet for no moment's space
Envies the all-regarded place.
Beautiful eyes meet his ; and he
Bears to admire uncravingly :
They pass ; he, mingled with the crowd,
Is in their far-off triumphs proud.
From some high station he looks down,
At sunset, on a populous town ;
Surveys each happy group that fleets,
Toil ended, through the shining streets ;
Each with some errand of its own ;—
And does not say, " I am alone."
He sees the gentle stir of birth
When Morning purifies the earth ;
. He leans upon a gate, and sees
The pastures, and the quiet trees.
Low woody hill, with gracious bound,
Folds the still valley almost round ;
The cuckoo, loud on some high lawn,
Is answer'd from the depth of dawn ;
In the hedge straggling to the stream,
Pale, dew-drench'd, half-shut roses gleam :

The Strayed Reveller

But where the further side slopes down
He sees the drowsy new-wak'd clown
In his white quaint-embroider'd frock
Make, whistling, towards his mist-wreath'd flock ;
Slowly, behind the heavy tread,
The wet flower'd grass heaves up its head.—
Lean'd on his gate, he gazes : tears
Are in his eyes, and in his ears
The murmur of a thousand years :
Before him he sees Life unroll,
A placid and continuous whole ;
That general Life, which does not cease,
Whose secret is not joy, but peace ;
That Life, whose dumb wish is not miss'd
If birth proceeds, if things subsist :
The Life of plants, and stones, and rain :
The Life he craves ; if not in vain
Fate gave, what Chance shall not controul,
His sad lucidity of soul.

You listen :—but that wandering smile,
Fausta, betrays you cold the while.
Your eyes pursue the bells of foam
Wash'd, eddying, from this bank, their home.
"Those Gipsies," so your thoughts I scan,
" Are less, the Poet more, than man.
They feel not, though they move and see :
Deeply the Poet feels ; but he
Breathes, when he will, immortal air,
Where Orpheus and where Homer are.
In the day's life, whose iron round
Hems us all in, he is not bound.

and Other Poems.

He escapes thence, but we abide.
Not deep the Poet sees, but wide."

The World in which we live and move
Outlasts aversion, outlasts love.
Outlasts each effort, interest, hope,
Remorse, grief, joy :—and were the scope
Of these affections wider made,
Man still would see, and see dismay'd,
Beyond his passion's widest range
Far regions of eternal change.
Nay, and since death, which wipes out man,
Finds him with many an unsolv'd plan,
With much unknown, and much untried,
Wonder not dead, and thirst not dried,
Still gazing on the ever full
Eternal mundane spectacle ;
This World in which we draw our breath,
In some sense, Fausta, outlasts death.

Blame thou not therefore him, who dares
Judge vain beforehand human cares.
Whose natural insight can discern
What through experience others learn.
Who needs not love and power, to know
Love transient, power an unreal show.
Who treads at ease life's uncheer'd ways :—
Him blame not, Fausta, rather praise.
Rather thyself for some aim pray
Nobler than this—to fill the day.
Rather, that heart, which burns in thee,
Ask, not to amuse, but to set free.

The Strayed Reveller

Be passionate hopes not ill resign'd
For quiet, and a fearless mind.
And though Fate grudge to thee and me
The Poet's rapt security,
Yet they, believe me, who await
No gifts from Chance, have conquer'd Fate.
They, winning room to see and hear,
And to men's business not too near,
Through clouds of individual strife
Draw homewards to the general Life.
Like leaves by suns not yet uncurl'd :
To the wise, foolish ; to the world,
Weak : yet not weak, I might reply,
Not foolish, Fausta, in His eye,
Each moment as it flies, to whom,
Crowd as we will its neutral room,
Is but a quiet watershed
Whence, equally, the Seas of Life and Death are fed.

Enough, we live :—and if a life,
With large results so little rife,
Though bearable, seem hardly worth
This pomp of worlds, this pain of birth ;
Yet, Fausta, the mute turf we tread,
The solemn hills around us spread,
This stream that falls incessantly,
The strange-scrawl'd rocks, the lonely sky,
If I might lend their life a voice,
Seem to bear rather than rejoice.
And even could the intemperate prayer
Man iterates, while these forbear,

For movement, for an ampler sphere,
Pierce Fate's impenetrable ear ;
Not milder is the general lot
Because our spirits have forgot,
In action's dizzying eddy whirl'd,
The something that infects the world.

.   .

SONNET TO THE HUNGARIAN NATION.

"Examiner," July 21st, 1849.[1]

NOT in sunk Spain's prolong'd death agony;
Not in rich England, bent but to make pour
The flood of the world's commerce on her shore;
Not in that madhouse, France, from whence the cry
Afflicts grave Heaven with its long senseless roar;
Not in American vulgarity,
Nor wordy German imbecility—
Lies any hope of heroism more.
Hungarians! Save the world! Renew the stories
Of men who against hope repell'd the chain,
And make the world's dead spirit leap again!
On land renew that Greek exploit, whose glories
Hallow the Salaminian promontories,
And the Armada flung to the fierce main.

[1] Discovered by a reference in "Letters of Matthew Arnold, 1848-1888." Collected and arranged by George W. E. Russell. Macmillan, 1895. Vol. I., page 11.

EMPEDOCLES ON ETNA

AND

OTHER POEMS

By A.

BIBLIOGRAPHICAL NOTE.

Empedocles on Etna and Other Poems. By A. London: B. Fellowes, Ludgate Street, 1852. Two poems in this volume—"Destiny" and "Courage"—have not been reprinted.

Σοφώτατον, χρόνος· ἀνευρίσκει γὰρ πάντα.

CONTENTS.

Contents.

EMPEDOCLES ON ETNA.

A Dramatic Poem.

PERSONS.

EMPEDOCLES.

PAUSANIAS, *a Physician*.

CALLICLES, *a young Harp-player*.

The Scene of the Poem is on Mount Etna; at first in the forest region, afterwards on the summit of the mountain.

Empedocles on Etna.

FIRST ACT: FIRST SCENE.

A Pass in the forest region of Etna. Morning.
CALLICLES, *alone, resting on a rock by the path.*

CALLICLES.

THE mules, I think, will not be here this hour.
    They feel the cool wet turf under their feet
By the stream side, after the dusty lanes
In which they have toil'd all night from Catana,
And scarcely will they budge a yard.   O Pan !
How gracious is the mountain at this hour !
A thousand times have I been here alone
Or with the revellers from the mountain towns,
But never on so fair a morn :—the sun
Is shining on the brilliant mountain crests,
And on the highest pines : but further down
Here in the valley is in shade ; the sward
Is dark, and on the stream the mist still hangs :
One sees one's foot-prints crush'd in the wet grass,
One's breath curls in the air ; and on these pines
That climb from the stream's edge, the long grey tufts,
Which the goats love, are jewell'd thick with dew.
Here will I stay till the slow litter comes.

113

Empedocles on Etna.

I have my harp too—that is well.—Apollo!
What mortal could be sick or sorry here?
I know not in what mind Empedocles,
Whose mules I follow'd, may be coming up,
But if, as most men say, he is half mad
With exile, and with brooding on his wrongs,
Pausanias, his sage friend, who mounts with him,
Could scarce have lighted on a lovelier cure.
The mules must be below, far down: I hear
Their tinkling bells, mix'd with the song of birds,
Rise faintly to me—now it stops!—Who's here?
Pausanias! and on foot? alone?

PAUSANIAS.

And thou, then?

I left thee supping with Pisianax,
With thy head full of wine, and thy hair crown'd,
Touching thy harp as the whim came on thee,
And prais'd and spoil'd by master and by guests
Almost as much as the new dancing girl.
Why hast thou follow'd us?

CALLICLES.

The night was hot,

And the feast past its prime: so we slipp'd out,
Some of us, to the portico to breathe:
Pisianax, thou know'st, drinks late: and then,
As I was lifting my soil'd garland off,
I saw the mules and litter in the court,
And in the litter sate Empedocles;
Thou, too, wert with him. Straightway I sped home;
I saddled my white mule, and all night long

Empedocles on Etna.

Through the cool lovely country follow'd you,
Pass'd you a little since as morning dawn'd,
And have this hour sate by the torrent here,
Till the slow mules should climb in sight again.
And now?

PAUSANIAS.

And now, back to the town with speed.
Crouch in the wood first, till the mules have pass'd:
They do but halt, they will be here anon.
Thou must be viewless to Empedocles;
Save mine, he must not meet a human eye.
One of his moods is on him that thou know'st:
I think, thou would'st not vex him.

CALLICLES.

No—and yet
I would fain stay and help thee tend him: once
He knew me well, and would oft notice me.
And still, I know not how, he draws me to him,
And I could watch him with his proud sad face,
His flowing locks and gold-encircled brow
And kingly gait, for ever: such a spell
In his severe looks, such a majesty
As drew of old the people after him,
In Agrigentum and Olympia,
When his star reign'd, before his banishment,
Is potent still on me in his decline.
But oh, Pausanias, he is chang'd of late:
There is a settled trouble in his air
Admits no momentary brightening now;
And when he comes among his friends at feasts,

Empedocles on Etna.

'Tis as an orphan among prosperous boys.
Thou know'st of old he loved this harp of mine,
When first he sojourn'd with Pisianax:
He is now always moody, and I fear him;
But I would serve him, soothe him, if I could,
Dar'd one but try.

PAUSANIAS.

Thou wert a kind child ever.
He loves thee, but he must not see thee now.
Thou hast indeed a rare touch on thy harp,
He loves that in thee too: there was a time
(But that is pass'd) he would have paid thy strain
With music to have drawn the stars from heaven.
He has his harp and laurel with him still,
But he has laid the use of music by,
And all which might relax his settled gloom.
Yet thou mayst try thy playing if thou wilt,
But thou must keep unseen: follow us on,
But at a distance; in these solitudes,
In this clear mountain air, a voice will rise,
Though from afar, distinctly: it may soothe him.
Play when we halt, and when the evening comes,
And I must leave him, (for his pleasure is
To be left musing these soft nights alone
In the high unfrequented mountain spots,)
Then watch him, for he ranges swift and far,
Sometimes to Etna's top, and to the cone;
But hide thee in the rocks a great way down,
And try thy noblest strains, my Callicles,
With the sweet night to help thy harmony.
Thou wilt earn my thanks sure, and perhaps his.

Empedocles on Etna.

CALLICLES.

More than a day and night, Pausanias,
Of this fair summer weather, on these hills,
Would I bestow to help Empedocles.
That needs no thanks : one is far better here
Than in the broiling city in these heats.
But tell me, how hast thou persuaded him
In this his present fierce, man-hating mood
To bring thee out with him alone on Etna?

PAUSANIAS.

Thou hast heard all men speaking of Panthea,
The woman who at Agrigentum lay
Thirty long days in a cold trance of death,
And whom Empedocles call'd back to life.
Thou art too young to note it, but his power
Swells with the swelling evil of this time,
And holds men mute to see where it will rise.
He could stay swift diseases in old days,
Chain madmen by the music of his lyre,
Cleanse to sweet airs the breath of poisonous streams,
And in the mountain chinks inter the winds.
This he could do of old, but now, since all
Clouds and grows daily worse in Sicily,
Since broils tear us in twain, since this new swarm
Of Sophists has got empire in our schools,
Where he was paramount, since he is banish'd,
And lives a lonely man in triple gloom,
He grasps the very reins of life and death.
I ask'd him of Panthea yesterday,
When we were gather'd with Pisianax,
And he made answer, I should come at night

Empedocles on Etna.

On Etna here, and be alone with him,
And he would tell me, as his old, tried friend,
Who still was faithful, what might profit me;
That is, the secret of this miracle.

CALLICLES.

Bah! Thou a doctor? Thou art superstitious.
Simple Pausanias, 'twas no miracle,
Panthea, for I know her kinsmen well,
Was subject to these trances from a girl.
Empedocles would say so, did he deign:
But he still lets the people, whom he scorns,
Gape and cry wizard at him, if they list.
But thou, thou art no company for him,
Thou art as cross, as sour'd as himself.
Thou hast some wrong from thine own citizens,
And then thy friend is banish'd, and on that
Straightway thou fallest to arraign the times,
As if the sky was impious not to fall.
The Sophists are no enemies of his;
I hear, Gorgias, their chief, speaks nobly of him,
As of his gifted master and once friend.
He is too scornful, too high-wrought, too bitter.
'Tis not the times, 'tis not the Sophists vex him:
There is some root of suffering in himself,
Some secret and unfollow'd vein of woe,
Which makes the times look black and sad to him.
Pester him not in this his sombre mood
With questionings about an idle tale,
But lead him through the lovely mountain paths,
And keep his mind from preying on itself,
And talk to him of things at hand, and common,

Empedocles on Etna.

Not miracles : thou art a learned man,
But credulous of fables as a girl.

PAUSANIAS.

And thou, a boy whose tongue outruns his knowledge,
And on whose lightness blame is thrown away.
Enough of this : I see the litter wind
Up by the torrent side, under the pines.
I must rejoin Empedocles.   Do thou
Crouch in the brush-wood till the mules have pass'd,
Then play thy kind part well.   Farewell till night.

SCENE SECOND.

*Noon.   A Glen on the highest skirts of the woody
regions of Etna.*

EMPEDOCLES.   PAUSANIAS.

PAUSANIAS.

The noon is hot : when we have cross'd the stream
We shall have left the woody tract, and come
Upon the open shoulder of the hill.
See how the giant spires of yellow bloom
Of the sun-loving gentian, in the heat,
Are shining on those naked slopes like flame.
Let us rest here : and now, Empedocles,
Panthea's history.

[*A harp note below is heard.*

Empedocles on Etna.

EMPEDOCLES.

Hark! what sound was that

Rose from below? If it were possible,
And we were not so far from human haunt,
I should have said that someone touch'd a harp.
Hark! there again!

PAUSANIAS.

'Tis the boy Callicles,

The sweetest harp player in Catana.
He is for ever coming on these hills,
In summer, to all country festivals,
With a gay revelling band: he breaks from them
Sometimes, and wanders far among the glens.
But heed him not, he will not mount to us;
I spoke with him this morning. Once more, therefore,
Instruct me of Panthea's story, Master,
As I have prayed thee.

EMPEDOCLES.

That? and to what end?

PAUSANIAS.

It is enough that all men speak of it.
But I will also say, that, when the Gods
Visit us as they do with sign and plague,
To know those spells of time that stay their hand
Were to live free'd from terror.

EMPEDOCLES.

Spells? Mistrust them.

Mind is the spell which governs earth and heaven.

Empedocles on Etna.

Man has a mind with which to plan his safety.
Know that, and help thyself.

PAUSANIAS.

But thy own words?
" The wit and counsel of man was never clear,
Troubles confuse the little wit he has."
Mind is a light which the Gods mock us with,
To lead those false who trust it.

[*The harp sounds again.*

EMPEDOCLES.

Hist ! once more !
Listen, Pausanias !—Ay, 'tis Callicles :
I know those notes among a thousand.   Hark !

CALLICLES *sings unseen, from below.*

The track winds down to the clear stream,
To cross the sparkling shallows : there
The cattle love to gather, on their way
To the high mountain pastures, and to stay,
Till the rough cow-herds drive them past,
Knee-deep in the cool ford : for 'tis the last
Of all the woody, high, well-water'd dells
Of Etna ; and the beam
Of noon is broken there by chestnut boughs
Down its steep verdant sides : the air
Is freshen'd by the leaping stream, which throws
Eternal showers of spray on the moss'd roots
Of trees, and veins of turf, and long dark shoots
Of ivy-plants, and fragrant hanging bells
Of hyacinths, and on late anemones,

Empedocles on Etna.

That muffle its wet banks : but glade,
And stream, and sward, and chestnut trees,
End here : Etna beyond, in the broad glare
Of the hot noon, without a shade,
Slope behind slope, up to the peak, lies bare ;
The peak, round which the white clouds play.

In such a glen, on such a day,
On Pelion, on the grassy ground,
Chiron, the aged Centaur, lay ;
The young Achilles standing by.
The Centaur taught him to explore
The mountains : where the glens are dry,
And the tir'd Centaurs come to rest,
And where the soaking springs abound,
And the straight ashes grow for spears,
And where the hill-goats come to feed,
And the sea-eagles build their nest.
He show'd him Phthia far away,
And said—O Boy, I taught this lore
To Peleus, in long distant years.—
He told him of the Gods, the stars,
The tides :—and then of mortal wars,
And of the life that Heroes lead
Before they reach the Elysian place
And rest in the immortal mead :
And all the wisdom of his race.

[*The music below ceases, and* Empedocles
*speaks, accompanying himself in a solemn
manner on his harp.*

Empedocles on Etna.

The howling void to span
A cord the Gods first slung,
And then the Soul of Man
There, like a mirror, hung,
And bade the winds through space impel the gusty toy.

Hither and thither spins
The wind-borne mirroring Soul :
A thousand glimpses wins,
And never sees a whole :
Looks once, and drives elsewhere, and leaves its last
    employ.

The Gods laugh in their sleeve
To watch man doubt and fear,
Who knows not what to believe
Where he sees nothing clear,
And dares stamp nothing false where he finds nothing
    sure.

Is this, Pausanias, so ?
And can our souls not strive,
But with the winds must go
And hurry where they drive ?
Is Fate indeed so strong, man's strength indeed so poor?

I will not judge : that man,
Howbeit, I judge as lost,
Whose mind allows a plan
Which would degrade it most :
And he treats doubt the best who tries to see least ill.

Empedocles on Etna.

Be not then, Fear's blind slave.
Thou art my friend ; to thee,
All knowledge that I have,
All skill I wield, are free.
Ask not the latest news of the last miracle ;

Ask not what days and nights
In trance Panthea lay,
But ask thou how such sights
May'st see without dismay.
Ask what most helps when known, thou son of Anchitus.

What ? hate, and awe, and shame
Fill thee to see our day ;
Thou feelest thy Soul's frame
Shaken and in dismay :
What ? life and time go hard with thee too, as with us ;

Thy citizens, 'tis said,
Envy thee and oppress,
Thy goodness no men aid,
All strive to make it less :
Tyranny, pride, and lust fill Sicily's abodes :

Heaven is with earth at strife,
Signs make thy soul afraid,
The dead return to life,
Rivers are dried, winds stay'd :
Scarce can one think in calm, so threatening are the
        Gods :

Empedocles on Etna.

And we feel, day and night,
The burden of ourselves?—
Well, then, the wiser wight
In his own bosom delves,
And asks what ails him so, and gets what cure he can.

The Sophist sneers—Fool, take
Thy pleasure, right or wrong.—
The pious wail—Forsake
A world these Sophists throng.—
Be neither Saint nor Sophist led, but be a man.

These hundred doctors try
To preach thee to their school.
We have the truth, they cry.
And yet their oracle,
Trumpet it as they will, is but the same as thine.

Once read thy own breast right,
And thou hast done with fears.
Man gets no other light,
Search he a thousand years.
Sink in thyself: there ask what ails thee, at that shrine.

What makes thee struggle and rave?
Why are men ill at ease?
'Tis that the lot they have
Fails their own will to please.
For man would make no murmuring, were his will
    obey'd.

Empedocles on Etna.

And why is it that still
Man with his lot thus fights?
'Tis that he makes this *will*
The measure of his *rights*,
And believes Nature outrag'd if his will's gainsaid.

Couldst thou, Pausanias, learn
How deep a fault is this;
Couldst thou but once discern
Thou hast no *right* to bliss,
No title from the Gods to welfare and repose;

Then, thou wouldst look less maz'd
Whene'er from bliss debarr'd,
Nor think the Gods were craz'd
When thy own lot went hard.
But we are all the same—the fools of our own woes.

For, from the first faint morn
Of life, the thirst for bliss
Deep in Man's heart is born,
And, sceptic as he is,
He fails not to judge clear if this is quench'd or no.

Nor is that thirst to blame.
Man errs not that he deems
His welfare his true aim.
He errs because he dreams
The world does but exist that welfare to bestow.

We mortals are no kings
For each of whom to sway

Empedocles on Etna.

A new-made world up-springs
Meant merely for his play.
No, we are strangers here : the world is from of old.

In vain our pent wills fret
And would the world subdue,
Limits we did not set
Condition all we do.
Born into life we are, and life must be our mould.

Born into life : who lists
May what is false maintain,
And for himself make mists
Through which to see less plain :
The world is what it is, for all our dust and din.

Born into life : in vain,
Opinions, those or these,
Unalter'd to retain
The obstinate mind decrees.
Experience, like a sea, soaks all-effacing in.

Born into life : 'tis we,
And not the world, are new.
Our cry for bliss, our plea,
Others have urg'd it too.
Our wants have all been felt, our errors made before.

No eye could be too sound
To observe a world so vast :
No patience too profound

Empedocles on Etna.

To sort what's here amass'd.
How man may here best live no care too great to
    explore.

    But we,—as some rude guest
    Would change, where'er he roam,
    The manners there profess'd
    To those he brings from home ;—
We mark not the world's ways, but would have *it*
    learn *ours.*

    The world proclaims the terms
    On which man wins content.
    Reason its voice confirms.
    We spurn them : and invent
False weakness in the world, and in ourselves false
    powers.

    Riches we wish to get,
    Yet remain spendthrifts still ;
    We would have health, and yet
    Still use our bodies ill :
Bafflers of our own prayers from youth to life's last scenes

    We would have inward peace,
    Yet will not look within :
    We would have misery cease,
    Yet will not cease from sin :
We want all pleasant ends, but will use no harsh means ;

    We do not what we ought ;
    What we ought not, we do ;

Empedocles on Etna.

And lean upon the thought
That Chance will bring us through.
But our own acts, for good or ill, are mightier powers.

Yet, even when man forsakes
All sin,—is just, is pure ;
Abandons all that makes
His welfare insecure ;
Other existences there are, which clash with ours.

Like us the lightning fires
Love to have scope and play.
The stream, like us, desires
An unimpeded way.
Like us, the Libyan wind delights to roam at large.

Streams will not curb their pride
The just man not to entomb,
Nor lightnings go aside
To leave his virtues room,
Nor is the wind less rough that blows a good man's
     barge.

Nature, with equal mind,
Sees all her sons at play,
Sees man control the wind,
The wind sweep man away ;
Allows the proudly-riding and the founder'd bark.

And, lastly, though of ours
No weakness spoil our lot ;
Though the non-human powers

Empedocles on Etna.

Of Nature harm us not ;
The ill-deeds of other men make often *our* life dark.

What were the wise man's plan ?
Through this sharp, toil-set life
To fight as best he can,
And win what's won by strife ;
But we an easier way to cheat our pains have found.

Scratch'd by a fall, with moans,
As children of weak age
Lend life to the dumb stones
Whereon to vent their rage,
And bend their little fists, and rate the senseless
ground ;

So, loath to suffer mute,
We, peopling the void air,
Make Gods to whom to impute
The ills we ought to bear ;
With God and Fate to rail at, suffering easily.

Yet grant—as Sense long miss'd
Things that are now perceiv'd,
And much may still exist
Which is not yet believ'd—
Grant that the world were full of Gods we cannot see—

All things the world that fill
Of but one stuff are spun,
That we who rail are still
With what we rail at one :

Empedocles on Etna.

One with the o'er-labour'd Power that through the breadth and length

    Of Earth, and Air, and Sea,
    In men, and plants, and stones,
    Has toil perpetually,
    And struggles, pants, and moans;
Fain would do all things well, but sometimes fails in strength.

    And, punctually exact,
    This universal God
    Alike to any act
    Proceeds at any nod,
And patiently declaims the cursings of himself.

    This is not what Man hates,
    Yet he can curse but this.
    Harsh Gods and hostile Fates
    Are dreams: this only *is*:
Is everywhere: sustains the wise, the foolish elf.

    Nor only, in the intent
    To attach blame elsewhere,
    Do we at will invent
    Stern Powers who make their care
To embitter human life, malignant Deities;

    But, next, we would reverse
    The scheme ourselves have spun,
    And what we made to curse
    We now would lean upon,

Empedocles on Etna.

And feign kind Gods who perfect what man vainly
    tries.

    Look, the world tempts our eye,
    And we would know it all.
    We map the starry sky,
    We mind this earthen ball,
We measure the sea-tides, we number the sea-sands :

    We scrutinize the dates
    Of long-past human things,
    The bounds of effac'd states,
    The lines of deceas'd kings :
We search out dead men's words, and works of dead
    men's hands :

    We shut our eyes, and muse
    How our own minds are made ;
    What springs of thought they use,
    How righten'd, how betray'd ;
And spend our wit to name what most employ un-
    nam'd :

    But still, as we proceed,
    The mass swells more and more
    Of volumes yet to read,
    Of secrets yet to explore.
Our hair grows grey, our eyes are dimm'd, our heat is
    tam'd—

    We rest our faculties,
    And thus address the Gods :—

Empedocles on Etna.

"True Science if there is,
It stays in your abodes.
Man's measures cannot span the illimitable All:

"You only can take in
The world's immense design.
Our desperate search was sin,
Which henceforth we resign:
Sure only that *your* mind sees all things which befall."

Fools! that in man's brief term
He cannot all things view,
Affords no ground to affirm
That there are Gods who do:
Nor does being weary prove that he has where to rest.

Again: our youthful blood
Claims rapture as its right.
The world, a rolling flood
Of newness and delight,
Draws in the enamour'd gazer to its shining breast;

Pleasure to our hot grasp
Gives flowers after flowers;
With passionate warmth we clasp
Hand after hand in ours:
Nor do we soon perceive how fast our youth is spent.

At once our eyes grow clear:
We see in blank dismay

Empedocles on Etna.

Year posting after year,
Sense after sense decay;
Our shivering heart is min'd by secret discontent:

Yet still, in spite of truth,
In spite of hopes entomb'd
That longing of our youth
Burns ever unconsum'd:
Still hungrier for delight, as delights grow more rare.

We pause; we hush our heart,
And then address the Gods :—
"The world hath fail'd to impart
The joy our youth forbodes,
Fail'd to fill up the void which in our breasts we bear.

"Changeful till now, we still
Look'd on to something new :
Let us, with changeless will,
Henceforth look on to you ;
To find with you the joy we in vain *here* require."

Fools ! that so often here
Happiness mock'd our prayer,
I think, might make us fear
A like event elsewhere :
Make us not fly to dreams, but moderate desire.

And yet, for those who know
Themselves, who wisely take

Empedocles on Etna.

Their way through life, and bow
To what they cannot break,—
Why should I say that life need yield but *moderate*
    bliss?

Shall we, with tempers spoil'd,
Health sapp'd by living ill,
And judgments all embroil'd
By sadness and self-will,
Shall we judge what for man is not high bliss or is?

Is it so small a thing
To have enjoy'd the sun,
To have liv'd light in the spring,
To have lov'd, to have thought, to have done;
To have advanc'd true friends, and beat down baffling
    foes;

That we must feign a bliss
Of doubtful future date,
And while we dream on this
Lose all our present state,
And relegate to worlds yet distant our repose?

Not much, I know, you prize
What pleasures may be had,
Who look on life with eyes
Estrang'd, like mine, and sad:
And yet the village churl feels the truth more than you.

Who's loth to leave this life
Which to him little yields:

Empedocles on Etna.

His hard-task'd sunburnt wife,
His often-labour'd fields;
The boors with whom he talk'd, the country spots he
    knew.

But thou, because thou hear'st
Men scoff at Heaven and Fate;
Because the Gods thou fear'st
Fail to make blest thy state,
Tremblest, and wilt not dare to trust the joys there are.

I say, Fear not! life still
Leaves human effort scope.
But, since life teems with ill,
Nurse no extravagant hope.
Because thou must not dream, thou need'st not then
    despair.

Far, far from here,
The Adriatic breaks in a warm bay
Among the green Illyrian hills; and there
The sunshine in the happy glens is fair,
And by the sea, and in the brakes.
The grass is cool, the sea-side air
Buoyant and fresh, the mountain flowers
As virginal and sweet as ours.
And there, they say, two bright and aged snakes,
Who once were Cadmus and Harmonia,

Empedocles on Etna.

Bask in the glens or on the warm sea-shore,
In breathless quiet, after all their ills.
Nor do they see their country, nor the place
Where the Sphinx liv'd among the frowning hills,
Nor the unhappy palace of their race,
Nor Thebes, nor the Ismenus, any more.

There those two live, far in the Illyrian brakes.
They had staid long enough to see,
In Thebes, the billow of calamity
Over their own dear children roll'd,
Curse upon curse, pang upon pang,
For years, they sitting helpless in their home,
A grey old man and woman : yet of old
The gods had to their marriage come,
And at the banquet all the Muses sang.

Therefore they did not end their days
In sight of blood ; but were rapt, far away,
To where the west wind plays,
And murmurs of the Adriatic come
To those untrodden mountain lawns : and there
Placed safely in chang'd forms, the Pair
Wholly forget their first sad life, and home,
And all that Theban woe, and stray
For ever through the glens, placid and dumb.

Empedocles.

That was my harp-player again—where is he?
Down by the stream?

Pausanias.

Yes, Master, in the wood.

Empedocles on Etna.

EMPEDOCLES.

He ever lov'd the Theban story well.
But the day wears.   Go now, Pausanias,
For I must be alone.   Leave me one mule;
Take down with thee the rest to Catana.
And for young Callicles, thank him from me;
Tell him I never fail'd to love his lyre:
But he must follow me no more to-night.

PAUSANIAS.

Thou wilt return to-morrow to the city?

EMPEDOCLES.

Either to-morrow or some other day,
In the sure revolutions of the world,
Good friend, I shall revisit Catana.
I have seen many cities in my time
Till my eyes ache with the long spectacle,
And I shall doubtless see them all again:
Thou know'st me for a wanderer from of old.
Meanwhile, stay me not now.   Farewell, Pausanias!
　　　　[He departs on his way up the mountain.

PAUSANIAS (*alone*).

I dare not urge him further; he must go:
But he is strangely wrought;—I will speed back
And bring Pisianax to him from the city:
His counsel could once soothe him.   But, Apollo!
How his brow lighten'd as the music rose!
Callicles must wait here, and play to him:
I saw him through the chestnuts far below,
Just since, down at the stream.—Ho! Callicles!
　　　　[He descends, calling.

Empedocles on Etna.

ACT SECOND.

Evening.   The Summit of Etna.

EMPEDOCLES.

Alone—
On this charr'd, blacken'd, melancholy waste,
Crown'd by the awful peak, Etna's great mouth,
Round which the sullen vapour rolls—alone.
Pausanias is far hence, and that is well,
For I must henceforth speak no more with man.
He has his lesson too, and that debt's paid:
And the good, learned, friendly, quiet man,
May bravelier front his life, and in himself
Find henceforth energy and heart:—but I,
The weary man, the banish'd citizen,
Whose banishment is not his greatest ill,
Whose weariness no energy can reach,
And for whose hurt courage is not the cure—
What should I do with life and living more?

No, thou art come too late, Empedocles!
And the world hath the day, and must break thee,
Not thou the world.   With men thou canst not live;
Their thoughts, their ways, their wishes, are not thine:
And being lonely thou art miserable,
For something has impair'd thy spirit's strength,
And dried its self-sufficing fount of joy.

Empedocles on Etna.

Thou canst not live with men nor with thyself—
Oh sage ! oh sage !—Take then the one way left,
And turn thee to the Elements, thy friends,
Thy well-tried friends, thy willing ministers,
And say,—Ye servants, hear Empedocles,
Who asks this final service at your hands.
Before the Sophist brood hath overlaid
The last spark of man's consciousness with words—
Ere quite the being of man, ere quite the world
Be disarray'd of their divinity—
Before the soul lose all her solemn joys,
And awe be dead, and hope impossible,
And the soul's deep eternal night come on,
Receive me, hide me, quench me, take me home !

      [*He advances to the edge of the crater. Smoke
        and fire break forth with a loud noise,
        and* CALLICLES *is heard below, singing* :—

The lyre's voice is lovely everywhere.
In the courts of Gods, in the city of men,
And in the lonely rock-strewn mountain glen,
In the still mountain air.

Only to Typho, it sounds hatefully,
Only to Typho, the rebel o'erthrown,
Through whose heart Etna drives her roots of stone,
To imbed them in the sea.

Wherefore dost thou groan so loud ?
Wherefore do thy nostrils flash,
Through the dark night, suddenly,
Typho, such red jets of flame ?

Empedocles on Etna.

Is thy tortur'd heart still proud?
Is thy fire-scath'd arm still rash?
Still alert thy stone-crush'd frame?
Does thy fierce soul still deplore
Thy ancient rout by the Cilician hills,
And that curst treachery on the Mount of Gore?
Do thy bloodshot eyes still see
The fight that crown'd thy ills,
Thy last defeat in this Sicilian sea?
Hast thou sworn, in thy sad lair,
Where erst the strong sea-currents suck'd thee down,
Never to cease to writhe, and try to sleep
Letting the sea-stream wander through thy hair?
That thy groans, like thunder deep,
Begin to roll, and almost drown
The sweet notes, whose lulling spell
Gods and the race of mortals love so well,
When through thy caves thou hearest music swell?

But an awful pleasure bland
Spreading o'er the Thunderer's face,
When the sound climbs near his seat,
The Olympian Council sees;
As he lets his lax right hand,
Which the lightnings doth embrace,
Sink upon his mighty knees.
And the eagle, at the beck
Of the appeasing gracious harmony,
Droops all his sheeny, brown, deep-feather'd neck,
Nestling nearer to Jove's feet:
While o'er his sovereign eye
The curtains of the blue films slowly meet,

Empedocles on Etna.

And the white Olympus peaks
Rosily brighten, and the sooth'd Gods smile
At one another from their golden chairs;
And no one round the charmed circle speaks.
Only the lov'd Hebe bears
The cup about, whose draughts beguile
Pain and care, with a dark store
Of fresh-pull'd violets wreath'd and nodding o'er;
And her flush'd feet glow on the marble floor.

EMPEDOCLES.

He fables, yet speaks truth.
The brave impetuous hand yields everywhere
To the subtle, contriving head.
Great qualities are trodden down,
And littleness united
Is become invincible.

These rumblings are not Typho's groans, I know.
These angry smoke-bursts
Are not the passionate breath
Of the mountain-crush'd, tortur'd, intractable Titan king.
But over all the world
What suffering is there not seen
Of plainness oppress'd by cunning,
As the well-counsell'd Zeus oppress'd
The self-helping son of Earth?
What anguish of greatness
Rail'd and hunted from the world
Because its simplicity rebukes
This envious, miserable age!

Empedocles on Etna.

I am weary of it !
Lie there, ye ensigns
Of my unloved pre-eminence
In an age like this !
Among a people of children,
Who throng'd me in their cities,
Who worshipp'd me in their houses,
And ask'd, not wisdom,
But drugs to charm with,
But spells to mutter—
All the fool's armoury of magic—Lie there,
My golden circlet !
My purple robe !

CALLICLES (*from below*).
As the sky-brightening south wind clears the day,
And makes the mass'd clouds roll,
The music of the lyre blows away
The clouds that wrap the soul.

Oh, that Fate had let me see
That triumph of the sweet persuasive lyre,
That famous, final victory
When jealous Pan with Marsyas did conspire ;

When, from far Parnassus' side,
Young Apollo, all the pride
Of the Phrygian flutes to tame,
To the Phrygian highlands came.
Where the long green reed-beds sway
In the rippled waters grey

Empedocles on Etna.

Of that solitary lake
Where Mæander's springs are born.
Where the ridg'd pine-darken'd roots
Of Messogis westward, break,
Mounting westward, high and higher.
There was held the famous strife ;
There the Phrygian brought his flutes,
And Apollo brought his lyre,
And, when now the westering sun
Touch'd the hills, the strife was done,
And the attentive Muses said,
Marsyas ! thou art vanquished.
Then Apollo's minister
Hang'd upon a branching fir
Marsyas that unhappy Faun,
And began to whet his knife.
But the Mænads, who were there,
Left their friend, and with robes flowing
In the wind, and loose dark hair
O'er their polish'd bosoms blowing,
Each her ribbon'd tambourine
Flinging on the mountain sod,
With a lovely frighten'd mien
Came about the youthful God.
But he turned his beauteous face
Haughtily another way,
From the grassy sun-warmed place,
Where in proud repose he lay,
With one arm over his head,
Watching how the whetting sped.

But aloof, on the lake strand,

Empedocles on Etna.

Did the young Olympus stand,
Weeping at his master's end ;
For the Faun had been his friend.
For he taught him how to sing,
And he taught him flute-playing.
Many a morning had they gone
To the glimmering mountain lakes,
And had torn up by the roots
The tall crested water reeds
With long plumes, and soft brown seeds,
And had carv'd them into flutes,
Sitting on a tabled stone
Where the shoreward ripple breaks.
And he taught him how to please
The red-snooded Phrygian girls,
Whom the summer evening sees
Flashing in the dance's whirls
Underneath the starlit trees
In the mountain villages.
Therefore now Olympus stands,
At his master's piteous cries,
Pressing fast with both his hands
His white garment to his eyes,
Not to see Apollo's scorn.
Ah, poor Faun, poor Faun ! ah, poor Faun !

EMPEDOCLES.

And lie thou there,
My laurel bough !
Though thou hast been my shade in the world's heat—
Though I have lov'd thee, liv'd in honouring thee—

145

Empedocles on Etna.

Yet lie thou there,
My laurel bough !

I am weary of thee.
I am weary of the solitude
Where he who bears thee must abide.
Of the rocks of Parnassus,
Of the gorge of Delphi,
Of the moonlit peaks, and the caves,
Thou guardest them, Apollo !
Over the grave of the slain Pytho,
Though young, intolerably severe.
Thou keepest aloof the profane,
But the solitude oppresses thy votary.
The jars of men reach him not in thy valley—
But can life reach him ?
Thou fencest him from the multitude—
Who will fence him from himself ?
He hears nothing but the cry of the torrents
And the beating of his own heart.
The air is thin, the veins swell—
The temples tighten and throb there—
Air ! air !

Take thy bough ; set me free from my solitude !
I have been enough alone.
    Where shall thy votary fly then ? back to men ?
But they will gladly welcome him once more,
And help him to unbend his too tense thought,
And rid him of the presence of himself,
And keep their friendly chatter at his ear,
And haunt him, till the absence from himself,

Empedocles on Etna.

That other torment, grow unbearable :
And he will fly to solitude again,
And he will find its air too keen for him,
And so change back : and many thousand times
Be miserably bandied to and fro
Like a sea wave, betwixt the world and thee,
Thou young, implacable God ! and only death
Shall cut his oscillations short, and so
Bring him to poise.   There is no other way.

And yet what days were those, Parmenides !
When we were young, when we could number friends
In all the Italian cities like ourselves,
When with elated hearts we join'd your train,
Ye Sun-born virgins ! on the road of Truth.
Then we could still enjoy, then neither thought
Nor outward things were clos'd and dead to us,
But we receiv'd the shock of mighty thoughts
On simple minds with a pure natural joy ;
And if the sacred load oppress'd our brain,
We had the power to feel the pressure eas'd,
The brow unbound, the thought flow free again,
In the delightful commerce of the world.
We had not lost our balance then, nor grown
Thought's slaves, and dead to every natural joy.
The smallest thing could give us pleasure then—
The sports of the country people ;
A flute note from the woods ;
Sunset over the sea ;
Seed-time and harvest ;
The reapers in the corn ;
The vinedresser in his vineyard ;

Empedocles on Etna.

The village-girl at her wheel.

Fulness of life and power of feeling, ye
Are for the happy, for the souls at ease,
Who dwell on a firm basis of content.
But he who has outliv'd his prosperous days,
But he, whose youth fell on a different world
From that on which his exil'd age is thrown ;
Whose mind was fed on other food, was train'd
By other rules than are in vogue to-day ;
Whose habit of thought is fix'd, who will not change,
But in a world he loves not must subsist
In ceaseless opposition, be the guard
Of his own breast, fetter'd to what he guards,
That the world win no mastery over him ;
Who has no friend, no fellow left, not one ;
Who has no minute's breathing space allow'd
To nurse his dwindling faculty of joy ;—
Joy and the outward world must die to him
As they are dead to me.

> [*A long pause, during which* EMPEDOCLES
> *remains motionless, plunged in thought.*
> *The night deepens. He moves forward*
> *and gazes round him, and proceeds :—*

And you, ye Stars !
Who slowly begin to marshal,
As of old, in the fields of heaven,
Your distant, melancholy lines—
Have you, too, surviv'd yourselves ?
Are you, too, what I fear to become ?
You too once liv'd—

Empedocles on Etna.

You too mov'd joyfully
Among august companions
In an older world, peopled by Gods,
In a mightier order,
The radiant, rejoicing, intelligent Sons of Heaven !
But now, you kindle
Your lonely, cold-shining lights,
Unwilling lingerers
In the heavenly wilderness,
For a younger, ignoble world.
And renew, by necessity,
Night after night your courses,
In echoing unnear'd silence,
Above a race you know not.
Uncaring and undelighted,
Without friend and without home.
Weary like us, though not
Weary with our weariness.

No, no, ye Stars ! there is no death with you,
No languor, no decay ! Languor and death,
They are with me, not you ! ye are alive !
Ye and the pure dark ether where ye ride
Brilliant above me ! And thou, fiery world !
That sapp'st the vitals of this terrible mount
Upon whose charr'd and quaking crust I stand,
Thou, too, brimmest with life ;—the sea of cloud
That heaves its white and billowy vapours up
To moat this isle of ashes from the world,
Lives ;—and that other fainter sea, far down,
O'er whose lit floor a road of moonbeam leads
To Etna's Liparean sister fires

Empedocles on Etna.

And the long dusky line of Italy—
That mild and luminous floor of waters lives,
With held-in joy swelling its heart :—I only,
Whose spring of hope is dried, whose spirit has fail'd—
I, who have not, like these, in solitude
Maintain'd courage and force, and in myself,
Nurs'd an immortal vigour—I alone
Am dead to life and joy ; therefore I read
In all things my own deadness.

> [*A long silence.   He continues :*

Oh, that I could glow like this mountain !
Oh, that my heart bounded with the swell of the sea !
Oh, that my soul were full of light as the stars !
Oh, that it brooded over the world like the air !

But no, this heart will glow no more : thou art
A living man no more, Empedocles !
Nothing but a devouring flame of thought—
But a naked, eternally restless mind.

> [*After a pause :*—

To the elements it came from
Everything will return.
Our bodies to Earth ;
Our blood to Water ;
Heat to Fire ;
Breath to Air.
They were well born, they will be well entomb'd.
But mind !—

And we might gladly share the fruitful stir
Down on our mother Earth's miraculous womb.
Well would it be

Empedocles on Etna.

With what roll'd of us in the stormy deep.
We should have joy, blent with the all-bathing Air.
Or with the active radiant life of Fire.

But Mind—but Thought—
If these have been the master part of us—
Where will *they* find their parent element?
What will receive *them*, who will call *them* home?
But we shall still be in them, and they in us,
And we shall be the strangers of the world,
And they will be our lords, as they are now;
And keep us prisoners of our consciousness,
And never let us clasp and feel the All
But through their forms, and modes, and stifling veils.
And we shall be unsatisfied as now,
And we shall feel the agony of thirst,
The ineffable longing for the life of life
Baffled for ever: and still Thought and Mind
Will hurry us with them on their homeless march,
Over the unallied unopening Earth,
Over the unrecognizing Sea: while Air
Will blow us fiercely back to Sea and Earth,
And Fire repel us from its living waves.
And then we shall unwillingly return
Back to this meadow of calamity,
This uncongenial place, this human life.
And in our individual human state
Go through the sad probation all again,
To see if we will poise our life at last,
To see if we will now at last be true
To our own only true deep-buried selves,
Being one with which we are one with the whole world;

Empedocles on Etna.

Or whether we will once more fall away
Into some bondage of the flesh or mind,
Some slough of sense, or some fantastic maze
Forg'd by the imperious lonely Thinking-Power.
And each succeeding age in which we are born
Will have more peril for us than the last;
Will goad our senses with a sharper spur,
Will fret our minds to an intenser play,
Will make ourselves harder to be discern'd.
And we shall struggle awhile, gasp and rebel :
And we shall fly for refuge to past times.
Their soul of unworn youth, their breath of greatness :
And the reality will pluck us back,
Knead us in its hot hand, and change our nature.
And we shall feel our powers of effort flag,
And rally them for one last fight—and fail.
And we shall sink in the impossible strife,
And be astray for ever.

       Slave of Sense
I have in no wise been : but slave of Thought ?—
 And who can say,—I have been always free,
Liv'd ever in the light of my own soul ?—
I cannot : I have liv'd in wrath and gloom,
Fierce, disputatious, ever at war with man,
Far from my own soul, far from warmth and light.
But I have not grown easy in these bonds—
But I have not denied what bonds these were.
Yea, I take myself to witness,
That I have lov'd no darkness,
Sophisticated no truth,
Nurs'd no delusion,
Allow'd no fear.

Empedocles on Etna.

And therefore, O ye Elements, I know—
Ye know it too—it hath been granted me
Not to die wholly, not to be all enslav'd.
I feel it in this hour.   The numbing cloud
Mounts off my soul: I feel it, I breathe free.

Is it but for a moment?
Ah ! boil up, ye vapours !
Leap and roar, thou Sea of Fire !
My soul glows to meet you.
Ere it flag, ere the mists
Of despondency and gloom
Rush over it again,
Receive me ! save me !   [*He plunges into the crater.*

CALLICLES (*from below*).
Through the black, rushing smoke-bursts,
Thick breaks the red flame.
All Etna heaves fiercely
Her forest-cloth'd frame.

Not here, O Apollo !
Are haunts meet for thee.
But, where Helicon breaks down
In cliff to the sea.

Where the moon-silver'd inlets
Send far their light voice
Up the still vale of Thisbe,
O speed, and rejoice !

Empedocles on Etna.

On the sward, at the cliff-top,
Lie strewn the white flocks;
On the cliff-side, the pigeons
Roost deep in the rocks.

In the moonlight the shepherds,
Soft lull'd by the rills,
Lie wrapt in their blankets,
Asleep on the hills.

—What Forms are these coming
So white through the gloom?
What garments out-glistening
The gold-flower'd broom?

What sweet-breathing Presence
Out-perfumes the thyme?
What voices enrapture
The night's balmy prime?—

'Tis Apollo comes leading
His choir, The Nine.
—The Leader is fairest,
But all are divine.

They are lost in the hollows,
They stream up again.
What seeks on this mountain
The glorified train? —

They bathe on this mountain,
In the spring by their road.

Empedocles on Etna.

Then on to Olympus,
Their endless abode.

—Whose praise do they mention,
Of what is it told ?—
What will be for ever,
What was from of old.

First hymn they the Father
Of all things : and then
The rest of Immortals,
The action of men.

The Day in its hotness,
The strife with the palm ;
The Night in its silence,
The Stars in their calm.

.

POEMS.

THE RIVER.

STILL glides the stream, slow drops the boat
 Under the rustling poplars' shade;
Silent the swans beside us float:
None speaks, none heeds—ah, turn thy head.

Let those arch eyes now softly shine,
That mocking mouth grow sweetly bland:
Ah, let them rest, those eyes, on mine;
On mine let rest that lovely hand.

My pent up tears oppress my brain,
My heart is swoln with love unsaid:
Ah, let me weep, and tell my pain,
And on thy shoulder rest my head.

Before I die, before the soul,
Which now is mine, must re-attain
Immunity from my control,
And wander round the world again:

Before this teas'd o'er-labour'd heart
For ever leaves its vain employ,
Dead to its deep habitual smart,
And dead to hopes of future joy.

Poems.

EXCUSE.

I TOO have suffer'd : yet I know
She is not cold, though she seems so :
She is not cold, she is not light ;
But our ignoble souls lack might.

She smiles and smiles, and will not sigh,
While we for hopeless passion die ;
Yet she could love, those eyes declare,
Were but men nobler than they are.

Eagerly once her gracious ken
Was turn'd upon the sons of men.
But light the serious visage grew—
She look'd, and smil'd, and saw them through.

Our petty souls, our strutting wits,
Our labour'd puny passion-fits—
Ah, may she scorn them still, till we
Scorn them as bitterly as she !

Yet oh, that Fate would let her see
One of some better race than we ;
One for whose sake she once might prove
How deeply she who scorns can love.

His eyes be like the starry lights—
His voice like sounds of summer nights—
In all his lovely mien let pierce
The magic of the universe.

Poems.

And she to him will reach her hand,
And gazing in his eyes will stand,
And know her friend, and weep for glee,
And cry—Long, long I've look'd for thee.—

Then will she weep—with smiles, till then,
Coldly she mocks the sons of men.
Till then her lovely eyes maintain
Their gay, unwavering, deep disdain.

INDIFFERENCE.

I must not say that thou wert true,
Yet let me say that thou wert fair.
And they that lovely face who view,
They will not ask if truth be there.

Truth—what is truth? Two bleeding hearts
Wounded by men, by Fortune tried,
Outwearied with their lonely parts,
Vow to beat henceforth side by side.

The world to them was stern and drear;
Their lot was but to weep and moan.
Ah, let them keep their faith sincere,
For neither could subsist alone!

But souls whom some benignant breath
Has charm'd at birth from gloom and care,
These ask no love—these plight no faith,
For they are happy as they are.

M

Poems.

The world to them may homage make,
And garlands for their forehead weave.
And what the world can give, they take :
But they bring more than they receive.

They smile upon the world : their ears
To one demand alone are coy.
They will not give us love and tears—
They bring us light, and warmth, and joy.

It was not love that heav'd thy breast,
Fair child ! it was the bliss within.
Adieu ! and say that one, at least,
Was just to what he did not win.

TOO LATE.

Each on his own strict line we move,
And some find death ere they find love :
So far apart their lives are thrown
From the twin soul that halves their own.

And sometimes, by still harder fate,
The lovers meet, but meet too late.
—Thy heart is mine !—True, true ! ah true !
Then, love, thy hand !—Ah no ! adieu !

Poems.

ON THE RHINE.

VAIN is the effort to forget.
Some day I shall be cold, I know,
As is the eternal moonlit snow
Of the high Alps, to which I go :
But ah, not yet ! not yet !

Vain is the agony of grief.
'Tis true, indeed, an iron knot
Ties straightly up from mine thy lot,
And were it snapt—thou lov'st me not !
But is despair relief ?

Awhile let me with thought have done.
And as this brimm'd unwrinkled Rhine
And that far purple mountain line
Lie sweetly in the look divine
Of the slow-sinking sun ;

So let me lie, and calm as they
Let beam upon my inward view
Those eyes of deep, soft, lucent hue—
Eyes too expressive to be blue,
Too lovely to be grey.

Ah, Quiet, all things feel thy balm !
Those blue hills too, this river's flow,
Were restless once, but long ago.
Tam'd is their turbulent youthful glow :
Their joy is in their calm.

Poems.

LONGING.

Come to me in my dreams, and then
By day I shall be well again.
For then the night will more than pay
The hopeless longing of the day.

Come, as thou cam'st a thousand times
A messenger from the radiant climes,
And smile on thy new world, and be
As kind to all the rest as me.

Or, as thou never cam'st in sooth,
Come now, and let me dream it truth.
And part my hair, and kiss my brow,
And say—My love ! why sufferest thou ?

Come to me in my dreams, and then
By day I shall be well again.
For then the night will more than pay
The hopeless longing of the day.

THE LAKE.

Again I see my bliss at hand ;
The town, the lake are here.
My Marguerite smiles upon the strand
Unalter'd with the year.

Poems.

I know that graceful figure fair,
That cheek of languid hue;
I know that soft enkerchief'd hair,
And those sweet eyes of blue.

Again I spring to make my choice;
Again in tones of ire
I hear a God's tremendous voice—
"Be counsell'd, and retire!"

Ye guiding Powers, who join and part,
What would ye have with me?
Ah, warn some more ambitious heart,
And let the peaceful be!

PARTING.

Ye storm-winds of Autumn
Who rush by, who shake
The window, and ruffle
The gleam-lighted lake;
Who cross to the hill-side
Thin-sprinkled with farms,
Where the high woods strip sadly
Their yellowing arms;—
  Ye are bound for the mountains—
Ah, with you let me go
Where your cold distant barrier,
The vast range of snow,
Through the loose clouds lifts dimly

Poems.

Its white peaks in air—
How deep is their stillness!
Ah! would I were there!

But on the stairs what voice is this I hear,
Buoyant as morning, and as morning clear?
Say, has some wet bird-haunted English lawn
Lent it the music of its trees at dawn?
Or was it from some sun-fleck'd mountain-brook
That the sweet voice its upland clearness took?
Ah! it comes nearer—
Sweet notes, this way!

Hark! fast by the window
The rushing winds go,
To the ice-cumber'd gorges,
The vast seas of snow.
There the torrents drive upward
Their rock-strangled hum,
There the avalanche thunders
The hoarse torrent dumb.
—I come, O ye mountains!
Ye torrents, I come!

But who is this, by the half-open'd door,
Whose figure casts a shadow on the floor?
The sweet blue eyes—the soft, ash-colour'd hair—
The cheeks that still their gentle paleness wear—
The lovely lips, with their arch smile, that tells
The unconquer'd joy in which her spirit dwells—
Ah! they bend nearer—
Sweet lips, this way!

Poems.

Hark ! the wind rushes past us—
Ah ! with that let me go
To the clear waning hill-side
Unspotted by snow,
There to watch, o'er the sunk vale,
The frore mountain wall,
Where the nich'd snow-bed sprays down
Its powdery fall.
There its dusky blue clusters
The aconite spreads ;
There the pines slope, the cloud-strips
Hung soft in their heads.
No life but, at moments,
The mountain-bee's hum.
—I come, O ye mountains !
Ye pine-woods, I come !

Forgive me ! forgive me !
Ah, Marguerite, fain
Would these arms reach to clasp thee :—
But see ! 'tis in vain.

In the void air towards thee
My strain'd arms are cast.
But a sea rolls between us—
Our different past.

To the lips, ah ! of others,
Those lips have been prest,
And others, ere I was,
Were clasp'd to that breast ;

Poems.

Far, far from each other
Our spirits have grown.
And what heart knows another?
Ah! who knows his own?

Blow, ye winds! lift me with you!
I come to the wild.
Fold closely, O Nature!
Thine arms round thy child.

To thee only God granted
A heart ever new:
To all always open;
To all always true.

Ah, calm me! restore me!
And dry up my tears
On thy high mountain platforms,
Where Morn first appears,

Where the white mists, for ever,
Are spread and unfurl'd;
In the stir of the forces
Whence issued the world.

ABSENCE.

In this fair stranger's eyes of grey
Thine eyes, my love, I see.
I shudder: for the passing day
Had borne me far from thee.

Poems.

This is the curse of life: that not
A nobler, calmer train
Of wiser thoughts and feelings blot
Our passions from our brain;

But each day brings its petty dust
Our soon-chok'd souls to fill,
And we forget because we must,
And not because we will.

I struggle towards the light; and ye,
Once long'd-for storms of love!
If with the light ye cannot be,
I bear that ye remove.

I struggle towards the light; but oh,
While yet the night is chill,
Upon Time's barren, stormy flow,
Stay with me, Marguerite, still!

DESTINY.

Why each is striving, from of old,
To love more deeply than he can?
Still would be true, yet still grows cold?
—Ask of the Powers that sport with man!

They yok'd in him, for endless strife,
A heart of ice, a soul of fire;
And hurl'd him on the Field of Life,
An aimless unallay'd Desire.

TO MARGUERITE.

In returning a volume of the letters of Ortis.

YES: in the sea of life enisl'd,
With echoing straits between us thrown,
Dotting the shoreless watery wild,
We mortal millions live *alone*.
    The islands feel the enclasping flow,
And then their endless bounds they know.

But when the moon their hollows lights
And they are swept by balms of spring,
And in their glens, on starry nights,
The nightingales divinely sing,
And lovely notes, from shore to shore,
Across the sounds and channels pour;

Oh then a longing like despair
Is to their farthest caverns sent;
—For surely once, they feel, we were
Parts of a single continent.
Now round us spreads the watery plain—
Oh might our marges meet again!

Who order'd, that their longing's fire
Should be, as soon as kindled, cool'd?
Who renders vain their deep desire?
    A God, a God their severance rul'd;
And bade betwixt their shores to be
The unplumb'd, salt, estranging sea.

Poems.

HUMAN LIFE.

WHAT mortal, when he saw,
Life's voyage done, his Heavenly Friend,
Could ever yet dare tell him fearlessly,
"I have kept unfring'd my nature's law.
The inly-written chart thou gavest me
To guide me, I have steer'd by to the end?"

Ah! let us make no claim
On life's incognizable sea
To too exact a steering of our way.
Let us not fret and fear to miss our aim
If some fair coast has lur'd us to make stay,
Or some friend hail'd us to keep company.

Ay, we would each fain drive
At random, and not steer by rule.
Weakness! and worse, weakness bestow'd in vain!
Winds from our side the unsuiting consort rive:
We rush by coasts where we had lief remain.
Man cannot, though he would, live Chance's fool.

No! as the foaming swathe
Of torn-up water, on the main,
Falls heavily away with long-drawn roar
On either side the black deep-furrow'd path
Cut by an onward-labouring vessel's prore,
And never touches the ship-side again;

Poems.

Even so we leave behind,
As, charter'd by some unknown Powers,
We stem across the sea of life by night,
The joys which were not for our use design'd.
The friends to whom we had no natural right :
The homes that were not destin'd to be ours.

DESPONDENCY.

THE thoughts that rain their steady glow
Like stars on life's cold sea,
Which others know, or say they know—
They never shone for me.

Thoughts light, like gleams, my spirit's sky,
But they will not remain ;
They light me once, they hurry by,
And never come again.

SONNET.

WHEN I shall be divorc'd, some ten years hence,
From this poor present self which I am now ;
When youth has done its tedious vain expense
Of passions that for ever ebb and flow ;
Shall I not joy youth's heats are left behind,
And breathe more happy in an even clime ?

Ah no, for then I shall begin to find
A thousand virtues in this hated time.
Then I shall wish its agitations back,
And all its thwarting currents of desire;
Then I shall praise the heat which then I lack,
And call this hurrying fever, generous fire,
And sigh that one thing only has been lent
To youth and age in common—discontent.

SELF-DECEPTION.

Say, what binds us, that we claim the glory
Of possessing powers not our share?—
Since man woke on earth, he knows his story,
But, before we woke on earth, we were.

Long, long since, undower'd yet, our spirit
Roam'd, ere birth, the treasuries of God:
Saw the gifts, the powers it might inherit;
Ask'd an outfit for its earthly road.

Then, as now, this tremulous, eager being
Strain'd, and long'd, and grasp'd each gift it saw.
Then, as now, a Power beyond our seeing
Stav'd us back, and gave our choice the law.

Ah, whose hand that day through heaven guided
Man's new spirit, since it was not we?
Ah, who sway'd our choice, and who decided
What the parts, and what the whole should be?

For, alas ! he left us each retaining
Shreds of gifts which he refus'd in full.
Still these waste us with their hopeless straining—
Still the attempt to use them proves them null.

And on earth we wander, groping, reeling ;
Powers stir in us, stir and disappear.
Ah, and he, who placed our master-feeling,
Fail'd to place that master-feeling clear.

We but dream we have our wish'd-for powers.
Ends we seek we never shall attain.
Ah, *some* power exists there, which is ours?
Some end is there, we indeed may gain?

LINES WRITTEN BY A DEATH-BED.

YES, now the longing is o'erpast,
Which, dogg'd by fear and fought by shame,
Shook her weak bosom day and night,
Consum'd her beauty like a flame,
And dimm'd it like the desert blast.
And though the curtains hide her face,
Yet were it lifted to the light
The sweet expression of her brow
Would charm the gazer, till his thought
Eras'd the ravages of time,
Fill'd up the hollow cheek, and brought
A freshness back as of her prime—

Poems.

So healing is her quiet now.
So perfectly the lines express
A placid, settled loveliness ;
Her youngest rival's freshest grace.

But ah, though peace indeed is here,
And ease from shame, and rest from fear ;
Though nothing can dismarble now
The smoothness of that limpid brow ;
Yet is a calm like this, in truth,
The crowning end of life and youth?
And when this boon rewards the dead,
Are all debts paid, has all been said?
And is the heart of youth so light,
Its step so firm, its eye so bright,
Because on its hot brow there blows
A wind of promise and repose
From the far grave, to which it goes?
Because it has the hope to come,
One day, to harbour in the tomb?
Ah no, the bliss youth dreams is one
For daylight, for the cheerful sun,
For feeling nerves and living breath—
Youth dreams a bliss on this side death.
It dreams a rest, if not more deep,
More grateful than this marble sleep.
It hears a voice within it tell—
"Calm's not life's crown, though calm is well."
'Tis all perhaps which man acquires :
But 'tis not what our youth desires.

TRISTRAM AND ISEULT.

Tristram and Iseult.

I.

TRISTRAM.

TRISTRAM.

IS she not come? The messenger was sure.
  Prop me upon the pillows once again—
Raise me, my page : this cannot long endure.
Christ! what a night! how the sleet whips the pane!
  What lights will those out to the northward be?

THE PAGE.

The lanterns of the fishing-boats at sea.

TRISTRAM.

Soft—who is that stands by the dying fire?

THE PAGE.

Iseult.

TRISTRAM.

Ah! not the Iseult I desire.

What knight is this, so weak and pale,
Though the locks are yet brown on his noble head,

Tristram and Iseult.

Propt on pillows in his bed,
Gazing seawards for the light
Of some ship that fights the gale
On this wild December night ?
Over the sick man's feet is spread
A dark green forest dress.
A gold harp leans against the bed,
Ruddy in the fire's light.
    I know him by his harp of gold,
Famous in Arthur's court of old :
I know him by his forest dress.
    The peerless hunter, harper, knight—
Tristram of Lyoness.

What lady is this whose silk attire
Gleams so rich in the light of the fire ?
Never surely has been seen
So slight a form in so rich a dress.
The ringlets on her shoulders lying
In their flitting lustre vying
With the clasp of burnish'd gold
Which her heavy robe doth hold.
But her cheeks are sunk and pale.
    Is it that the bleak sea-gale
Beating from the Atlantic sea
On this coast of Brittany,
Nips too keenly the sweet flower ?
    Is it that a deep fatigue
Hath come on her, a chilly fear,
Passing all her youthful hour
Spinning with her maidens here,
Listlessly through the window bars

Tristram and Iseult.

Gazing seawards many a league
From her lonely shore-built tower,
While the knights are at the wars?
Or, perhaps, has her young heart
Felt already some deeper smart,
Of those that in secret the heart-strings rive,
Leaving her sunk and pale, though fair?
  Who is this snowdrop by the sea?
I know her by her golden hair,
I know her by her rich silk dress,
And her fragile loveliness.
The sweetest Christian soul alive,
Iseult of Brittany.

Loud howls the wind, sharp patters the rain,
And the knight sinks back on his pillows again.
He is weak with fever and pain,
And his spirit is not clear.
Hark! he mutters in his sleep,
As he wanders far from here,
Changes place and time of year,
And his closed eye doth sweep
O'er some fair unwintry sea,
Not this fierce Atlantic deep,
  As he mutters brokenly—

TRISTRAM.

The calm sea shines, loose hang the vessel's sails—
Before us are the sweet green fields of Wales,
And overhead the cloudless sky of May.—
" Ah, would I were in those green fields at play,

Tristram and Iseult.

Not pent on ship-board this delicious day.
Tristram, I pray thee, of thy courtesy,
Reach me my golden cup that stands by thee,
And pledge me in it first for courtesy.—"
—Ha! dost thou start? are thy lips blanch'd like
    mine?
Child, 'tis no water this, 'tis poison'd wine.—
Iseult! . . . .

     Ah, sweet angels, let him dream!
Keep his eyelids! let him seem
Not this fever-wasted wight
Thinn'd and pal'd before his time,
But the brilliant youthful knight
In the glory of his prime,
Sitting in the gilded barge,
At thy side, thou lovely charge!
Bending gaily o'er thy hand,
Iseult of Ireland!
And she too, that princess fair,
If her bloom be now less rare,
Let her have her youth again—
   Let her be as she was then!
Let her have her proud dark eyes,
And her petulant quick replies,
Let her sweep her dazzling hand
With its gesture of command,
And shake back her raven hair
With the old imperious air.
As of old, so let her be,
That first Iseult, princess bright,
Chatting with her youthful knight

Tristram and Iseult.

As he steers her o'er the sea,
Quitting at her father's will
The green isle where she was bred,
   And her bower in Ireland,
For the surge-beat Cornish strand,
Where the prince whom she must wed
Keeps his court in Tyntagil,
Fast beside the sounding sea.
And that golden cup her mother
Gave her, that her lord and she
Might drink it on their marriage day,
And for ever love each other,
   Let her, as she sits on board,
Ah, sweet saints, unwittingly,
See it shine, and take it up,
And to Tristram laughing say—
" Sir Tristram, of thy courtesy
Pledge me in my golden cup!"
Let them drink it—let their hands
Tremble, and their cheeks be flame,
As they feel the fatal bands
Of a love they dare not name,
With a wild delicious pain
   Twine about their hearts again.
Let the early summer be
Once more round them, and the sea
Blue, and o'er its mirror kind
Let the breath of the May wind,
Wandering through their drooping sails,
   Die on the green fields of Wales.
Let a dream like this restore
What his eye must see no more.

Tristram and Iseult.

TRISTRAM.

Chill blows the wind, the pleasaunce walks are drear.
Madcap, what jest was this, to meet me here
Were feet like those made for so wild a way ?
The southern winter-parlour, by my fay,
Had been the likeliest trysting place to-day.
' Tristram !—nay, nay—thou must not take my hand—
Tristram—sweet love—we are betray'd—out-plann'd.
Fly—save thyself—save me.   I dare not stay."—
One last kiss first !—"'Tis vain—to horse—away !"

>Ah, sweet saints, his dream doth move
>Faster surely than it should,
>From the fever in his blood.
>All the spring-time of his love
>Is already gone and past,
>And instead thereof is seen
>Its winter, which endureth still—
>The palace towers of Tyntagil,
>The pleasaunce walks, the weeping queen,
>The flying leaves, the straining blast,
>And that long, wild kiss—their last.
>And this rough December night
>And his burning fever pain
>Mingle with his hurrying dream
>Till they rule it, till he seem
>The press'd fugitive again,
>The love-desperate banish'd knight
>With a fire in his brain
>Flying o'er the stormy main.
>   Whither does he wander now ?
>Haply in his dreams the wind

Tristram and Iseult.

Wafts him here, and lets him find
The lovely orphan child again
In her castle by the coast,
The youngest, fairest chatelaine,
That this realm of France can boast,
   Our snowdrop by the Atlantic sea,
Iseult of Brittany.
And—for through the haggard air,
The stain'd arms, the matted hair
Of that stranger knight ill-starr'd,
There gleam'd something that recall'd
The Tristram who in better days
Was Launcelot's guest at Joyous Gard—
Welcom'd here, and here install'd,
Tended of his fever here,
Haply he seems again to move
His young guardian's heart with love;
   In his exil'd loneliness,
In his stately deep distress,
Without a word, without a tear.—
   Ah, 'tis well he should retrace
His tranquil life in this lone place;
His gentle bearing at the side
Of his timid youthful bride;
His long rambles by the shore
On winter evenings, when the roar
Of the near waves came, sadly grand,
Through the dark, up the drown'd sand:
   Or his endless reveries
In the woods, where the gleams play
On the grass under the trees,
Passing the long summer's day

Tristram and Iseult.

Idle as a mossy stone
In the forest depths alone ;
The chase neglected, and his hound
Couch'd beside him on the ground.—
   Ah, what trouble 's on his brow ?
Hither let him wander now,
Hither, to the quiet hours
Pass'd among these heaths of ours
By the grey Atlantic sea.
   Hours, if not of ecstasy,
From violent anguish surely free.

TRISTRAM.

All red with blood the whirling river flows,
The wide plain rings, the daz'd air throbs with blows.
Upon us are the chivalry of Rome—
Their spears are down, their steeds are bath'd in foam.
" Up, Tristram, up," men cry, " thou moonstruck
   knight !
What foul fiend rides thee ? On into the fight ! "
   Above the din her voice is in my ears—
I see her form glide through the crossing spears.—
Iseult ! . . . .

Ah, he wanders forth again ;
   We cannot keep him ; now as then
There's a secret in his breast
   That will never let him rest.
These musing fits in the green wood
They cloud the brain, they dull the blood.
   His sword is sharp—his horse is good—

Tristram and Iseult.

Beyond the mountains will he see
The famous towns of Italy,
And label with the blessed sign
The heathen Saxons on the Rhine.
At Arthur's side he fights once more
With the Roman Emperor.
There's many a gay knight where he goes
Will help him to forget his care.
The march—the leaguer—Heaven's blithe air—
The neighing steeds—the ringing blows;
    Sick pining comes not where these are.
Ah, what boots it, that the jest
Lightens every other brow,
What, that every other breast
Dances as the trumpets blow,
If one's own heart beats not light
In the waves of the toss'd fight,
If oneself cannot get free
From the clog of misery?
    Thy lovely youthful wife grows pale
Watching by the salt sea tide
With her children at her side
For the gleam of thy white sail.
Home, Tristram, to thy halls again !
To our lonely sea complain,
    To our forests tell thy pain.

TRISTRAM.

All round the forest sweeps off, black in shade,
But it is moonlight in the open glade:
And in the bottom of the glade shine clear

Tristram and Iseult.

The forest chapel and the fountain near.
  I think, I have a fever in my blood :
Come, let me leave the shadow of this wood,
Ride down, and bathe my hot brow in the flood.
  Mild shines the cold spring in the moon's clear light.
God ! 'tis *her* face plays in the waters bright.
" Fair love," she says, " canst thou forget so soon,
At this soft hour, under this sweet moon ? "
Iseult ! . . . .

  Ah poor soul, if this be so,
  Only death can balm thy woe.
  The solitudes of the green wood
  Had no medicine for thy mood.
    The rushing battle clear'd thy blood
  As little as did solitude.
    Ah, his eyelids slowly break
  Their hot seals, and let him wake.
  What new change shall we now see ?
    A happier ? Worse it cannot be.

TRISTRAM.

Is my page here ? Come, turn me to the fire.
Upon the window panes the moon shines bright ;
The wind is down : but she'll not come to-night.
Ah no—she is asleep in Tyntagil
Far hence—her dreams are fair—her sleep is still.
Of me she recks not, nor of my desire.
  I have had dreams, I have had dreams, my page,
Would take a score years from a strong man's age,
And with a blood like mine, will leave, I fear,

Tristram and Iseult.

Scant leisure for a second messenger.
  My princess, art thou there?   Sweet, 'tis too late.
To bed, and sleep: my fever is gone by:
To-night my page shall keep me company.
Where do the children sleep? kiss them for me.
Poor child, thou art almost as pale as I :
This comes of nursing long and watching late.
To bed—good night !

She left the gleam-lit fire-place,
    She came to the bed-side.
She took his hands in hers : her tears
Down on her slender fingers rain'd.
She rais'd her eyes upon his face—
Not with a look of wounded pride,
A look as if the heart complain'd :—
    Her look was like a sad embrace ;
The gaze of one who can divine
A grief, and sympathise.
Sweet flower, thy children's eyes
    Are not more innocent than thine.
    But they sleep in shelter'd rest,
Like helpless birds in the warm nest,
On the castle's southern side ;
Where feebly comes the mournful roar
Of buffeting wind and surging tide
Through many a room and corridor.
Full on their window the moon's ray
Makes their chamber as bright as day ;
It shines upon the blank white walls
And on the snowy pillow falls,

Tristram and Iseult.

And on two angel-heads doth play
Turn'd to each other :—the eyes clos'd—
  The lashes on the cheeks repos'd.
Round each sweet brow the cap close-set
Hardly lets peep the golden hair ;
Through the soft-open'd lips the air
Scarcely moves the coverlet.
One little wandering arm is thrown
At random on the counterpane,
And often the fingers close in haste
As if their baby owner chas'd
The butterflies again.
This stir they have and this alone ;
But else they are so still.
  Ah, tired madcaps, you lie still.
But were you at the window now
To look forth on the fairy sight
Of your illumin'd haunts by night ;
To see the park-glades where you play
Far lovelier than they are by day ;
To see the sparkle on the eaves,
And upon every giant bough
Of those old oaks, whose wet red leaves
Are jewell'd with bright drops of rain—
  How would your voices run again !
And far beyond the sparkling trees
Of the castle park one sees
The bare heaths spreading, clear as day,
Moor behind moor, far, far away,
Into the heart of Brittany.
And here and there, lock'd by the land,
Long inlets of smooth glittering sea,

Tristram and Iseult.

And many a stretch of watery sand
All shining in the white moon-beams.
But you see fairer in your dreams.

What voices are these on the clear night air?
What lights in the court? what steps on the stair?

Tristram and Iseult.

II.

ISEULT OF IRELAND.

TRISTRAM.

RAISE the light, my page, that I may see her.—
Thou art come at last then, haughty Queen !
Long I've waited, long I've fought my fever :
Late thou comest, cruel thou hast been.

ISEULT.

Blame me not, poor sufferer, that I tarried :
I was bound, I could not break the band.
Chide not with the past, but feel the present :
I am here—we meet—I hold thy hand.

TRISTRAM.

Thou art come, indeed—thou hast rejoin'd me ;
Thou hast dar'd it : but too late to save.
Fear not now that men should tax thy honour.
I am dying : build—(thou may'st)—my grave !

Tristram and Iseult.

ISEULT.

Tristram, for the love of Heaven, speak kindly!
What, I hear these bitter words from thee?
Sick with grief I am, and faint with travel—
Take my hand—dear Tristram, look on me!

TRISTRAM.

I forgot, thou comest from thy voyage.
Yes, the spray is on thy cloak and hair.
But thy dark eyes are not dimm'd, proud Iseult!
And thy beauty never was more fair.

ISEULT.

Ah, harsh flatterer! let alone my beauty.
I, like thee, have left my youth afar.
Take my hand, and touch these wasted fingers—
See my cheek and lips, how white they are.

TRISTRAM.

Thou art paler:—but thy sweet charm, Iseult!
Would not fade with the dull years away.
Ah, how fair thou standest in the moonlight!
I forgive thee, Iseult!—thou wilt stay?

ISEULT.

Fear me not, I will be always with thee;
I will watch thee, tend thee, soothe thy pain;
Sing thee tales of true long-parted lovers
Join'd at evening of their days again.

Tristram and Iseult.

TRISTRAM.

No, thou shalt not speak ; I should be finding
Something alter'd in thy courtly tone.
Sit—sit by me : I will think, we've liv'd so
In the greenwood, all our lives, alone.

ISEULT.

Alter'd, Tristram ? Not in courts, believe me,
Love like mine is alter'd in the breast.
Courtly life is light and cannot reach it.
Ah, it lives, because so deep suppress'd.

What, thou think'st, men speak in courtly chambers
Words by which the wretched are consol'd ?
What, thou think'st, this aching brow was cooler,
Circled, Tristram, by a band of gold ?

Ah, on which, if both our lots were balanc'd,
Was indeed the heaviest burden thrown,
Thee, a weeping exile in thy forest—
Me, a smiling queen upon my throne ?

Vain and strange debate, where both have suffer'd ;
Both have pass'd a youth constrain'd and sad ;
Both have brought their anxious day to evening,
And have now short space for being glad.

Join'd we are henceforth: nor will thy people
Nor thy younger Iseult take it ill
That an ancient rival shares her office,
When she sees her humbled, pale, and still.

Tristram and Iseult.

I, a faded watcher by thy pillow,
I, a statue on thy chapel floor,
Pour'd in grief before the Virgin Mother,
Rouse no anger, make no rivals more.

She will say—" Is this the form I dreaded?
This his idol? this that royal bride?
Ah, an hour of health would purge his eyesight:
Stay, pale queen! for ever by my side."

Hush, no words! that smile, I see, forgives me.
I am now thy nurse, I bid thee sleep.
Close thine eyes—this flooding moonlight blinds
        them—
Nay, all's well again: thou must not weep.

TRISTRAM.

I am happy: yet I feel, there's something
Swells my heart, and takes my breath away:
Through a mist I see thee: near!—come nearer!
Bend—bend down—I yet have much to say.

ISEULT.

Heaven! his head sinks back upon the pillow!—
Tristram! Tristram! let thy heart not fail.
Call on God and on the holy angels!
What, love, courage!—Christ! he is so pale.

TRISTRAM.

Hush, 'tis vain, I feel my end approaching.
This is what my mother said should be,
When the fierce pains took her in the forest,
The deep draughts of death, in bearing me.

Tristram and Iseult.

"Son," she said, "thy name shall be of sorrow!
Tristram art thou call'd for my death's sake!"
So she said, and died in the drear forest.
Grief since then his home with me doth make.

I am dying.—Start not, nor look wildly!
Me, thy living friend, thou canst not save.
But, since living we were ununited,
Go not far, O Iseult! from my grave.

Rise, go hence, and seek the princess Iseult:
Speak her fair, she is of royal blood.
Say, I charg'd her, that ye live together:—
She will grant it—she is kind and good.

Now stand clear before me in the moonlight.
Fare, farewell, thou long, thou deeply lov'd!

ISEULT.
Tristram!—Tristram—stay—I come! Ah Sorrow—
Fool! thou missest—we are both unmov'd!

You see them clear: the moon shines bright.
Slow—slow and softly, where she stood,
She sinks upon the ground: her hood
Had fallen back: her arms outspread
Still hold her lover's hands: her head
Is bow'd, half-buried, on the bed.
O'er the blanch'd sheet her raven hair
Lies in disorder'd streams; and there,
Strung like white stars, the pearls still are,

Tristram and Iseult.

And the golden bracelets heavy and rare
Flash on her white arms still.
The very same which yesternight
Flash'd in the silver sconces' light,
When the feast was loud and the laughter shril
In the banquet-hall of Tyntagil.
But then they deck'd a restless ghost
With hot-flush'd cheeks and brilliant eyes
And quivering lips on which the tide
Of courtly speech abruptly died,
And a glance that over the crowded floor,
The dancers, and the festive host,
Flew ever to the door.
That the knights eyed her in surprise,
And the dames whisper'd scoffingly—
" Her moods, good lack, they pass like showers !
But yesternight and she would be
As pale and still as wither'd flowers,
And now to-night she laughs and speaks
And has a colour in her cheeks.
Heaven keep us from such fantasy !"—
    The air of the December night
Steals coldly around the chamber bright,
Swinging with it, in the light
Shines the ghostlike tapestry.
And there upon the wall you see
A stately huntsman, clad in green,
And round him a fresh forest scene.
'Tis noon with him, and yet he stays
With his pack round him, and delays,
As rooted to the earth, nor sounds
His lifted horn, nor cheers his hounds

Tristram and Iseult.

Into the tangled glen below.
Yet in the sedgy bottom there
Where the deep forest stream creeps slow
Fring'd with dead leaves and mosses rare,
The wild boar harbours close, and feeds.

    He gazes down into the room
With heated cheeks and flurried air—
Who is that kneeling lady fair?
And on his pillows that pale knight
Who seems of marble on a tomb?
How comes it here, this chamber bright,
Through whose mullion'd windows clear
The castle court all wet with rain,
The drawbridge, and the moat appear,
And then the beach, and mark'd with spray
The sunken reefs, and far away
The unquiet bright Atlantic plain?—

    He stares and stares, with troubled face
At the huge gleam-lit fireplace,
At the bright iron-figur'd door,
And the blown rushes on the floor.

    Has then some glamour made him sleep,
And sent him with his dogs to sweep,
By night, with boisterous bugle peal,
Through some old, sea-side, knightly hall,
Not in the free greenwood at all?
That knight's asleep, and at her prayer
That lady by the bed doth kneel:
Then hush, thou boisterous bugle peal!
The wild boar rustles in his lair—
The fierce hounds snuff the tainted air—
But lord and hounds keep rooted there.

Tristram and Iseult.

Cheer, cheer thy dogs into the brake,
O hunter ! and without a fear
Thy golden-tassell'd bugle blow,
And through the glades thy pastime take !
　For thou wilt rouse no sleepers here.
For these thou seest are unmov'd ;
Cold, cold as those who liv'd and lov d
A thousand years ago.

Tristram and Iseult.

III.

ISEULT OF BRITTANY.

A YEAR had flown, and in the chapel old
Lay Tristram and queen Iseult dead and cold.
The young surviving Iseult, one bright day,
Had wander'd forth : her children were at play
In a green circular hollow in the heath
Which borders the sea-shore ; a country path
Creeps over it from the till'd fields behind.
The hollow's grassy banks are soft inclin'd,
And to one standing on them, far and near
The lone unbroken view spreads bright and clear
Over the waste :—This ring of open ground
Is light and green ; the heather, which all round
Creeps thickly, grows not here ; but the pale grass
Is strewn with rocks, and many a shiver'd mass
Of vein'd white-gleaming quartz, and here and there
Dotted with holly trees and juniper.
In the smooth centre of the opening stood
Three hollies side by side, and made a screen
Warm with the winter sun, of burnish'd green,

Tristram and Iseult.

With scarlet berries gemm'd, the fell-fare's food.
Under the glittering hollies Iseult stands
Watching her children play: their little hands
Are busy gathering spars of quartz, and streams
Of stagshorn for their hats: anon, with screams
Of mad delight they drop their spoils, and bound
Among the holly clumps and broken ground,
Racing full speed, and startling in their rush
The fell-fares and the speckled missel-thrush
Out of their glossy coverts: but when now
Their cheeks were flush'd, and over each hot brow
Under the feather'd hats of the sweet pair
In blinding masses shower'd the golden hair—
Then Iseult called them to her, and the three
Cluster'd under the holly screen, and she
Told them an old-world Breton history.

Warm in their mantles wrapt, the three stood there,
Under the hollies, in the clear still air—
Mantles with those rich furs deep glistering
Which Venice ships do from swart Egypt bring.
Long they staid still—then, pacing at their ease,
Mov'd up and down under the glossy trees;
But still as they pursued their warm dry road
From Iseult's lips the unbroken story flow'd,
And still the children listen'd, their blue eyes
Fix'd on their mother's face in wide surprise;
Nor did their looks stray once to the sea-side,
Nor to the brown heaths round them, bright and wide,
Nor to the snow which, though 'twas all away
From the open heath, still by the hedgerows lay,
Nor to the shining sea-fowl that with screams

Tristram and Iseult.

Bore up from where the bright Atlantic gleams,
Swooping to landward; nor to where, quite clear,
The fell-fares settled on the thickets near.
And they would still have listen'd, till dark night
Came keen and chill down on the heather bright;
But, when the red glow on the sea grew cold,
And the grey turrets of the castle old
Look'd sternly through the frosty evening air,—
Then Iseult took by the hand those children fair,
And brought her tale to an end, and found the path,
And led them home over the darkening heath.

And is she happy? Does she see unmov'd
The days in which she might have liv'd and lov'd
Slip without bringing bliss slowly away,
One after one, to-morrow like to-day?
Joy has not found her yet, nor ever will :—
Is it this thought that makes her mien so still,
Her features so fatigued, her eyes, though sweet,
So sunk, so rarely lifted save to meet
Her children's? She moves slow: her voice alone
Has yet an infantine and silver tone,
But even that comes languidly : in truth,
She seems one dying in a mask of youth.
And now she will go home, and softly lay
Her laughing children in their beds, and play
Awhile with them before they sleep; and then
She'll light her silver lamp, which fishermen
Dragging their nets through the rough waves, afar,
Along this iron coast, know like a star,
And take her broidery frame, and there she'll sit
Hour after hour, her gold curls sweeping it,

Tristram and Iseult.

Lifting her soft-bent head only to mind
Her children, or to listen to the wind.
And when the clock peals midnight, she will move
Her work away, and let her fingers rove
Across the shaggy brows of Tristram's hound
Who lies, guarding her feet, along the ground :
Or else she will fall musing, her blue eyes
Fix'd, her slight hands clasp'd on her lap ; then rise,
And at her prie-dieu kneel, until she have told
Her rosary beads of ebony tipp'd with gold,
Then to her soft sleep : and to-morrow 'll be
To-day's exact repeated effigy.

　　Yes, it is lonely for her in her hall.
The children, and the grey-hair'd seneschal,
Her women, and Sir Tristram's aged hound,
Are there the sole companions to be found.
But these she loves ; and noisier life than this
She would find ill to bear, weak as she is :
She has her children too, and night and day
Is with them; and the wide heaths where they play,
The hollies, and the cliff, and the sea-shore,
The sand, the sea birds, and the distant sails,
These are to her dear as to them : the tales
With which this day the children she beguil'd
She glean'd from Breton grandames when a child
In every hut along this sea-coast wild.
She herself loves them still, and, when they are told,
Can forget all to hear them, as of old.

　　Dear saints, it is not sorrow, as I hear,
Not suffering, that shuts up eye and ear

Tristram and Iseult.

To all which has delighted them before,
And lets us be what we were once no more.
No : we may suffer deeply, yet retain
Power to be mov'd and sooth'd, for all our pain,
By what of old pleas'd us, and will again.
No : 'tis the gradual furnace of the world,
In whose hot air our spirits are upcurl'd
Until they crumble, or else grow like steel—
Which kills in us the bloom, the youth, the spring—
Which leaves the fierce necessity to feel,
But takes away the power—this can avail,
By drying up our joy in everything,
To make our former pleasures all seem stale.
This, or some tyrannous single thought, some fit
Of passion, which subdues our souls to it,
Till for its sake alone we live and move—
Call it ambition, or remorse, or love—
This too can change us wholly, and make seem
All that we did before, shadow and dream.

  And yet, I swear, it angers me to see
How this fool passion gulls men potently ;
Being in truth but a diseas'd unrest
And an unnatural overheat at best.
How they are full of languor and distress
Not having it ; which when they do possess
They straightway are burnt up with fume and care,
And spend their lives in posting here and there
Where this plague drives them ; and have little ease,
Can never end their tasks, are hard to please.
Like that bald Cæsar, the fam'd Roman wight,
Who wept at reading of a Grecian knight

Tristram and Iseult.

Who made a name at younger years than he :
Or that renown'd mirror of chivalry,
Prince Alexander, Philip's peerless son,
Who carried the great war from Macedon
Into the Soudan's realm, and thunder'd on
To die at thirty-five in Babylon.

What tale did Iseult to the children say,
Under the hollies, that bright winter's day?

She told them of the fairy-haunted land
Away the other side of Brittany,
Beyond the heaths, edg'd by the lonely sea ;
Of the deep forest-glades of Broce-liande,
Through whose green boughs the golden sunshine
        creeps,
Where Merlin by the enchanted thorn-tree sleeps.
For here he came with the fay Vivian,
One April, when the warm days first began ;
He was on foot, and that false fay, his friend,
On her white palfrey : here he met his end,
In these lone sylvan glades, that April day.
This tale of Merlin and the lovely fay
Was the one Iseult chose, and she brought clear
Before the children's fancy him and her.

Blowing between the stems the forest air
Had loosen'd the brown curls of Vivian's hair,
Which play'd on her flush'd cheek, and her blue eyes
Sparkled with mocking glee and exercise.
Her palfrey's flanks were mired and bath'd in sweat,
For they had travell'd far and not stopp'd yet.

Tristram and Iseult.

A briar in that tangled wilderness
Had scor'd her white right hand, which she allows
To rest unglov'd on her green riding-dress;
The other warded off the drooping boughs.
But still she chatted on, with her blue eyes
Fix'd full on Merlin's face, her stately prize:
Her 'haviour had the morning's fresh clear grace,
The spirit of the woods was in her face;
She look'd so witching fair, that learned wight
Forgot his craft, and his best wits took flight,
And he grew fond, and eager to obey
His mistress, use her empire as she may.

They came to where the brushwood ceas'd, and day
Peer'd 'twixt the stems; and the ground broke away
In a slop'd sward down to a brawling brook,
And up as high as where they stood to look
On the brook's further side was clear; but then
The underwood and trees began again.
This open glen was studded thick with thorns
Then white with blossom; and you saw the horns,
Through the green fern, of the shy fallow-deer
Which come at noon down to the water here.
You saw the bright-eyed squirrels dart along
Under the thorns on the green sward; and strong
The blackbird whistled from the dingles near,
And the light chipping of the woodpecker
Rang lonelily and sharp: the sky was fair,
And a fresh breath of spring stirr'd everywhere.
Merlin and Vivian stopp'd on the slope's brow
To gaze on the green sea of leaf and bough
Which glistering lay all round them, lone and mild,

Tristram and Iseult.

As if to itself the quiet forest smil'd.
Upon the brow-top grew a thorn ; and here
The grass was dry and moss'd, and you saw clear
Across the hollow : white anemones
Starr'd the cool turf, and clumps of primroses
Ran out from the dark underwood behind.
No fairer resting-place a man could find.
" Here let us halt," said Merlin then ; and she
Nodded, and tied her palfrey to a tree.

They sate them down together, and a sleep
Fell upon Merlin, more like death, so deep.
Her finger on her lips, then Vivian rose,
And from her brown-lock'd head the wimple throws,
And takes it in her hand, and waves it over
The blossom'd thorn-tree and her sleeping lover.
Nine times she wav'd the fluttering wimple round,
And made a little plot of magic ground.
And in that daisied circle, as men say,
Is Merlin prisoner till the judgment-day,
But she herself whither she will can rove,
For she was passing weary of his love.

POEMS.

MEMORIAL VERSES.

April, 1850.

GOETHE in Weimar sleeps, and Greece,
Long since, saw Byron's struggle cease.
But one such death remain'd to come.
The last poetic verse is dumb.
What shall be said o'er Wordsworth's tomb?

When Byron's eyes were shut in death,
We bow'd our head and held our breath.
He taught us little : but our soul
Had *felt* him like the thunder's roll.
With shivering heart the strife we saw
Of Passion with Eternal Law.
And yet with reverential awe
We watch'd the fount of fiery life
Which serv'd for that Titanic strife.

When Goethe's death was told, we said—
Sunk, then, is Europe's sagest head.
Physician of the Iron Age
Goethe has done his pilgrimage.

Poems.

He took the suffering human race,
He read each wound, each weakness clear—
And struck his finger on the place
And said—Thou ailest here, and here.—
He look'd on Europe's dying hour
Of fitful dream and feverish power ;
His eye plung'd down the weltering strife,
The turmoil of expiring life ;
He said—The end is everywhere :
Art still has truth, take refuge there.—
And he was happy, if to know
Causes of things, and far below
His feet to see the lurid flow
Of terror, and insane distress,
And headlong fate, be happiness.

And Wordsworth !—Ah, pale ghosts ! rejoice !
For never has such soothing voice
Been to your shadowy world convey'd,
Since erst, at morn, some wandering shade
Heard the clear song of Orpheus come
Through Hades, and the mournful gloom.
Wordsworth is gone from us—and ye,
Ah, may ye feel his voice as we.
He too upon the wintry clime
Had fallen—on this iron time
Of doubts, disputes, distractions, fears.
He found us when the age had bound
Our souls in its benumbing round :
He spoke, and loos'd our heart in tears.
He laid us as we lay at birth
On the cool flowery lap of earth ;

Poems.

Smiles broke from us and we had ease.
The hills were round us, and the breeze
Went o'er the sun-lit fields again:
Our foreheads felt the wind and rain.
Our youth return'd: for there was shed
On spirits that had long been dead,
Spirits dried up and closely-furl'd,
The freshness of the early world.

Ah, since dark days still bring to light
Man's prudence and man's fiery might,
Time may restore us in his course
Goethe's sage mind and Byron's force:
But where will Europe's latter hour
Again find Wordsworth's healing power?
Others will teach us how to dare,
And against fear our breast to steel;
Others will strengthen us to bear—
But who, ah who, will make us feel?
The cloud of mortal destiny,
Others will front it fearlessly—
But who, like him, will put it by?

Keep fresh the grass upon his grave,
O Rotha! with thy living wave.
Sing him thy best! for few or none
Hears thy voice right, now he is gone.

Poems.

COURAGE.

'TRUE, we must tame our rebel will :
True, we must bow to Nature's law :
Must bear in silence many an ill ;
Must learn to wail, renounce, withdraw.

Yet now, when boldest wills give place.
When Fate and Circumstance are strong,
And in their rush the human race
Are swept, like huddling sheep, along :

Those sterner spirits let me prize,
Who, though the tendence of the whole
They less than us might recognize,
Kept, more than us, their strength of soul.

Yes, be the second Cato prais'd !
Not that he took the course to die—
But that, when 'gainst himself he rais'd
His arm, he rais'd it dauntlessly.

And, Byron ! let us dare admire
If not thy fierce and turbid song,
Yet that, in anguish, doubt, desire,
Thy fiery courage still was strong.

The sun that on thy tossing pain
Did with such cold derision shine,
He crush'd thee not with his disdain—
He had his glow, and thou hadst thine.

Poems.

Our bane, disguise it as we may,
Is weakness, is a faltering course.
Oh that past times could give our day,
Join'd to its clearness, of their force !

SELF DEPENDENCE.

WEARY of myself, and sick of asking
What I am, and what I ought to be,
At the vessel's prow I stand, which bears me
Forwards, forwards, o'er the star-lit sea.

And a look of passionate desire
O'er the sea and to the stars I send :
"Ye who from my childhood up have calm'd me,
Calm me, ah, compose me to the end.

"Ah, once more," I cried, "Ye Stars, ye Waters,
On my heart your mighty charm renew :
Still, still, let me, as I gaze upon you,
Feel my soul becoming vast like you."

From the intense, clear, star-sown vault of heaven,
Over the lit sea's unquiet way,
In the rustling night-air came the answer—
"Wouldst thou *be* as these are ? *live* as they.

"Unaffrighted by the silence round them,
Undistracted by the sights they see,
These demand not that the things without them
Yield them love, amusement, sympathy.

Poems.

"And with joy the stars perform their shining,
And the sea its long moon-silver'd roll.
For alone they live, nor pine with noting
All the fever of some differing soul.

"Bounded by themselves, and unobservant
In what state God's other works may be,
In their own tasks all their powers pouring,
These attain the mighty life you see."

O air-born Voice! long since, severely clear,
A cry like thine in my own heart I hear.
"Resolve to be thyself: and know, that he
Who finds himself, loses his misery."

A SUMMER NIGHT.

IN the deserted moon-blanch'd street
How lonely rings the echo of my feet!
Those windows, which I gaze at, frown,
Silent and white, unopening down,
Repellent as the world:—but see!
A break between the housetops shows
The moon, and, lost behind her, fading dim
Into the dewy dark obscurity
Down at the far horizon's rim,
    Doth a whole tract of heaven disclose.

Poems.

And to my mind the thought
Is on a sudden brought
Of a past night, and a far different scene.
Headlands stood out into the moon-lit deep
As clearly as at noon;
The spring-tide's brimming flow
Heav'd dazzlingly between;
Houses with long white sweep
Girdled the glistening bay:
Behind, through the soft air,
The blue haze-cradled mountains spread away.
    That night was far more fair;
But the same restless pacings to and fro,
And the same agitated heart was there,
And the same bright calm moon.

And the calm moonlight seems to say—
—" Hast thou then still the old unquiet breast
That neither deadens into rest
Nor ever feels the fiery glow
That whirls the spirit from itself away,
But fluctuates to and fro
Never by passion quite possess'd,
And never quite benumb'd by the world's sway?"—
And I, I know not if to pray
Still to be what I am, or yield, and be
Like all the other men I see.

For most men in a brazen prison live,
Where in the sun's hot eye,
With heads bent o'er their toil, they languidly
Their lives to some unmeaning taskwork give,

Poems.

Dreaming of nought beyond their prison wall.
And as, year after year,
Fresh products of their barren labour fall
From their tired hands, and rest
Never yet comes more near,
Gloom settles slowly down over their breast.
And while they try to stem
The waves of mournful thought by which they are prest,
Death in their prison reaches them
Unfreed, having seen nothing, still unblest.

And the rest, a few,
Escape their prison, and depart
On the wide Ocean of Life anew.
There the freed prisoner, where'er his heart
Listeth, will sail ;
Nor does he know how there prevail,
Despotic on life's sea,
Trade-winds that cross it from eternity.
Awhile he holds some false way, undebarr'd
By thwarting signs, and braves
The freshening wind and blackening waves.
And then the tempest strikes him, and between
The lightning bursts is seen
Only a driving wreck,
And the pale Master on his spar-strewn deck
With anguish'd face and flying hair
Grasping the rudder hard,
Still bent to make some port he knows not where,
Still standing for some false impossible shore.
And sterner comes the roar

Of sea and wind, and through the deepening gloom
Fainter and fainter wreck and helmsman loom,
And he too disappears, and comes no more.
　　Is there no life, but these alone?
Madman or slave, must man be one?

Plainness and clearness without shadow of stain,
Clearness divine!
Ye Heavens, whose pure dark regions have no sign
Of languor, though so calm, and though so great
Are yet untroubled and unpassionate:
Who, though so noble, share in the world's toil,
And though so task'd, keep free from dust and soil:
I will not say that your mild deeps retain
A tinge, it may be, of their silent pain
Who have long'd deeply once, and long'd in vain;
But I will rather say that you remain
A world above man's head, to let him see
How boundless might his soul's horizon be,
How vast, yet of what clear transparency.
How it were good to sink there, and breathe free.
　　How high a lot to fill
Is left to each man still.

THE BURIED LIFE.

Light flows our war of mocking words, and yet,
Behold, with tears my eyes are wet.
I feel a nameless sadness o'er me roll.
　　Yes, yes, we know that we can jest,

Poems.

We know, we know that we can smile ;
But there's a something in this breast
To which thy light words bring no rest,
And thy gay smiles no anodyne.
  Give me thy hand, and hush awhile,
And turn those limpid eyes on mine,
And let me read there, love, thy inmost soul.

Alas, is even Love too weak
To unlock the heart and let it speak ?
Are even lovers powerless to reveal
To one another what indeed they feel ?
I knew the mass of men conceal'd
Their thoughts, for fear that if reveal'd
They would by other men be met
With blank indifference, or with blame reprov'd :
I knew they liv'd and mov'd
Trick'd in disguises, alien to the rest
Of men, and alien to themselves—and yet
  There beats one heart in every human breast.
But we, my love—does a like spell benumb
Our hearts—our voices ?—must we too be dumb ?

Ah, well for us, if even we,
Even for a moment, can get free
Our heart, and have our lips unchain'd :
  For that which seals them hath been deep ordain'd.

Fate, which foresaw
How frivolous a baby man would be,
By what distractions he would be possess'd,
How he would pour himself in every strife,

Poems.

And well-nigh change his own identity ;
That it might keep from his capricious play
His genuine self, and force him to obey
Even in his own despite, his being's law,
Bade, through the deep recesses of our breast,
The unregarded river of our life
Pursue with indiscernible flow its way ;
And that we should not see
The buried stream, and seem to be
Eddying about in blind uncertainty,
Though driving on with it eternally.
But often in the world's most crowded streets,
But often, in the din of strife,
There rises an unspeakable desire
After the knowledge of our buried life,
A thirst to spend our fire and restless force
In tracking out our true, original course ;
A longing to enquire
Into the mystery of this heart that beats
So wild, so deep in us, to know
Whence our thoughts come, and where they go.
And many a man in his own breast then delves,
But deep enough, alas, none ever mines :
And we have been on many thousand lines,
And we have shown on each talent and power,
But hardly have we, for one little hour,
Been on our own line, have we been ourselves ;
Hardly had skill to utter one of all
The nameless feelings that course through our breast,
But they course on for ever unexpress'd.
And long we try in vain to speak and act
Our hidden self, and what we say and do

Poems.

Is eloquent, is well—but 'tis not true :
   And then we will no more be rack'd
With inward striving, and demand
Of all the thousand things of the hour
Their stupifying power,
Ah yes, and they benumb us at our call ;
Yet still, from time to time, vague and forlorn,
From the soul's subterranean depth upborne
As from an infinitely distant land,
Come airs, and floating echoes, and convey
A melancholy into all our day.

Only—but this is rare—
When a beloved hand is laid in ours,
When, jaded with the rush and glare
Of the interminable hours,
Our eyes can in another's eyes read clear,
When our world-deafen'd ear
Is by the tones of a loved voice caress'd,
   A bolt is shot back somewhere in our breast
And a lost pulse of feeling stirs again :
The eye sinks inward, and the heart lies plain,
And what we mean, we say, and what we would, we
       know.
A man becomes aware of his life's flow
And hears its winding murmur, and he sees
The meadows where it glides, the sun, the breeze.

And there arrives a lull in the hot race
Wherein he doth for ever chase
That flying and elusive shadow, Rest.
An air of coolness plays upon his face,

Poems.

And an unwonted calm pervades his breast.
  And then he thinks he knows
The Hills where his life rose,
And the Sea where it goes.

A FAREWELL.

My horse's feet beside the lake,
Where sweet the unbroken moonbeams lay,
Sent echoes through the night to wake
Each glistening strand, each heath-fring'd bay.

The poplar avenue was pass'd,
And the roof'd bridge that spans the stream.
Up the steep street I hurried fast,
Lit by thy taper's starlike beam.

I came, I saw thee rise;—the blood
Came flooding to thy languid cheek.
Lock'd in each other's arms we stood,
In tears, with hearts too full to speak.

Days flew: ah, soon I could discern
A trouble in thine alter'd air.
Thy hand lay languidly in mine—
Thy cheek was grave, thy speech grew rare.

I blame thee not :—this heart, I know
To be long lov'd was never fram'd ;
For something in its depths doth glow
Too strange, too restless, too untam'd.

Poems.

And women—things that live and move
Min'd by the fever of the soul—
They seek to find in those they love
Stern strength, and promise of control.

They ask not kindness, gentle ways ;
These they themselves have tried and known :
They ask a soul that never sways
With the blind gusts which shake their own.

I too have felt the load I bore
In a too strong emotion's sway ;
I too have wish'd, no woman more,
This starting, feverish heart away.

I too have long'd for trenchant force,
And will like a dividing spear ;
Have praised the keen, unscrupulous course,
Which knows no doubt, which feels no fear.

But in the world I learnt, what there
Thou too wilt surely one day prove,
That will, that energy, though rare,
Are yet far far less rare than love.

Go, then ! till Time and Fate impress
This truth on thee, be mine no more !
They will : for thou, I feel, no less
Than I, wert destin'd to this lore.

We school our manners, act our parts :
But He, who sees us through and through,

Knows that the bent of both our hearts
Was to be gentle, tranquil, true.

And though we wear out life, alas !
Distracted as a homeless wind,
In beating where we must not pass,
In seeking what we shall not find ;

Yet we shall one day gain, life past,
Clear prospect o'er our being's whole :
Shall see ourselves, and learn at last
Our true affinities of soul.

We shall not then deny a course
To every thought the mass ignore :
We shall not then call hardness force,
Nor lightness wisdom any more.

Then, in the eternal Father's smile,
Our sooth'd, encourag'd souls will dare
To seem as free from pride and guile,
As good, as generous, as they are.

Then we shall know our friends : though much
Will have been lost—the help in strife ;
The thousand sweet still joys of such
As hand in hand face earthly life—

Though these be lost, there will be yet
A sympathy august and pure ;
Ennobled by a vast regret,
And by contrition seal'd thrice sure.

Poems.

And we, whose ways were unlike here,
May then more neighbouring courses ply,
May to each other be brought near,
And greet across infinity.

How sweet, unreach'd by earthly jars,
My sister! to behold with thee
The hush among the shining stars,
The calm upon the moonlit sea.

How sweet to feel, on the boon air,
All our unquiet pulses cease—
To feel that nothing can impair
The gentleness, the thirst for peace—

The gentleness too rudely hurl'd
On this wild earth of hate and fear:
The thirst for peace a raving world
Would never let us satiate here.

STANZAS

In memory of the author of " Obermann."

In front the awful Alpine track
Crawls up its rocky stair;
The autumn storm-winds drive the rack
Close o'er it, in the air.

Behind are the abandoned baths
Mute in their meadows lone;

Poems.

The leaves are on the valley paths ;
The mists are on the Rhone—

The white mists rolling like a sea.
I hear the torrents roar.
—Yes, Obermann, all speaks of thee !
I feel thee near once more.

I turn thy leaves : I feel their breath
Once more upon me roll ;
That air of languor, cold, and death,
Which brooded o'er thy soul.

Fly hence, poor Wretch, whoe'er thou art,
Condemn'd to cast about,
All shipwreck in thy own weak heart,
For comfort from without :

A fever in these pages burns
Beneath the calm they feign ;
A wounded human spirit turns
Here on its bed of pain.

Yes, though the virgin mountain air
Fresh through these pages blows,
Though to these leaves the glaciers spare
The soul of their mute snows,

Though here a mountain murmur swells
Of many a dark-bough'd pine,
Though, as you read, you hear the bells
Of the high-pasturing kine—

Poems.

Yet, through the hum of torrent lone,
And brooding mountain bee,
There sobs I know not what ground tone
Of human agony.

Is it for this, because the sound
Is fraught too deep with pain,
That, Obermann! the world around
So little loves thy strain?

Some secrets may the poet tell,
For the world loves new ways.
To tell too deep ones is not well;
It knows not what he says.

Yet of the spirits who have reign'd
In this our troubled day,
I know but two, who have attain'd,
Save thee, to see their way.

By England's lakes, in grey old age,
His quiet home one keeps;[1]
And one, the strong much-toiling Sage,
In German Weimar sleeps.

But Wordsworth's eyes avert their ken
From half of human fate;
And Goethe's course few sons of man
May think to emulate.

[1] Written in November, 1849.

Poems.

For he pursued a lonely road,
His eye on nature's plan ;
Neither made man too much a God,
Nor God too much a man.

Strong was he, with a spirit free
From mists, and sane, and clear ;
Clearer, how much ! than ours : yet we
Have a worse course to steer.

For though his manhood bore the blast
Of a tremendous time,
Yet in a tranquil world was pass'd
His tenderer youthful prime.

But we, brought forth and rear'd in hours
Of change, alarm, surprise—
What shelter to grow ripe is ours ?
What leisure to grow wise ?

Like children bathing on the shore,
Buried a wave beneath,
The second wave succeeds, before
We have had time to breathe.

Too fast we live, too much are tried,
Too harass'd to attain
Wordsworth's sweet calm, or Goethe's wide
And luminous view to gain.

And then we turn, thou sadder sage !
To thee : we feel thy spell.

Poems.

The hopeless tangle of our age—
Thou too hast scann'd it well.

Immovable thou sittest; still
As death; compos'd to bear.
Thy head is clear, thy feeling chill—
And icy thy despair.

Yes, as the Son of Thetis said,
One hears thee saying now—
"Greater by far than thou art dead:
Strive not: die also thou."—

Ah! Two desires toss about
The poet's feverish blood.
One drives him to the world without,
And one to solitude.

The glow of thought, the thrill of life—
Where, where do these abound?
Not in the world, not in the strife
Of men, shall they be found.

He who hath watch'd, not shar'd, the strife,
Knows how the day hath gone;
He only lives with the world's life
Who hath renounc'd his own.

To thee we come, then. Clouds are roll'd
Where thou, O Seer, art set;
Thy realm of thought is drear and cold—
The world is colder yet!

And thou hast pleasures too to share
With those who come to thee:
Balms floating on thy mountain air,
And healing sights to see.

How often, where the slopes are green
On Jaman, hast thou sate
By some high chalet door and seen
The summer day grow late,

And darkness steal o'er the wet grass
With the pale crocus starr'd,
And reach that glimmering sheet of glass
Beneath the piny sward,

Lake Leman's waters, far below:
And watch'd the rosy light
Fade from the distant peaks of snow:
And on the air of night

Heard accents of the eternal tongue
Through the pine branches play:
Listen'd, and felt thyself grow young;
Listen'd, and wept—Away!

Away the dreams that but deceive!
And thou, sad Guide, adieu!
I go; Fate drives me: but I leave
Half of my life with you.

We, in some unknown Power's employ,
Move on a rigorous line:

Can neither, when we will, enjoy ;
Nor, when we will, resign.

I in the world must live :—but thou,
Thy melancholy Shade !
Wilt not, if thou can'st see me now,
Condemn me, nor upbraid.

For thou art gone away from earth,
And place with those dost claim,
The Children of the Second Birth
Whom the world could not tame ;

And with that small transfigur'd Band,
Whom many a different way
Conducted to their common land,
Thou learn'st to think as they.

Christian and pagan, king and slave,
Soldier and anchorite,
Distinctions we esteem so grave,
Are nothing in their sight.

They do not ask, who pin'd unseen,
Who was on action hurl'd,
Whose one bond is, that all have been
Unspotted by the world.

There without anger thou wilt see
Him who obeys thy spell
No more, so he but rest, like thee,
Unsoil'd :—and so, Farewell !

Poems.

Farewell !—Whether thou now liest near
That much-lov'd inland sea,,
The ripples of whose blue waves cheer
Vevey and Meillerie,

And in that gracious region bland,
Where with clear-rustling wave
The scented pines of Switzerland
Stand dark round thy green grave,

Between the dusty vineyard walls
Issuing on that green place,
The early peasant still recalls
The pensive stranger's face,

And stoops to clear thy moss-grown date
Ere he plods on again :
Or whether, by maligner fate,
Among the swarms of men,

Where between granite terraces
The Seine conducts her wave,
The Capital of Pleasure sees
Thy hardly heard of grave—

Farewell ! Under the sky we part,
In this stern Alpine dell.
O unstrung will ! O broken heart !
A last, a last farewell !

Poems.

CONSOLATION.

Mɪsᴛ clogs the sunshine.
Smoky dwarf houses
Hem me round everywhere.
    A vague dejection
Weighs down my soul.

Yet, while I languish,
Everywhere, countless
Prospects unroll themselves
    And countless beings
Pass countless moods.

Far hence, in Asia,
On the smooth convent-roofs,
On the gold terraces
    Of holy Lassa,
Bright shines the sun.

Grey time-worn marbles
Hold the pure Muses.
In their cool gallery,
    By yellow Tiber,
They still look fair.

Strange unlov'd uproar [1]
Shrills round their portal.
Yet not on Helicon
    Kept they more cloudless
Their noble calm.

[1] Written during the siege of Rome by the French.

Through sun-proof alleys,
In a lone, sand-hemm'd
City of Africa,
  A blind, led beggar,
Age-bow'd, asks alms.

No bolder Robber
Erst abode ambush'd
Deep in the sandy waste:
  No clearer eyesight
Spied prey afar.

Saharan sand-winds
Sear'd his keen eyeballs.
Spent is the spoil he won,
  For him the present
Holds only pain.

Two young, fair lovers,
Where the warm June wind,
Fresh from the summer fields,
  Plays fondly round them,
Stand, tranc'd in joy.

With sweet, join'd voices,
And with eyes brimming—
"Ah," they cry, "Destiny
  Prolong the present!
Time! stand still here!"

Poems.

The prompt stern Goddess
Shakes her head, frowning.
Time gives his hour glass
    Its due reversal.
Their hour is gone.

With weak indulgence
Did the just Goddess
Lengthen their happiness,
    She lengthen'd also
Distress elsewhere.

The hour, whose happy
Unalloy'd moments
I would eternalize,
    Ten thousand mourners
Well pleas'd see end.

The bleak stern hour,
Whose severe moments
I would annihilate,
    Is pass'd by others
In warmth, light, joy.

Time, so complain'd of,
Who to no one man
Shows partiality,
    Brings round to all men
Some undimm'd hours.

Poems.

LINES

Written in Kensington Gardens.

In this lone open glade I lie,
Screen'd by dark trees on either hand ;
And at its head, to stay the eye,
Those black-topp'd, red-bol'd pine-trees stand.

The clouded sky is still and grey,
Through silken rifts soft peers the sun,
Light the green-foliag'd chestnuts play,
The darker elms stand grave and dun.

The birds sing sweetly in these trees
Across the girdling city's hum ;
How green under the boughs it is !
How thick the tremulous sheep-cries come !

Sometimes a child will cross the glade
To take his nurse his broken toy :
Sometimes a thrush flit overhead
Deep in her unknown day's employ.

Here at my feet what wonders pass,
What endless active life is here !
What blowing daisies, fragrant grass !
An air-stirr'd forest, fresh and clear.

Poems.

Scarce fresher is the mountain sod
Where the tired angler lies, stretch'd out,
And, eas'd of basket and of rod,
Counts his day's spoil, the spotted trout.

I, on men's impious uproar hurl'd,
Think sometimes, as I hear them rave,
That peace has left the upper world,
And now keeps only in the grave.

Yet here is peace for ever new.
When I, who watch them, am away,
Still all things in this glade go through
The changes of their quiet day.

Then to their happy rest they pass.
The flowers close, the birds are fed :
The night comes down upon the grass :
The child sleeps warmly in his bed.

Calm Soul of all things ! make it mine
To feel, amid the city's jar,
That there abides a peace of thine,
Man did not make, and cannot mar.

The will to neither strive nor cry,
The power to feel with others give.
Calm, calm me more ; not let me die
Before I have begun to live.

Poems.

SONNET.[1]

So far as I conceive the World's rebuke
To him address'd who would recast her new,
Not from herself her fame of strength she took,
But from their weakness, who would work her rue.
  " Behold, she cries, so many rages lull'd,
So many fiery spirits quite cool'd down :
Look how so many valours, long undull'd,
After short commerce with me, fear my frown.
Thou too, when thou against my crimes wouldst cry,
Let thy foreboded homage check thy tongue."—
The World speaks well : yet might her foe reply—
  " Are wills so weak ? then let not mine wait long.
Hast thou so rare a poison ? let me be
Keener to slay thee, lest thou poison me."

THE SECOND BEST.

MODERATE tasks and moderate leisure ;
Quiet living, strict-kept measure
Both in suffering and in pleasure,
  'Tis for this thy nature yearns.

But so many books thou readest,
But so many schemes thou breedest,
But so many wishes feedest,
  That thy poor head almost turns.

[1] In the " Poems," 1853, this sonnet is entitled " The World's Triumphs."—ED.

Poems.

And, (the world's so madly jangled,
Human things so fast entangled)
Nature's wish must now be strangled
   For that best which she discerns.

So it must be : yet, while leading
A strain'd life, while overfeeding,
Like the rest, his wit with reading,
   No small profit that man earns,

Who through all he meets can steer him,
Can reject what cannot clear him,
Cling to what can truly cheer him :
   Who each day more surely learns

That an impulse, from the distance
Of his deepest, best existence,
To the words " Hope, Light, Persistance,"
   Strongly stirs and truly burns.

REVOLUTIONS.

Before Man parted for this earthly strand,
While yet upon the verge of heaven he stood,
God put a heap of letters in his hand,
And bade him make with them what word he could.

And Man has turn'd them many times : made Greece,
Rome, England, France :—yes, nor in vain essay'd
Way after way, changes that never cease.
The letters have combin'd : something was made.

Poems.

But ah, an inextinguishable sense
Haunts him that he has not made what he should.
That he has still, though old, to recommence,
Since he has not yet found the word God would.

And Empire after Empire, at their height
Of sway, have felt this boding sense come on.
Have felt their huge frames not constructed right,
And droop'd, and slowly died upon their throne.

One day, thou say'st, there will at last appear
The word, the order, which God meant should be.
Ah, we shall know *that* well when it comes near.
The band will quit Man's heart :—he will breathe free.

THE YOUTH OF NATURE.

Rais'd are the dripping oars—
Silent the boat : the lake,
Lovely and soft as a dream,
Swims in the sheen of the moon.
The mountains stand at its head
Clear in the pure June night,
But the valleys are flooded with haze.
Rydal and Fairfield are there ;
In the shadow Wordsworth lies dead.
So it is, so it will be for aye.
    Nature is fresh as of old,
Is lovely : a mortal is dead.

The spots which recall him survive,
For he lent a new life to these hills.
The Pillar still broods o'er the fields
That border Ennerdale Lake,
And Egremont sleeps by the sea.
The gleam of the Evening Star
Twinkles on Grasmere no more,
But ruin'd and solemn and grey
The sheepfold of Michael survives,
And far to the south, the heath
Still blows in the Quantock coombs,
    By the favourite waters of Ruth.
These survive : yet not without pain,
Pain and dejection to-night,
Can I feel that their Poet is gone.

He grew old in an age he condemn'd.
He look'd on the rushing decay
Of the times which had shelter'd his youth.
Felt the dissolving throes
Of a social order he lov'd.
Outliv'd his brethren, his peers.
And, like the Theban seer,
    Died in his enemies' day.

Cold bubbled the spring of Tilphusa.
Copais lay bright in the moon.
Helicon glass'd in the lake
Its firs, and afar, rose the peaks
Of Parnassus, snowily clear.
Thebes was behind him in flames,

Poems.

And the clang of arms in his ear,
When his awe-struck captors led
The Theban seer to the spring.
  Tiresias drank and died.
Nor did reviving Thebes
See such a prophet again.

Well, may we mourn, when the head
Of a sacred poet lies low
In an age which can rear them no more.
The complaining millions of men
Darken in labour and pain;
But he was a priest to us all
Of the wonder and bloom of the world,
Which we saw with his eyes, and were glad.
  He is dead, and the fruit-bearing day
Of his race is past on the earth;
And darkness returns to our eyes.

For oh, is it you, is it you,
Moonlight, and shadow, and lake,
And mountains, that fills us with joy,
Or the Poet who sings you so well?
Is it you, O Beauty, O Grace,
O Charm, O Romance, that we feel,
Or the voice which reveals what you are?
Are ye, like daylight and sun,
Shar'd and rejoic'd in by all?
Or are ye immers'd in the mass
Of matter, and hard to extract,
Or sunk at the core of the world
Too deep for the most to discern?

Poems.

Like stars in the deep of the sky,
Which arise on the glass of the sage,
But are lost when their watcher is gone.

"They are here"—I heard, as men heard
In Mysian Ida the voice
Of the Mighty Mother, or Crete,
The murmur of Nature reply—
"Loveliness, Magic, and Grace,
They are here—they are set in the world—
They abide—and the finest of souls
Has not been thrill'd by them all,
Nor the dullest been dead to them quite.
The poet who sings them may die,
But they are immortal, and live,
For they are the life of the world.
    Will ye not learn it, and know,
When ye mourn that a poet is dead,
That the singer was less than his themes,
    Life, and Emotion, and I?

"More than the singer are these.
Weak is the tremor of pain
That thrills in his mournfullest chord
To that which once ran through his soul.
Cold the elation of joy
In his gladdest, airiest song,
To that which of old in his youth
Fill'd him and made him divine.
Hardly his voice at its best
Gives us a sense of the awe,

Poems.

The vastness, the grandeur, the gloom
Of the unlit gulf of himself.

"Ye know not yourselves—and your bards,
The clearest, the best, who have read
Most in themselves, have beheld
Less than they left unreveal'd.
Ye express not yourselves—can ye make
With marble, with colour, with word
What charm'd you in others re-live?
Can thy pencil, O Artist, restore
The figure, the bloom of thy love,
As she was in her morning of spring?
Canst thou paint the ineffable smile
Of her eyes as they rested on thine?
Can the image of life have the glow,
The motion of life itself?

"Yourselves and your fellows ye know not—and me
The mateless, the one, will ye know?
Will ye scan me, and read me, and tell
Of the thoughts that ferment in my breast,
My longing, my sadness, my joy?
Will ye claim for your great ones the gift
To have render'd the gleam of my skies,
To have echoed the moan of my seas,
Utter'd the voice of my hills?
When your great ones depart, will ye say—
   "All things have suffer'd a loss—
Nature is hid in their grave?"

" Race after race, man after man,
Have dream'd that my secret was theirs,
Have thought that I liv'd but for them,
That they were my glory and joy.—
They are dust, they are chang'd, they are gone.
      I remain."

THE YOUTH OF MAN.

WE, O Nature, depart,
Thou survivest us : this,
This, I know, is the law.
Yes, but more than this,
Thou who seest us die
Seest us change while we live ;
Seest our dreams one by one,
Seest our errors depart :
   Watchest us, Nature, throughout,
Mild and inscrutably calm.

Well for us that we change !
Well for us that the Power
Which in our morning prime,
Saw the mistakes of our youth,
Sweet, and forgiving, and good,
Sees the contrition of age !

Behold, O Nature, this pair !
See them to-night where they stand,

Poems.

Not with the halo of youth
Crowning their brows with its light,
Not with the sunshine of hope,
Not with the rapture of spring,
Which they had of old, when they stood
Years ago at my side
In this self-same garden, and said;
"We are young, and the world is ours,
For man is the king of the world.
Fools that these mystics are
Who prate of Nature! but she
Has neither beauty, nor warmth,
Nor life, nor emotion, nor power.
But Man has a thousand gifts,
And the generous dreamer invests
The senseless world with them all.
   Nature is nothing! her charm
Lives in our eyes which can paint,
Lives in our hearts which can feel!"

Thou, O Nature, wert mute,
Mute as of old: days flew,
Days and years; and Time
With the ceaseless stroke of his wings
Brush'd off the bloom from their soul.
Clouded and dim grew their eye,
Languid their heart; for Youth
Quicken'd its pulses no more.
Slowly within the walls
Of an ever-narrowing world
They droop'd, they grew blind, they grew old.

Poems.

Thee and their Youth in thee,
Nature, they saw no more.

    Murmur of living!
Stir of existence!
Soul of the world!
Make, oh make yourselves felt
To the dying spirit of Youth.
Come, like the breath of the spring.
Leave not a human soul
To grow old in darkness and pain.
    Only the living can feel you:
But leave us not while we live.

Here they stand to-night—
Here, where this grey balustrade
Crowns the still valley: behind
Is the castled house with its woods
Which shelter'd their childhood, the sun
On its ivied windows; a scent
From the grey-wall'd gardens, a breath
Of the fragrant stock and the pink
Perfumes the evening air.
    Their children play on the lawns.
They stand and listen: they hear
The children's shouts, and, at times,
Faintly, the bark of a dog
From a distant farm in the hills:—
Nothing besides: in front
The wide, wide valley outspreads
To the dim horizon, repos'd
In the twilight, and bath'd in dew,

Poems.

Corn-field and hamlet and copse
Darkening fast ; but a light,
Far off, a glory of day,
Still plays on the city spires :
And there in the dusk by the walls,
With the grey mist marking its course
Though the silent flowery land,
On, to the plains, to the sea,
Floats the imperial Stream.

Well I know what they feel.
They gaze, and the evening wind
Plays on their faces : they gaze ;
Airs from the Eden of Youth,
Awake and stir in their soul :
The past returns ; they feel
What they are, alas ! what they were.
They, not Nature, are chang'd.
Well I know what they feel.

Hush ! for tears
Begin to steal to their eyes.
Hush ! for fruit
Grows from such sorrow as theirs.

And they remember
With piercing untold anguish
The proud boasting of their youth.
And they feel how Nature was fair.
And the mists of delusion,
And the scales of habit,
Fall away from their eyes.

And they see, for a moment,
Stretching out, like the desert
In its weary, unprofitable length,
    Their faded ignoble lives.

While the locks are yet brown on thy head,
While the soul still looks through thine eyes,
While the heart still pours
The mantling blood to thy cheek,
    Sink, O Youth, in thy soul !
Yearn to the greatness of Nature !
Rally the good in the depths of thyself.

MORALITY.

We cannot kindle when we will
The fire that in the heart resides
The spirit bloweth and is still,
In mystery our soul abides :
    But tasks in hours of insight will'd
Can be through hours of gloom fulfill'd.

With aching hands and bleeding feet
We dig and heap, lay stone on stone ;
We bear the burden and the heat
Of the long day, and wish 'twere done.
    Not till the hours of light return
All we have built do we discern.

Poems.

Then, when the clouds are off the soul,
When thou dost bask in Nature's eye,
Ask, how *she* view'd thy self-control,
Thy struggling task'd morality.
   Nature, whose free, light, cheerful air,
Oft made thee, in thy gloom, despair.

And she, whose censure thou dost dread,
Whose eyes thou wert afraid to seek,
See, on her face a glow is spread,
A strong emotion on her cheek.
   " Ah child," she cries, " that strife divine—
Whence was it, for it is not mine?

" 'There is no effort on *my* brow—
I do not strive, I do not weep.
I rush with the swift spheres, and glow
In joy, and, when I will, I sleep.—
   Yet that severe, that earnest air,
I saw, I felt it once—but where?

" I knew not yet the gauge of Time,
Nor wore the manacles of Space.
I felt it in some other clime—
I saw it in some other place.
   —'Twas when the heavenly house I trod.
And lay upon the breast of God."

Poems.

PROGRESS.

THE Master stood upon the Mount, and taught.
He saw a fire in his Disciples' eyes.
" The old Law," they said, "is wholly come to nought ;
   Behold the new world rise ! "

" Was it," the Lord then said, "with scorn ye saw
The old Law observed by Scribes and Pharisees?
I say unto you, see *ye* keep that Law
   More faithfully than these.

" Too hasty heads for ordering worlds, alas !
Think not that I to annul the Law have will'd.
No jot, no tittle from the Law shall pass,
   Till all shall be fulfill'd."

So Christ said eighteen hundred years ago.
And what then shall be said to those to-day
Who cry aloud to lay the old world low
   To clear the new world's way?

"Religious fervours ! ardour misapplied !
Hence, hence," they cry, " ye do but keep man blind !
But keep him self-immers'd, preoccupied,
   And lame the active mind."

Ah, from the old world let some one answer give—
" Scorn ye this world, their tears, their inward cares?
I say unto you, see that *your* souls live
   A deeper life than theirs.

Poems.

"Say ye,—The spirit of man has found new roads;
And we must leave the old faiths, and walk therein?—
Quench then the altar fires of your old Gods!
    Quench not the fire within!

"Bright else, and fast, the stream of life may roll,
And no man may the other's hurt behold.
Yet each will have one anguish—his own soul
    Which perishes of cold."

Here let that voice make end : then, let a strain
From a far lonelier distance, like the wind
Be heard, floating through heaven, and fill again
    These men's profoundest mind—

"Children of men! the unseen Power, whose eye
Ever accompanies the march of man,
Hath without pain seen *no* religion die,
    Since first the world began.

"That man must still to some new worship press
Hath in his eye ever but serv'd to show
The depth of that consuming restlessness
    Which makes man's greatest woe.

"Which has not taught weak wills how much they can,
Which has not fall'n on the dry heart like rain?
Which has not cried to sunk self-weary man,
    'Thou must be born again?'

Poems.

"Children of men ! not that your age excel
In pride of life the ages of your sires ;
But that you too feel deeply, bear fruit well,
  The Friend of man desires."

THE FUTURE.

A WANDERER is man from his birth.
He was born in a ship
On the breast of the River of Time.
Brimming with wonder and joy
He spreads out his arms to the light,
Rivets his gaze on the banks of the stream.

As what he sees is, so have his thoughts been.
Whether he wakes
Where the snowy mountainous pass
Echoing the screams of the eagles
Hems in its gorges the bed
  Of the new-born clear-flowing stream :

Whether he first sees light
Where the river in gleaming rings
  Sluggishly winds through the plain :
Whether in sound of the swallowing sea :—
  As is the world on the banks
So is the mind of the man.

Poems.

Vainly does each as he glides
Fable and dream
Of the lands which the River of Time
Had left ere he woke on its breast,
Or shall reach when his eyes have been clos'd.
Only the tract where he sails
He wots of: only the thoughts,
Rais'd by the objects he passes, are his.

Who can see the green Earth any more
As she was by the sources of Time?
Who imagines her fields as they lay
In the sunshine, unworn by the plough?
Who thinks as they thought,
The tribes who then liv'd on her breast,
   Her vigorous primitive sons?

   What girl
Now reads in her bosom as clear
As Rebekah read, when she sate
At eve by the palm-shaded well?
Who guards in her breast
As deep, as pellucid a spring
Of feeling, as tranquil, as sure?

   What Bard,
At the height of his vision, can deem
Of God, of the world, of the soul,
With a plainness as near,
As flashing as Moses felt,

When he lay in the night by his flock
On the starlit Arabian waste?
Can rise and obey
The beck of the Spirit like him?

This tract which the River of Time
Now flows through with us, is the Plain.
Gone is the calm of its earlier shore.
Border'd by cities and hoarse
With a thousand cries is its stream.
And we on its breast, our minds
Are confus'd as the cries which we hear,
Changing and shot as the sights which we see.

And we say that repose has fled
For ever the course of the River of Time.
That cities will crowd to its edge
In a blacker incessanter line;
That the din will be more on its banks,
Denser the trade on its stream,
Flatter the plain where it flows,
Fiercer the sun overhead.
That never will those on its breast
See an ennobling sight,
Drink of the feeling of quiet again.

But what was before us we know not,
And we know not what shall succeed.

Haply, the River of Time,
As it grows, as the towns on its marge

Poems.

Fling their wavering lights
On a wider statelier stream—
May acquire, if not the calm
Of its early mountainous shore,
    Yet a solemn peace of its own.

And the width of the waters, the hush
Of the grey expanse where he floats,
Freshening its current and spotted with foam
As it draws to the Ocean, may strike
Peace to the soul of the man on its breast :
    As the pale waste widens around him—
As the banks fade dimmer away—
As the stars come out, and the night-wind
Brings up the stream
Murmurs and scents of the infinite Sea.

POEMS

BY

MATTHEW ARNOLD.

A NEW EDITION.

BIBLIOGRAPHICAL NOTE.

Poems by Matthew Arnold. A New Edition. London: Longman, Brown, Green, and Longmans, 1853. This volume contains many poems from the "Empedocles" and "Strayed Reveller" volumes, and the following nine poems, one of which, "Thekla's Answer," is printed in this volume only.

Preface.

In two small volumes of Poems, published anony-
mously, one in 1849, the other in 1852, many of the
Poems which compose the present volume have already
appeared. The rest are now published for the first
time.

I have, in the present collection, omitted the Poem
from which the volume published in 1852 took its
title. I have done so, not because the subject of it
was a Sicilian Greek born between two and three
thousand years ago, although many persons would
think this a sufficient reason. Neither have I done so
because I had, in my own opinion, failed in the de-
lineation which I intended to effect. I intended to
delineate the feelings of one of the last of the Greek
religious philosophers, one of the family of Orpheus
and Musæus, having survived his fellows, living on into
a time when the habits of Greek thought and feeling
had begun fast to change, character to dwindle, the
influence of the Sophists to prevail. Into the feelings
of a man so situated there entered much that we are
accustomed to consider as exclusively modern ; how
much, the fragments of Empedocles himself which
remain to us are sufficient at least to indicate. What
those who are familiar only with the great monuments

of early Greek genius suppose to be its exclusive characteristics, have disappeared ; the calm, the cheerfulness, the disinterested objectivity have disappeared : the dialogue of the mind with itself has commenced ; modern problems have presented themselves ; we hear already the doubts, we witness the discouragement, of Hamlet and of Faust.

The representation of such a man's feelings must be interesting, if consistently drawn. We all naturally take pleasure, says Aristotle, in any imitation or representation whatever : this is the basis of our love of Poetry : and we take pleasure in them, he adds, because all knowledge is naturally agreeable to us ; not to the philosopher only, but to mankind at large. Every representation therefore which is consistently drawn may be supposed to be interesting, inasmuch as it gratifies this natural interest in knowledge of all kinds. What is *not* interesting, is that which does not add to our knowledge of any kind ; that which is vaguely conceived and loosely drawn ; a representation which is general, indeterminate, and faint, instead of being particular, precise, and firm.

Any accurate representation may therefore be expected to be interesting ; but, if the representation be a poetical one, more than this is demanded. It is demanded, not only that it shall interest, but also that it shall inspirit and rejoice the reader : that it shall convey a charm, and infuse delight. For the Muses, as Hesiod says, were born that they might be " a forgetfulness of evils, and a truce from cares : " and it is not enough that the Poet should add to the knowledge of men, it is required of him also that he should add to their happiness. "All Art," says Schiller," is dedicated to Joy, and there is no higher and no more serious problem, than how to make men happy. The right Art is that alone, which creates the highest enjoyment."

A poetical work, therefore, is not yet justified when it has been shown to be an accurate, and therefore interesting representation; it has to be shown also that it is a representation from which men can derive enjoyment. In presence of the most tragic circumstances, represented in a work of Art, the feeling of enjoyment, as is well known, may still subsist: the representation of the most utter calamity, of the liveliest anguish, is not sufficient to destroy it: the more tragic the situation, the deeper becomes the enjoyment; and the situation is more tragic in proportion as it becomes more terrible.

What then are the situations, from the representation of which, though accurate, no poetical enjoyment can be derived? They are those in which the suffering finds no vent in action; in which a continuous state of mental distress is prolonged, unrelieved by incident, hope, or resistance; in which there is everything to be endured, nothing to be done. In such situations there is inevitably something morbid, in the description of them something monotonous. When they occur in actual life, they are painful, not tragic; the representation of them in poetry is painful also.

To this class of situations, poetically faulty as it appears to me, that of Empedocles, as I have endeavoured to represent him, belongs; and I have therefore excluded the Poem from the present collection.

Preface.

And why, it may be asked, have I entered into this explanation respecting a matter so unimportant as the admission or exclusion of the Poem in question? I have done so, because I was anxious to avow that the sole reason for its exclusion was that which has been stated above; and that it has not been excluded in deference to the opinion which many critics of the present day appear to entertain against subjects chosen from distant times and countries: against the choice, in short, of any subjects but modern ones.

"The Poet," it is said, and by an apparently intelligent critic, "the Poet who would really fix the public attention must leave the exhausted past, and draw his subjects from matters of present import, and *therefore* both of interest and novelty."

Now this view I believe to be completely false. It is worth examining, inasmuch as it is a fair sample of a class of critical dicta everywhere current at the present day, having a philosophical form and air, but no real basis in fact; and which are calculated to vitiate the judgment of readers of poetry, while they exert, so far as they are adopted, a misleading influence on the practice of those who write it.

What are the eternal objects of Poetry, among all nations, and at all times? They are actions; human actions; possessing an inherent interest in themselves, and which are to be communicated in an interesting manner by the art of the Poet. Vainly will the latter imagine that he has everything in his own power; that he can make an intrinsically inferior action equally delightful with a more excellent one by his treatment of it: he may indeed compel us to admire his skill, but his work will possess, within itself, an incurable defect.

The Poet, then, has in the first place to select an excellent action; and what actions are the most excellent? Those, certainly, which most powerfully appeal to the great primary human affections: to those elementary feelings which subsist permanently in the race, and which are independent of time. These feelings are permanent and the same; that which interests them is permanent and the same also. The modernness or antiquity of an action, therefore, has nothing to do with its fitness for poetical representation; this depends upon its inherent qualities. To the elementary part of our nature, to our passions, that which is great and passionate is eternally interesting; and interesting solely in proportion to its greatness and to its passion. A great human action of a thousand years ago is more interesting to it than a smaller human action of to-day, even though upon the representation of this last the most consummate skill may have been expended, and though it has the advantage of appealing by its modern language, familiar manners, and contemporary allusions, to all our transient feelings and interests. These, however, have no right to demand of a poetical work that it shall satisfy them; their claims are to be directed elsewhere. Poetical works belong to the domain of our permanent passions: let them interest these, and the voice of all subordinate claims upon them is at once silenced.

Achilles, Prometheus, Clytemnestra, Dido—what modern poem presents personages as interesting, even to us moderns, as these personages of an "exhausted

Preface.

past ?" We have the domestic epic dealing with the details of modern life which pass daily under our eyes; we have poems representing modern personages in contact with the problems of modern life, moral, intellectual, and social; these works have been produced by poets the most distinguished of their nation and time; yet I fearlessly assert that Hermann and Dorothea, Childe Harold, Jocelyn, The Excursion, leave the reader cold in comparison with the effect produced upon him by the latter books of the Iliad, by the Orestea, or by the episode of Dido. And why is this? Simply because in the three latter cases the action is greater, the personages nobler, the situations more intense : and this is the true basis of the interest in a poetical work, and this alone.

It may be urged, however, that past actions may be interesting in themselves, but that they are not to be adopted by the modern Poet, because it is impossible for him to have them clearly present to his own mind, and he cannot therefore feel them deeply, nor represent them forcibly. But this is not necessarily the case. The externals of a past action, indeed, he cannot know with the precision of a contemporary; but his business is with its essentials. The outward man of Œdipus or of Macbeth, the houses in which they lived, the ceremonies of their courts, he cannot accurately figure to himself; but neither do they essentially concern him. His business is with their inward man; with their feelings and behaviour in certain tragic situations, which engage their passions as men; these have in them nothing local and casual; they are as accessible to the modern Poet as to a contemporary.

Preface.

The date of an action, then, signifies nothing: the action itself, its selection and construction, this is what is all-important. This the Greeks understood far more clearly than we do. The radical difference between their poetical theory and ours consists, as it appears to me, in this: that, with them, the poetical character of the action in itself, and the conduct of it, was the first consideration; with us, attention is fixed mainly on the value of the separate thoughts and images which occur in the treatment of an action. They regarded the whole; we regard the parts. With them, the action predominated over the expression of it; with us, the expression predominates over the action. Not that they failed in expression, or were inattentive to it; on the contrary, they are the highest models of expression, the unapproached masters of the *grand style:* but their expression is so excellent because it is so admirably kept in its right degree of prominence; because it is so simple and so well subordinated; because it draws its force directly from the pregnancy of the matter which it conveys. For what reason was the Greek tragic poet confined to so limited a range of subjects? Because there are so few actions which unite in themselves, in the highest degree, the conditions of excellence: and it was not thought that on any but an excellent subject could an excellent Poem be constructed. A few actions, therefore, eminently adapted for tragedy, maintained almost exclusive possession of the Greek tragic stage; their significance appeared inexhaustible; they were as permanent problems, perpetually offered to the genius of every fresh poet. This too is the reason of what appears to us moderns

a certain baldness of expression in Greek tragedy; of
the triviality with which we often reproach the remarks
of the chorus, where it takes part in the dialogue:
that the action itself, the situation of Orestes, or
Merope, or Alcmæon, was to stand the central point
of interest, unforgotten, absorbing, principal; that no
accessories were for a moment to distract the spectator's attention from this; that the tone of the parts
was to be perpetually kept down, in order not to impair the grandiose effect of the whole. The terrible
old mythic story on which the drama was founded
stood, before he entered the theatre, traced in its bare
outlines upon the spectator's mind; it stood in his
memory, as a group of statuary, faintly seen, at the
end of a long and dark vista: then came the Poet,
embodying outlines, developing situations, not a word
wasted, not a sentiment capriciously thrown in: stroke
upon stroke, the drama proceeded: the light deepened
upon the group; more and more it revealed itself to
the rivetted gaze of the spectator: until at last, when
the final words were spoken, it stood before him in
broad sunlight, a model of immortal beauty.

This was what a Greek critic demanded; this was
what a Greek poet endeavoured to effect. It signified
nothing to what time an action belonged; we do not
find that the Persæ occupied a particularly high rank
among the dramas of Æschylus, because it represented
a matter of contemporary interest: this was not what
a cultivated Athenian required; he required that the
permanent elements of his nature should be moved;
and dramas of which the action, though taken from a
long-distant mythic time, yet was calculated to accom-

plish this in a higher degree than that of the Persæ,
stood higher in his estimation accordingly. The Greeks
felt, no doubt, with their exquisite sagacity of taste,
that an action of present times was too near them, too
much mixed up with what was accidental and passing,
to form a sufficiently grand, detached, and self-subsis-
tent object for a tragic poem : such objects belonged
to the domain of the comic poet, and of the lighter
kinds of poetry. For the more serious kinds, for *prag-
matic* poetry, to use an excellent expression of Polybius,
they were more difficult and severe in the range of
subjects which they permitted. But for all kinds of
poetry alike there was one point on which they were
rigidly exacting; the adaptability of the subject to the
kind of poetry selected, and the careful construction
of the poem. Their theory and practice alike, the
admirable treatise of Aristotle, and the unrivalled
works of their poets, exclaim with a thousand tongues
—"All depends upon the subject; choose a fitting
action, penetrate yourself with the feeling of its situations ; this done, everything else will follow."

How different a way of thinking from this is ours !
We can hardly at the present day understand what
Menander meant, when he told a man who enquired
as to the progress of his comedy that he had finished
it, not having yet written a single line, because he had
constructed the action of it in his mind. A modern
critic would have assured him that the merit of his
piece depended on the brilliant things which arose
under his pen as he went along. We have poems
which seem to exist merely for the sake of single lines
and passages ; not for the sake of producing any total-

impression.   We have critics who seem to direct their attention merely to detached expressions, to the language about the action, not to the action itself.   I verily think that the majority of them do not in their hearts believe that there is such a thing as a total-impression to be derived from a poem at all, or to be demanded from a poet; they think the term a common-place of metaphysical criticism.   They will permit the Poet to select any action he pleases, and to suffer that action to go as it will, provided he gratifies them with occasional bursts of fine writing, and with a shower of isolated thoughts and images.   That is, they permit him to leave their poetical sense ungratified, provided that he gratifies their rhetorical sense and their curiosity. Of his neglecting to gratify these, there is little danger; he needs rather to be warned against the danger of attempting to gratify these alone; he needs rather to be perpetually reminded to prefer his action to every-thing else; so to treat this, as to permit its inherent excellences to develope themselves, without interruption from the intrusion of his personal peculiarities: most fortunate, when he most entirely succeeds in effacing himself, and in enabling a noble action to subsist as it did in nature.

But the modern critic not only permits a false practice; he absolutely prescribes false aims.—"A true allegory of the state of one's own mind in a repre-sentative history," the Poet is told, "is perhaps the highest thing that one can attempt in the way of poetry." —And accordingly he attempts it.   An allegory of the state of one's own mind, the highest problem of an art which imitates actions!   No assuredly, it is not, it never can be so : no great poetical work has ever been produced with such an aim. Faust itself, in which something of the kind is attempted, wonderful passages as it contains, and in spite of the unsurpassed beauty of the scenes which relate to Margaret, Faust itself, judged as a whole, and judged strictly as a poetical work, is defective : its illustrious author, the greatest poet of modern times, the greatest critic of all times, would have been the first to acknowledge it ; he only defended his work, indeed, by asserting it to be " something incommensurable."

The confusion of the present times is great, the multitude of voices counselling different things bewildering, the number of existing works capable of attracting a young writer's attention and of becoming his models, immense : what he wants is a hand to guide him through the confusion, a voice to prescribe to him the aim which he should keep in view, and to explain to him that the value of the literary works which offer themselves to his attention is relative to their power of helping him forward on his road towards this aim. Such a guide the English writer at the present day will nowhere find. Failing this, all, that can be looked for, all indeed that can be desired, is, that his attention should be fixed on excellent models ; that he may reproduce, at any rate, something of their excellence, by penetrating himself with their works and by catching their spirit, if he cannot be taught to produce what is excellent independently.

Foremost among these models for the English writer stands Shakspeare : a name the greatest perhaps of all poetical names ; a name never to be mentioned without reverence. I will venture, however, to express a doubt, whether the influence of his works, excellent and fruitful for the readers of poetry, for the great majority, has been of unmixed advantage to the writers of it. Shakspeare indeed chose excellent subjects; the world could afford no better than Macbeth, or Romeo and Juliet, or Othello: he had no theory respecting the necessity of choosing subjects of present import, or the paramount interest attaching to allegories of the state of one's own mind; like all great poets, he knew well what constituted a poetical action; like them, wherever he found such an action, he took it; like them, too, he found his best in past times. But to these general characteristics of all great poets he added a special one of his own; a gift, namely, of happy, abundant, and ingenious expression, eminent and unrivalled: so eminent as irresistibly to strike the attention first in him, and even to throw into comparative shade his other excellences as a poet. Here has been the mischief. These other excellences were his fundamental excellences *as a poet;* what distinguishes the artist from the mere amateur, says Goethe, is *Architectonicè* in the highest sense; that power of execution, which creates, forms, and constitutes: not the profoundness of single thoughts, not the richness of imagery, not the abundance of illustration. But these attractive accessories of a poetical work being more easily seized than the spirit of the whole, and their accessories being possessed by Shakspeare in an unequal degree, a young writer having recourse to Shakspeare as his model runs great risk of being vanquished and absorbed by them, and, in consequence, of reproducing, according to the measure of his power, these, and these alone. Of this preponderating quality of Shakspeare's genius, accordingly, almost the whole of modern English poetry has, it appears to me, felt the influence. To the exclusive attention on the part of his imitators to this it is in a great degree owing, that of the majority of modern poetical works the details alone are valuable, the composition worthless. In reading them one is perpetually reminded of that terrible sentence on a modern French poet—*il dit tout ce qu'il veut, mais malheureusement il n'a rien à dire.*

Let me give an instance of what I mean. I will take it from the works of the very chief among those who seem to have been formed in the school of Shakspeare : of one whose exquisite genius and pathetic death render him for ever interesting. I will take the poem of Isabella, or the Pot of Basil, by Keats. I choose this rather than the Endymion, because the latter work, (which a modern critic has classed with the Fairy Queen !) although undoubtedly there blows through it the breath of genius, is yet as a whole so utterly incoherent, as not strictly to merit the name of a poem at all. The poem of Isabella, then, is a perfect treasure-house of graceful and felicitous words and images : almost in every stanza there occurs one of those vivid and picturesque turns of expression, by which the object is made to flash upon the eye of the mind, and which thrill the reader with a sudden delight. This one short poem contains, perhaps, a greater number of happy single expressions which one could quote than all the extant tragedies of Sophocles. But the action, the story? The action in itself is an excellent

Preface.

one; but so feebly is it conceived by the Poet, so loosely constructed, that the effect produced by it, in and for itself, is absolutely null. Let the reader, after he has finished the poem of Keats, turn to the same story in the Decameron: he will then feel how pregnant and interesting the same action has become in the hands of a great artist, who above all things delineates his object; who subordinates expression to that which it is designed to express.

I have said that the imitators of Shakspeare, fixing their attention on his wonderful gift of expression, have directed their imitation to this, neglecting his other excellences. These excellences, the fundamental excellences of poetical art, Shakspeare no doubt possessed them—possessed many of them in a splendid degree; but it may perhaps be doubted whether even he himself did not sometimes give scope to his faculty of expression to the prejudice of a higher poetical duty. For we must never forget that Shakspeare is the great poet he is from his skill in discerning and firmly conceiving an excellent action, from his power of intensely feeling a situation, of intimately associating himself with a character; not from his gift of expression, which rather even leads him astray, degenerating sometimes into a fondness for curiosity of expression, into an irritability of fancy, which seems to make it impossible for him to say a thing plainly, even when the press of the action demands the very directest language, or its level character the very simplest. Mr. Hallam, than whom it is impossible to find a saner and more judicious critic, has had the courage (for at the present day it needs courage) to

remark, how extremely and faultily difficult Shakspeare's language often is. It is so: you may find
main scenes in some of his greatest tragedies, King
Lear for instance, where the language is so artificial,
so curiously tortured, and so difficult, that every speech
has to be read two or three times before its meaning can be comprehended. This over-curiousness of
expression is indeed but the excessive employment
of a wonderful gift—of the power of saying a thing in
a happier way than any other man; nevertheless, it is
carried so far that one understands what M. Guizot
meant, when he said that Shakspeare appears in his
language to have tried all styles except that of simplicity. He has not the severe and scrupulous self-
restraint of the ancients, partly no doubt, because he
had a far less cultivated and exacting audience: he
has indeed a far wider range than they had, a far richer
fertility of thought; in this respect he rises above
them: in his strong conception of his subject, in the
genuine way in which he is penetrated with it, he
resembles them, and is unlike the moderns: but in
the accurate limitation of it, the conscientious rejec-
tion of superfluities, the simple and rigorous development of it from the first line of his work to the last, he
falls below them, and comes nearer to the moderns.
In his chief works, besides what he has of his own, he
has the elementary soundness of the ancients; he has
their important action and their large and broad
manner: but he has not their purity of method. He
is therefore a less safe model; for what he has of his
own is personal, and inseparable from his own rich
nature; it may be imitated and exaggerated, it cannot

Preface.

be learned or applied as an art; he is above all suggestive; more valuable, therefore, to young writers as men
than as artists. But clearness of arrangement, rigour
of development, simplicity of style—these may to a
certain extent be learned: and these may, I am convinced, be learned best from the ancients, who although
infinitely less suggestive than Shakspeare, are thus, to
the artist, more instructive.

What then, it will be asked, are the ancients to be
our sole models? the ancients with their comparatively
narrow range of experience, and their widely different
circumstances? Not, certainly, that which is narrow
in the ancients, nor that in which we can no longer
sympathize. An action like the action of the Antigone
of Sophocles, which turns upon the conflict between
the heroine's duty to her brother's corpse and that to
the laws of her country, is no longer one in which
it is possible that we should feel a deep interest. I
am speaking too, it will be remembered, not of the
best sources of intellectual stimulus for the general
reader, but of the best models of instruction for the
individual writer. This last may certainly learn of the
ancients, better than anywhere else, three things which
it is vitally important for him to know :—the all-import-
ance of the choice of a subject; the necessity of
accurate construction; and the subordinate character
of expression. He will learn from them how unspeak-
ably superior is the effect of the one moral impression
left by a great action treated as a whole, to the effect
produced by the most striking single thought or by the
happiest image. As he penetrates into the spirit of the
great classical works, as he becomes gradually aware of

their intense significance, their noble simplicity, and their calm pathos, he will be convinced that it is this effect, unity and profoundness of moral impression, at which the ancients Poets aimed; that it is this which constitutes the grandeur of their works, and which makes them immortal. He will desire to direct his own efforts towards producing the same effect. Above all, he will deliver himself from the jargon of modern criticism, and escape the danger of producing poetical works conceived in the spirit of the passing time, and which partake of its transitoriness.

The present age makes great claims upon us: we owe it service, it will not be satisfied without our admiration. I know not how it is, but their commerce with the ancients appears to me to produce, in those who constantly practise it, a steadying and composing effect upon their judgment, not of literary works only, but of men and events in general. They are like persons who have had a very weighty and impressive experience: they are more truly than others under the empire of facts, and more independent of the language current among those with whom they live. They wish neither to applaud nor to revile their age: they wish to know what it is, what it can give them, and whether this is what they want. What they want, they know very well; they want to educe and cultivate what is best and noblest in themselves: they know, too, that this is no easy task—χαλεπὸν, as Pittacus said, χαλεπὸν ἐσθλὸν ἔμμεναι—and they ask themselves sincerely whether their age and its literature can assist them in the attempt. If they are endeavouring to practise any art, they remember the plain and simple proceedings of the old artists, who attained their grand results by penetrating themselves with some noble and significant action, not by inflating themselves with a belief in the preeminent importance and greatness of their own times. They do not talk of their mission, nor of interpreting their age, nor of the coming Poet; all this, they know, is the mere delirium of vanity; their business is not to praise their age, but to afford to the men who live in it the highest pleasure which they are capable of feeling. If asked to afford this by means of subjects drawn from the age itself, they ask what special fitness the present age has for supplying them: they are told that it is an era of progress, an age commissioned to carry out the great ideas of industrial development and social amelioration. They reply that with all this they can do nothing; that the elements they need for the exercise of their art are great actions, calculated powerfully and delightfully to affect what is permanent in the human soul; that so far as the present age can supply such actions, they will gladly make use of them; but that an age wanting in moral grandeur can with difficulty supply such, and an age of spiritual discomfort with difficulty be powerfully and delightfully affected by them.

A host of voices will indignantly rejoin that the present age is inferior to the past neither in moral grandeur nor in spiritual health. He who possesses the discipline I speak of will content himself with remembering the judgments passed upon the present age, in this respect, by the men of strongest head and widest culture whom it has produced; by Goethe and by Niebuhr. It will be sufficient for him that he knows

Preface.

the opinions held by these two great men respecting
the present age and its literature; and that he feels
assured in his own mind that their aims and demands
upon life were such as he would wish, at any rate, his
own to be; and their judgment as to what is impeding
and disabling such as he may safely follow. He will
not, however, maintain a hostile attitude towards the
false pretensions of his age; he will content himself
with not being overwhelmed by them. He will esteem
himself fortunate if he can succeed in banishing from
his mind all feelings of contradiction, and irritation,
and impatience; in order to delight himself with the
contemplation of some noble action of a heroic time,
and to enable others, through his representation of it,
to delight in it also.

I am far indeed from making any claim, for myself,
that I possess this discipline; or for the following
Poems, that they breathe its spirit. But I say, that
in the sincere endeavour to learn and practise, amid
the bewildering confusion of our times, what is sound
and true in poetical art, I seemed to myself to find the
only sure guidance, the only solid footing, among the
ancients. They, at any rate, knew what they wanted
in Art, and we do not. It is this uncertainty which is
disheartening, and not hostile criticism. How often
have I felt this when reading words of disparagement
or of cavil: that it is the uncertainty as to what is
really to be aimed at which makes our difficulty, not
the dissatisfaction of the critic, who himself suffers
from the same uncertainty. *Non me tua turbida terrent
Dicta: Dii me terrent, et Jupiter hostis.*

Two kinds of *dilettanti*, says Goethe, there are in

Preface.

poetry : he who neglects the indispensable mechanical part, and thinks he has done enough if he shows spirituality and feeling ; and he who seeks to arrive at poetry merely by mechanism, in which he can acquire an artisan's readiness, and is without soul and matter. And he adds, that the first does most harm to Art, and the last to himself. If we must be *dilettanti :* if it is impossible for us, under the circumstances amidst which we live, to think clearly, to feel nobly, and to delineate firmly : if we cannot attain to the mastery of the great artists—let us, at least, have so much respect for our Art as to prefer it to ourselves : let us not bewilder our successors : let us transmit to them the practice of Poetry, with its boundaries and wholesome regulative laws, under which excellent works may again, perhaps, at some future time, be produced, not yet fallen into oblivion through our neglect, not yet condemned and cancelled by the influence of their eternal enemy, Caprice.

Fox How, Ambleside,
  October 1, 1853.

CONTENTS.

SOHRAB AND RUSTUM.

Sohrab and Rustum.

AN EPISODE.

AND the first grey of morning fill'd the east,
   And the fog rose out of the Oxus stream.
But all the Tartar camp along the stream
Was hush'd, and still the men were plunged in sleep:
Sohrab alone, he slept not: all night long
He had lain wakeful, tossing on his bed;
But when the grey dawn stole into his tent,
He rose, and clad himself, and girt his sword,
And took his horseman's cloak, and left his tent,
And went abroad into the cold wet fog,
Through the dim camp to Peran-Wisa's tent.
   Through the black Tartar tents he pass'd, which stood
Clustering like bee-hives on the low flat strand
Of Oxus, where the summer floods o'erflow
When the sun melts the snows in high Pamere:
Through the black tents he pass'd, o'er that low strand,
And to a hillock came, a little back
From the stream's brink, the spot where first a boat,
Crossing the stream in summer, scrapes the land.
The men of former times had crown'd the top
With a clay fort: but that was fall'n; and now

285

Sohrab and Rustum.

The Tartars built there Peran-Wisa's tent,
A dome of laths, and o'er it felts were spread.
And Sohrab came there, and went in, and stood
Upon the thick-pil'd carpets in the tent,
And found the old man sleeping on his bed
Of rugs and felts, and near him lay his arms.
And Peran-Wisa heard him, though the step
Was dull'd; for he slept light, an old man's sleep;
And he rose quickly on one arm, and said :—

"Who art thou? for it is not yet clear dawn.
Speak! is there news, or any night alarm?"

But Sohrab came to the bedside, and said :—
"Thou know'st me, Peran-Wisa : it is I.
The sun is not yet risen, and the foe
Sleep; but I sleep not; all night long I lie
Tossing and wakeful, and I come to thee.
For so did King Afrasiab bid me seek
Thy counsel, and to heed thee as thy son,
In Samarcand, before the army march'd;
And I will tell thee what my heart desires.
Thou knowest if, since from Ader-baijan first
I came among the Tartars, and bore arms,
I have still serv'd Afrasiab well, and shown,
At my boy's years, the courage of a man.
This too thou know'st, that, while I still bear on
The conquering Tartar ensigns through the world,
And beat the Persians back on every field,
I seek one man, one man, and one alone.
Rustum, my father; who, I hop'd, should greet,
Should one day greet, upon some well-fought field
His not unworthy, not inglorious son.
So I long hop'd, but him I never find.

"

Sohrab and Rustum.

Come then, hear now, and grant me what I ask.
Let the two armies rest to-day : but I
Will challenge forth the bravest Persian lords
To meet me, man to man : if I prevail,
Rustum will surely hear it ; if I fall—
Old man, the dead need no one, claim no kin.
Dim is the rumour of a common fight,
Where host meets host, and many names are sunk :
But of a single combat Fame speaks clear.”

He spoke : and Peran-Wisa took the hand
Of the young man in his, and sigh'd, and said :—
   “ O Sohrab, an unquiet heart is thine !
Canst thou not rest among the Tartar chiefs,
And share the battle's common chance with us
Who love thee, but must press for ever first,
In single fight incurring single risk,
To find a father thou hast never seen ?
Or, if indeed this one desire rules all,
To seek out Rustum—seek him not through fight :
Seek him in peace, and carry to his arms,
O Sohrab, carry an unwounded son !
But far hence seek him, for he is not here.
For now it is not as when I was young,
When Rustum was in front of every fray :
But now he keeps apart, and sits at home,
In Seistan, with Zal, his father old.
Whether that his own mighty strength at last
Feels the abhorr'd approaches of old age ;
Or in some quarrel with the Persian King.
There go :—Thou wilt not? Yet my heart forebodes
Danger or death awaits thee on this field.
Fain would I know thee safe and well, though lost

Sohrab and Rustum.

To us : fain therefore send thee hence, in peace
To seek thy father, not seek single fights
In vain :—but who can keep the lion's cub
From ravening ? and who govern Rustum's son ?
Go : I will grant thee what thy heart desires."
   So said he, and dropp'd Sohrab's hand, and left
His bed, and the warm rugs whereon he lay,
And o'er his chilly limbs his woollen coat
He pass'd, and tied his sandals on his feet,
And threw a white cloak round him, and he took
In his right hand a ruler's staff, no sword ;
And on his head he plac'd his sheep-skin cap,
Black, glossy, curl'd, the fleece of Kara-Kul ;
And rais'd the curtain of his tent, and call'd
His herald to his side, and went abroad.
   The sun, by this, had risen, and clear'd the fog
From the broad Oxus and the glittering sands :
And from their tents the Tartar horsemen fil'd
Into the open plain ; so Haman bade ;
Haman, who next to Peran-Wisa rul'd
The host, and still was in his lusty prime.
From their black tents, long files of horse, they
     stream'd :
As when, some grey November morn, the files,
In marching order spread, of long-neck'd cranes,
Stream over Casbin, and the southern slopes
Of Elburz, from the Aralian estuaries,
Or some frore Caspian reed-bed, southward bound
For the warm Persian sea-board : so they stream'd.
The Tartars of the Oxus, the King's guard,
First with black sheep-skin caps and with long spears ;
Large men, large steeds ; who from Bokhara come

Sohrab and Rustum.   .

And Khiva, and ferment the milk of mares.
Next the more temperate Toorkmuns of the south,
The Tukas, and the lances of Salore,
And those from Attruck and the Caspian sands;
Light men, and on light steeds, who only drink
The acrid milk of camels, and their wells.
And then a swarm of wandering horse, who came
From far, and a more doubtful service own'd;
The Tartars of Ferghana, from the banks
Of the Jaxartes, men with scanty beards
And close-set skull-caps; and those wilder hordes
Who roam o'er Kipchak and the northern waste
Kalmuks and unkemp'd Kuzzaks, tribes who stray
Nearest the Pole, and wandering Kirghizzes,
Who come on shaggy ponies from Pamere.
These all fil'd out from camp into the plain.
And on the other side the Persians form'd:
First a light cloud of horse, Tartars they seem'd,
The Ilyats of Khorassan: and behind,
The royal troops of Persia, horse and foot,
Marshall'd battalions bright in burnished steel.
But Peran-Wisa with his herald came
Threading the Tartar squadrons to the front,
And with his staff kept back the foremost ranks.
And when Ferood, who led the Persians, saw
That Peran-Wisa kept the Tartars back,
He took his spear, and to the front he came,
And check'd his ranks, and fix'd them where they
      stood.
And the old Tartar came upon the sand
Betwixt the silent hosts, and spake, and said :—
  " Ferood, and ye, Persians and Tartars, hear!

                U

Sohrab and Rustum.

Let there be truce between the hosts to-day.
But choose a champion from the Persian lords
To fight our champion Sohrab, man to man."
    As, in the country, on a morn in June,
When the dew glistens on the pearled ears,
A shiver runs through the deep corn for joy—
So, when they heard what Peran-Wisa said,
A thrill through all the Tartar squadrons ran
Of pride and hope for Sohrab, whom they lov'd.
    But as a troop of pedlars, from Cabool,
Cross underneath the Indian Caucasus,
That vast sky-neighbouring mountain of milk snow ;
Winding so high, that, as they mount, they pass
Long flocks of travelling birds dead on the snow,
Chok'd by the air, and scarce can they themselves
Slake their parch'd throats with sugar'd mulberries—
In single file they move, and stop their breath,
For fear they should dislodge the o'erhanging snows—
So the pale Persians held their breath with fear.
    And to Ferood his brother Chiefs came up
To counsel : Gudurz and Zoarrah came,
And Feraburz, who rul'd the Persian host
Second, and was the uncle of the King :
These came and counsell'd ; and then Gudurz said :—
    "Ferood, shame bids us take their challenge up,
Yet champion have we none to match this youth.
He has the wild stag's foot, the lion's heart.
But Rustum came last night ; aloof he sits
And sullen, and has pitch'd his tents apart :
Him will I seek, and carry to his ear
The Tartar challenge, and this young man's name.
Haply he will forget his wrath, and fight.

Sohrab and Rustum.

Stand forth the while, and take their challenge up."
  So spake he; and Ferood stood forth and said :—
"Old man, be it agreed hast thou as said.
Let Sohrab arm, and we will find a man."
  He spoke; and Peran-Wisa turn'd, and strode
Back through the opening squadrons to his tent.
But through the anxious Persians Gudurz ran,
And cross'd the camp which lay behind, and reach'd,
Out on the sands beyond it, Rustum's tents.
Of scarlet cloth they were, and glittering gay,
Just pitch'd : the high pavilion in the midst
Was Rustum's, and his men lay camp'd around.
And Gudurz enter'd Rustum's tent, and found
Rustum : his morning meal was done, but still
The table stood beside him, charg'd with food ;
A side of roasted sheep, and cakes of bread,
And dark green melons; and there Rustum sate
Listless, and held a falcon on his wrist,
And play'd with it; but Gudurz came and stood
Before him; and he look'd, and saw him stand ;
And with a cry sprang up, and dropp'd the bird,
And greeted Gudurz with both hands, and said :—
  "Welcome! these eyes could see no better sight.
What news ? but sit down first, and eat and drink."
  But Gudurz stood in the tent door, and said :—
"Not now : a time will come to eat and drink,
But not to-day : to-day has other needs.
The armies are drawn out, and stand at gaze :
For from the Tartars is a challenge brought
To pick a champion from the Persian lords
To fight their champion—and thou know'st his name—
Sohrab men call him, but his birth is hid.

Sohrab and Rustum.

O Rustum, like thy might is this young man's !
He has the wild stag's foot, the lion's heart.
And he is young, and Iran's Chiefs are old,
Or else too weak ; and all eyes turn to thee.
Come down and help us, Rustum, or we lose."
   He spoke : but Rustum answer'd with a smile :—
" Go to ! if Iran's Chiefs, are old, then I
Am older : if the young are weak, the King
Errs strangely : for the King, for Kai Khosroo,
Himself is young, and honours younger men,
And lets the aged moulder to their graves.
Rustum he loves no more, but loves the young—
The young may rise at Sohrab's vaunts, not I.
For what care I, though all speak Sohrab's fame ?
For would that I myself had such a son,
And not that one slight helpless girl I have,
A son so fam'd, so brave, to send to war,
And I to tarry with the snow-hair'd Zal,
My father, whom the robber Afghans vex,
And clip his borders short, and drive his herds,
And he has none to guard his weak old age.
There would I go, and hang my armour up,
And with my great name fence that weak old man,
And spend the goodly treasures I have got,
And rest my age, and hear of Sohrab's fame,
And leave to death the hosts of thankless kings,
And with these slaughterous hands draw sword no
        more."
   He spoke, and smil'd ; and Gudurz made reply :—
" What then, O Rustum, will men say to this,
When Sohrab dares our bravest forth, and seeks
Thee most of all, and thou, whom most he seeks,

Sohrab and Rustum.

Hidest thy face? Take heed, lest men should say,
Like some old miser, Rustum hoards his fame,
And shuns to peril it with younger men."
And, greatly mov'd, then Rustum made reply :—
" O Gudurz, wherefore dost thou say such words?
Thou knowest better words than this to say.
What is one more, one less, obscure or fam'd,
Valiant or craven, young or old, to me?
Are not they mortal, am not I myself?
But who for men of nought would do great deeds?
Come, thou shalt see how Rustum hoards his fame.
But I will fight unknown, and in plain arms ;
Let not men say of Rustum, he was match'd
In single fight with any mortal man."
   He spoke, and frown'd ; and Gudurz turn'd, and ran
Back quickly through the camp in fear and joy,
Fear at his wrath, but joy that Rustum came.
But Rustum strode to his tent door, and call'd
His followers in, and bade them bring his arms,
And clad himself in steel : the arms he chose
Were plain, and on his shield was no device,
Only his helm was rich, inlaid with gold,
And from the fluted spine atop a plume
Of horsehair wav'd, a scarlet horsehair plume.
So arm'd he issued forth ; and Ruksh, his horse,
Follow'd him, like a faithful hound, at heel,
Ruksh, whose renown was nois'd through all the earth,
The horse, whom Rustum on a foray once
Did in Bokhara by the river find
A colt beneath its dam, and drove him home,
And rear'd him ; a bright bay, with lofty crest ;
Dight with a saddle-cloth of broider'd green

Sohrab and Rustum.

Crusted with gold, and on the ground were work'd
All beasts of chase, all beasts which hunters know:
So follow'd, Rustum left his tents, and cross'd
The camp, and to the Persian host appear'd.
And all the Persians knew him, and with shouts
Hail'd; but the Tartars knew not who he was.
And dear as the wet diver to the eyes
Of his pale wife who waits and weeps on shore,
By sandy Bahrein, in the Persian Gulf,
Plunging all day in the blue waves, at night,
Having made up his tale of precious pearls,
Rejoins her in their hut upon the sands—
So dear to the pale Persians Rustum came.

And Rustum to the Persian front advanc'd,
And Sohrab arm'd in Haman's tent, and came.
And as afield the reapers cut a swathe
Down through the middle of a rich man's corn,
And on each side are squares of standing corn,
And in the midst a stubble, short and bare;
So on each side were squares of men, with spears
Bristling, and in the midst, the open sand.
And Rustum came upon the sand, and cast
His eyes towards the Tartar tents, and saw
Sohrab come forth, and ey'd him as he came.

As some rich woman, on a winter's morn,
Eyes through her silken curtains the poor drudge
Who with numb blacken'd fingers makes her fire—
At cock-crow, on a starlit winter's morn,
When the frost flowers the whiten'd window panes—
And wonders how she lives, and what the thoughts
Of that poor drudge may be; so Rustum ey'd
The unknown adventurous Youth, who from afar

Sohrab and Rustum.

Came seeking Rustum, and defying forth
All the most valiant chiefs : long he perus'd
His spirited air, and wonder'd who he was.
For very young he seem'd, tenderly rear'd ;
Like some young cypress, tall, and dark, and straight,
Which in a queen's secluded garden throws
Its slight dark shadow on the moonlit turf,
By midnight, to a bubbling fountain's sound—
So slender Sohrab seem'd, so softly rear'd.
And a deep pity enter'd Rustum's soul
As he beheld him coming ; and he stood,
And beckon'd to him with his hand, and said :—
  "O thou young man, the air of Heaven is soft,
And warm, and pleasant ; but the grave is cold.
Heaven's air is better than the cold dead grave.
Behold me : I am vast, and clad in iron,
And tried ; and I have stood on many a field
Of blood, and I have fought with many a foe :
Never was that field lost, or that foe sav'd.
O Sohrab, wherefore wilt thou rush on death ?
Be govern'd : quit the Tartar host, and come
To Iran, and be as my son to me,
And fight beneath my banner till I die.
There are no youths in Iran brave as thou."
  So he spake, mildly : Sohrab heard his voice,
The mighty voice of Rustum ; and he saw
His giant figure planted on the sand,
Sole, like some single tower, which a chief
Has builded on the waste in former years
Against the robbers ; and he saw that head,
Streak'd with its first grey hairs : hope fill'd his soul ;
And he ran forwards and embrac'd his knees,

Sohrab and Rustum.

And clasp'd his hand within his own and said :—
  "Oh, by thy father's head ! by thine own soul !
Art thou not Rustum ? Speak ! art thou not he ?"
  But Rustum ey'd askance the kneeling youth,
And turn'd away, and spoke to his own soul :—
  "Ah me, I muse what this young fox may mean.
False, wily, boastful, are these Tartar boys.
For if I now confess this thing he asks,
And hide it not, but say—*Rustum is here*—
He will not yield indeed, nor quit our foes,
But he will find some pretext not to fight,
And praise my fame, and proffer courteous gifts,
A belt or sword perhaps, and go his way.
And on a feast day, in Afrasiab's hall,
In Samarcand, he will arise and cry—
' I challeng'd once, when the two armies camp'd
Beside the Oxus, all the Persian lords
To cope with me in single fight ; but they
Shrank ; only Rustum dar'd : then he and I
Chang'd gifts, and went on equal terms away.'
So will he speak, perhaps, while men applaud.
Then were the chiefs of Iran sham'd through me."
  And then he turn'd, and sternly spake aloud :—
" Rise ! wherefore dost thou vainly question thus
Of Rustum ?'I am here, whom thou hast call'd
By challenge forth : make good thy vaunt, or yield.
Is it with Rustum only thou wouldst fight ?
Rash boy, men look on Rustum's face and flee.
For well I know, that did great Rustum stand
Before thy face this day, and were reveal'd,
There would be then no talk of fighting more.
But being what I am, I tell thee this ;

Sohrab and Rustum.

Do thou record it in thine inmost soul:
Either thou shalt renounce thy vaunt, and yield;
Or else thy bones shall strew this sand, till winds
Bleach them, or Oxus with his summer floods,
Oxus in summer wash them all away."
    He spoke: and Sohrab answer'd, on his feet:—
"Art thou so fierce? Thou wilt not fright me so.
I am no girl, to be made pale by words.
Yet this thou hast said well, did Rustum stand
Here on this field, there were no fighting then.
But Rustum is far hence, and we stand here.
Begin: thou art more vast, more dread than I,
And thou art prov'd, I know, and I am young—
But yet Success sways with the breath of Heaven.
And though thou thinkest that thou knowest sure
Thy victory, yet thou canst not surely know.
For we are all, like swimmers in the sea,
Pois'd on the top of a huge wave of Fate,
Which hangs uncertain to which side to fall.
And whether it will heave us up to land,
Or whether it will roll us out to sea,
Back out to sea, to the deep waves of death,
We know not, and no search will make us know:
Only the event will teach us in its hour."
    He spoke; and Rustum answer'd not, but hurl'd
His spear: down from the shoulder, down it came,
As on some partridge in the corn a hawk
That long has tower'd in the airy clouds
Drops like a plummet: Sohrab saw it come,
And sprang aside, quick as a flash: the spear
Hiss'd, and went quivering down into the sand,
Which it sent flying wide:—then Sohrab threw

Sohrab and Rustum.

In turn, and full struck Rustum's shield: sharp rang,
The iron plates rang sharp, but turn'd the spear.
And Rustum seiz'd his club, which none but he
Could wield: an unlopp'd trunk it was, and huge,
Still rough; like those which men in treeless plains
To build them boats fish from the flooded rivers,
Hyphasis or Hydaspes, when, high up
By their dark springs, the wind in winter-time
Has made in Himalayan forests wrack,
And strewn the channels with torn boughs; so huge
The club which Rustum lifted now, and struck
One stroke; but again Sohrab sprang aside
Lithe as the glancing snake, and the club came
Thundering to earth, and leapt from Rustum's hand.
And Rustum follow'd his own blow, and fell
To his knees, and with his fingers clutch'd the sand:
And now might Sohrab have unsheath'd his sword,
And pierc'd the mighty Rustum while he lay
Dizzy, and on his knees, and chok'd with sand:
But he look'd on, and smil'd, nor bar'd his sword,
But courteously drew back, and spoke, and said:—

"Thou strik'st too hard: that club of thine will float
Upon the summer floods, and not my bones.
But rise, and be not wroth; not wroth am I:
No, when I see thee, wrath forsakes my soul.
Thou say'st, thou art not Rustum: be it so.
Who art thou then, that canst so touch my soul?
Boy as I am, I have seen battles too;
Have waded foremost in their bloody waves,
And heard their hollow roar of dying men;
But never was my heart thus touch'd before.
Are they from Heaven, these softenings of the heart?

Sohrab and Rustum.

O thou old warrior, let us yield to Heaven!
Come, plant we here in earth our angry spears,
And make a truce, and sit upon this sand,
And pledge each other in red wine, like friends
And thou shalt talk to me of Rustum's deeds.
There are enough foes in the Persian host
Whom I may meet, and strike, and feel no pang;
Champions enough Afrasiab has, whom thou
Mayst fight; fight them, when they confront thy spear.
But oh, let there be peace 'twixt thee and me!"

   He ceas'd: but while he spake, Rustum had risen,
And stood erect, trembling wtth rage: his club
He left to lie, but had regain'd his spear,
Whose fiery point now in his mail'd right-hand
Blaz'd bright and baleful, like that autumn Star,
The baleful sign of fevers: dust had soil'd
His stately crest, and dimm'd his glittering arms.
His breast heav'd; his lips foam'd; and twice his voice
Was chok'd with rage: at last these words broke way:—

   "Girl! nimble with thy feet, not with thy hands!
Curl'd minion, dancer, coiner of sweet words!
Fight; let me hear thy hateful voice no more!
Thou art not in Afrasiab's gardens now
With Tartar girls, with whom thou art wont to dance;
But on the Oxus sands, and in the dance
Of battle, and with me, who make no play
Of war: I fight it out, and hand to hand.
Speak not to me of truce, and pledge, and wine!
Remember all thy valour: try thy feints
And cunning: all the pity I had is gone:
Because thou hast sham'd me before both the hosts
With thy light skipping tricks, and thy girl's wiles.

Sohrab and Rustum.

He spoke; and Sohrab kindled at his taunts,
And he too drew his sword: at once they rush'd
Together, as two eagles on one prey
Come rushing down together from the clouds,
One from the east, one from the west: their shields
Dash'd with a clang together, and a din
Rose, such as that the sinewy woodcutters
Make often in the forest's heart at morn,
Of hewing axes, crashing trees: such blows
Rustum and Sohrab on each other hail'd.
And you would say that sun and stars took part
In that unnatural conflict; for a cloud
Grew suddenly in Heaven, and dark'd the sun
Over the fighters' heads; and a wind rose
Under their feet, and moaning swept the plain,
And in a sandy whirlwind wrapp'd the pair.
In gloom they twain were wrapp'd, and they alone;
For both the on-looking hosts on either hand
Stood in broad daylight, and the sky was pure,
And the sun sparkled on the Oxus stream.
But in the gloom they fought, with bloodshot eyes
And labouring breath; first Rustum struck the shield
Which Sohrab held stiff out: the steel-spik'd spear
Rent the tough plates, but fail'd to reach the skin,
And Rustum pluck'd it back with angry groan.
Then Sohrab with his sword smote Rustum's helm,
Nor clove its steel quite through; but all the crest
He shore away, and that proud horsehair plume,
Never till now defil'd, sunk to the dust;
And Rustum bow'd his head; but then the gloom
Grew blacker: thunder rumbled in the air,
And lightnings rent the cloud; and Ruksh, the horse,

Sohrab and Rustum.

Who stood at hand, utter'd a dreadful cry :
No horse's cry was that, most like the roar
Of some pain'd desert lion, who all day
Has trail'd the hunter's javelin in his side,
And comes at night to die upon the sand :—
The two hosts heard that cry, and quak'd for fear,
And Oxus curdled as it cross'd his stream.
But Sohrab heard, and quail'd not, but rush'd on,
And struck again ; and again Rustum bow'd
His head ; but this time all the blade, like glass,
Sprang in a thousand shivers on the helm,
And in his hand the hilt remain'd alone.
Then Rustum rais'd his head : his dreadful eyes
Glar'd, and he shook on high his menacing spear,
And shouted, *Rustum !* Sohrab heard that shout,
And shrank amaz'd : back he recoil'd one step,
And scann'd with blinking eyes the advancing Form :
And then he stood bewilder'd ; and he dropp'd
His covering shield, and the spear pierc'd his side.
He reel'd, and staggering back, sunk to the ground.
And then the gloom dispers'd, and the wind fell,
And the bright sun broke forth, and melted all
The cloud ; and the two armies saw the pair ;
Saw Rustum standing, safe upon his feet,
And Sohrab, wounded, on the bloody sand.
  Then, with a bitter smile, Rustum began :—
  Sohrab, thou thoughtest in thy mind to kill
A Persian lord this day, and strip his corpse,
And bear thy trophies to Afrasiab's tent.
Or else that the great Rustum would come down
Himself to fight, and that thy wiles would move
His heart to take a gift, and let thee go.

Sohrab and Rustum.

And then that all the Tartar host would praise
Thy courage or thy craft, and spread thy fame,
To glad thy father in his weak old age.
Fool ! thou art slain, and by an unknown man !
Dearer to the red jackals shalt thou be,
Than to thy friends, and to thy father old."
    And with a fearless mien Sohrab replied :—
" Unknown thou art ; yet thy fierce vaunt is vain.
Thou dost not slay me, proud and boastful man !
No ! Rustum slays me, and this filial heart.
For were I match'd with ten such men as thou,
And I were he who till to-day I was,
They should be lying here, I standing there.
But that beloved name unnerv'd my arm—
That name, and something, I confess, in thee,
Which troubles all my heart, and made my shield
Fall ; and thy spear transfix'd an unarm'd foe.
And now thou boastest, and insult'st my fate.
But hear thou this, fierce Man, tremble to hear !
The mighty Rustum shall avenge my death !
My father, whom I seek through all the world,
He shall avenge my death, and punish thee !"
    As when some hunter in the spring hath found
A breeding eagle sitting on her nest,
Upon the craggy isle of a hill lake,
And pierc'd her with an arrow as she rose,
And follow'd her to find her where she fell
Far off ;—anon her mate comes winging back
From hunting, and a great way off descries
His huddling young left sole ; at that, he checks
His pinion, and with short uneasy sweeps
Circles above his eyry, with loud screams

Sohrab and Rustum.

Chiding his mate back to her nest ; but she
Lies dying, with the arrow in her side,
In some far stony gorge out of his ken,
A heap of fluttering feathers : never more
Shall the lake glass her, flying over it ;
Never the black and dripping precipices
Echo her stormy scream as she sails by :—
As that poor bird flies home, nor knows his loss—
So Rustum knew not his own loss, but stood
Over his dying son, and knew him not.

    But with a cold, incredulous voice, he said :—
" What prate is this of fathers and revenge ?
The mighty Rustum never had a son."
    And, with a failing voice, Sohrab replied :—
" Ah yes, he had ! and that lost son am I.
Surely the news will one day reach his ear,
Reach Rustum, where he sits, and tarries long,
Somewhere, I know not where, but far from here ;
And pierce him like a stab, and make him leap
To arms, and cry for vengeance upon thee.
Fierce Man, bethink thee, for an only son !
What will that grief, what will that vengeance be !
Oh, could I live, till I that grief had seen !
Yet him I pity not so much, but her,
My mother, who in Ader-baijan dwells
With that old King, her father, who grows grey
With age, and rules over the valiant Koords.
Her most I pity, who no more will see
Sohrab returning from the Tartar camp,
With spoils and honour, when the war is done.
But a dark rumour will be bruited up,
From tribe to tribe, until it reach her ear ;

Sohrab and Rustum.

And then will that defenceless woman learn
That Sohrab will rejoice her sight no more ;
But that in battle with a nameless foe,
By the far distant Oxus, he is slain."
  He spoke ; and as he ceas'd he wept aloud,
Thinking of her he left, and his own death.
He spoke ; but Rustum listen'd, plung'd in thought.
Nor did he yet believe it was his son
Who spoke, although he call'd back names he knew ;
For he had had sure tidings that the babe,
Which was in Ader-baijan born to him,
Had been a puny girl, no boy at all :
So that sad mother sent him word, for fear
Rustum should take the boy, to train in arms ;
And so he deem'd that either Sohrab took,
By a false boast, the style of Rustum's son ;
Or that men gave it him, to swell his fame.
So deem'd he ; yet he listen'd, plung'd in thought ;
And his soul set to grief, as the vast tide
Of the bright rocking Ocean sets to shore
At the full moon : tears gathered in his eyes ;
For he remembered his own early youth,
And all its bounding rapture ; as, at dawn,
The Shepherd from his mountain lodge descries
A far bright City, smitten by the sun,
Through many rolling clouds ;—so Rustum saw
His youth ; saw Sohrab's mother, in her bloom ;
And that old King, her father, who lov'd well
His wandering guest, and gave him his fair child
With joy ; and all the pleasant life they led,
They three, in that long-distant summer-time—
The castle, and the dewy woods, and hunt

Sohrab and Rustum.

And hound, and morn on those delightful hills
In Ader-baijan.   And he saw that Youth,
Of age and looks to be his own dear son,
Piteous and lovely, lying on the sand,
Like some rich hyacinth, which by the scythe
Of an unskilful gardener has been cut,
Mowing the garden grass-plots near its bed,
And lies, a fragrant tower of purple bloom,
On the mown, dying grass ;—so Sohrab lay,
Lovely in death, upon the common sand.
And Rustum gaz'd on him with grief, and said :—

  "O Sohrab, thou indeed art such a son
Whom Rustum, wert thou his, might well have lov'd !
Yet here thou errest, Sohrab, or else men
Have told thee false ;—thou art not Rustum's son.
For Rustum had no son : one child he had—
But one—a girl : who with her mother now
Plies some light female task, nor dreams of us—
Of us she dreams not, nor of wounds, nor war."

  But Sohrab answer'd him in wrath ; for now
The anguish of the deep-fix'd spear grew fierce,
And he desired to draw forth the steel,
And let the blood flow free, and so to die ;
But first he would convince his stubborn foe—
And, rising sternly on one arm, he said :—

  "Man, who art thou who dost deny my words ?
Truth sits upon the lips of dying men,
And Falsehood, while I liv'd, was far from mine.
I tell thee, prick'd upon this arm I bear
That seal which Rustum to my mother gave,
That she might prick it on the babe she bore."

  He spoke : and all the blood left Rustum's cheeks ;

Sohrab and Rustum.

And his knees totter'd, and he smote his hand,
Against his breast, his heavy mailed hand,
That the hard iron corslet clank'd aloud :
And to his heart he press'd the other hand,
And in a hollow voice he spake, and said :—
 "Sohrab, that were a proof which could not lie.
If thou shew this, then art thou Rustum's son."
 Then, with weak hasty fingers, Sohrab loos'd
His belt, and near the shoulder bar'd his arm,
And shew'd a sign in faint vermilion points
Prick'd : as a cunning workman, in Pekin,
Pricks with vermilion some clear porcelain vase,
An emperor's gift—at early morn he paints,
And all day long, and, when night comes, the lamp
Lights up his studious forehead and thin hands :—
So delicately prick'd the sign appear'd
On Sohrab's arm, the sign of Rustum's seal.
It was that Griffin, which of old rear'd Zal,
Rustum's great father, whom they left to die,
A helpless babe, among the mountain rocks.
Him that kind Creature found, and rear'd, and lov'd—
Then Rustum took it for his glorious sign.
And Sohrab bar'd that figure on his arm,
And himself scann'd it long with mournful eyes,
And then he touch'd it with his hand and said :—
 "How say'st thou ? Is that sign the proper sign
Of Rustum's son, or of some other man's ?"
 He spoke : but Rustum gaz'd, and gaz'd, and stood
Speechless ; and then he utter'd one sharp cry—
O Boy—thy Father !—and his voice chok'd there.
And then a dark cloud pass'd before his eyes,
And his head swam, and he sunk down to earth

Sohrab and Rustum.

But Sohrab crawl'd to where he lay, and cast
His arms about his neck, and kiss'd his lips,
And with fond faltering fingers strok'd his cheeks,
Trying to call him back to life: and life
Came back to Rustum, and he op'd his eyes,
And they stood wide with horror; and he seiz'd
In both his hands the dust which lay around,
And threw it on his head, and smirch'd his hair,
His hair, and face, and beard, and glittering arms:
And strong convulsive groanings shook his breast,
And his sobs chok'd him; and he clutch'd his sword,
To draw it, and for ever let life out.
But Sohrab saw his thought, and held his hands,
And with a soothing voice he spoke, and said:—
   "Father, forbear: for I but meet to-day
The doom that at my birth was written down
In Heaven, and thou art Heaven's unconscious hand.
Surely my heart cried out that it was thou,
When first I saw thee; and thy heart spoke too,
I know it: but Fate trod those promptings down
Under its iron heel; Fate, Fate engag'd
The strife, and hurl'd me on my father's spear.
But let us speak no more of this: I find
My father; let me feel that I have found.
Come, sit beside me on this sand, and take
My head betwixt thy hands, and kiss my cheeks,
And wash them with thy tears, and say, 'My Son!'
Quick! quick! for number'd are my sands of life,
And swift; for like the lightning to this field
I came, and like the wind I go away—
Sudden, and swift, and like a passing wind.
But it was writ in Heaven that this should be."

Sohrab and Rustum.

So said he: and his voice releas'd the heart
Of Rustum, and his tears broke forth; he cast
His arms round his son's neck, and wept aloud,
And kiss'd him.   And awe fell on both the hosts
When they saw Rustum's grief: and Ruksh, the horse,
With his head bowing to the ground, and mane
Sweeping the dust, came near, and in mute woe
First to the one then to the other mov'd
His head, as if enquiring what their grief
Might mean; and from his dark, compassionate eyes,
The big warm tears roll'd down, and cak'd the sand.
But Rustum chid him with stern voice, and said :—

  "Ruksh, now thou grievest; but, O Ruksh, thy feet
Should then have rotted on thy nimble joints,
When first they bore thy Master to this field."

  But Sohrab look'd upon the horse and said :—
"Is this then Ruksh?   How often, in past days,
My mother told me of thee, thou brave Steed!
My terrible father's terrible horse; and said,
That I should one day find thy lord and thee.
Come, let me lay my hand upon thy mane.
O Ruksh, thou art more fortunate than I;
For thou hast gone where I shall never go,
And snuff'd the breezes of my father's home.
And thou hast trod the sands of Seistan,
And seen the River of Helmund, and the Lake
Of Zirrah; and the aged Zal himself
Has often strok'd thy neck, and given thee food,
Corn in a golden platter soak'd with wine,
And said—'O Ruksh! bear Rustum well!'—but I
Have never known my grandsire's furrow'd face,
Nor seen his lofty house in Seistan,

Sohrab and Rustum.

Nor slak'd my thirst at the clear Helmund stream :
But lodg'd among my father's foes, and seen
Afrasiab's cities only, Samarcand,
Bokhara, and lone Khiva in the waste,
And the black Toorkmun tents ; and only drunk
The desert rivers, Moorghab and Tejend,
Kohik, and where the Kalmuks feed their sheep,
The northern Sir ; and this great Oxus stream—
The yellow Oxus, by whose brink I die."

   And, with a heavy groan, Rustum replied :—
"Oh that its waves were flowing over me !
Oh that I saw its grains of yellow silt
Roll tumbling in the current o'er my head !"

   And, with a grave mild voice, Sohrab replied :—
" Desire not that, my father ; thou must live.
For some are born to do great deeds, and live,
As some are born to be obscur'd, and die.
Do thou the deeds I die too young to do,
And reap a second glory in thine age.
Thou art my father, and thy gain is mine.
But come : thou seest this great host of men
Which follow me ; I pray thee, slay not these :
Let me entreat for them : what have they done ?
They follow'd me, my hope, my fame, my star.
Let them all cross the Oxus back in peace.
But me thou must bear hence, not send with them,
But carry me with thee to Seistan,
And place me on a bed, and mourn for me,
Thou, and the snow-hair'd Zal, and all thy friends.
And thou must lay me in that lovely earth,
And heap a stately mound above my bones,
And plant a far-seen pillar over all :

Sohrab and Rustum.

That so the passing horseman on the waste
May see my tomb a great way off, and say—
Sohrab, the mighty Rustum's son, lies there,
Whom his great father did in ignorance kill—
And I be not forgotten in my grave."
      And, with a mournful voice, Rustum replied :—
" Fear not ; as thou hast said, Sohrab, my son,
So shall it be : for I will burn my tents,
And quit the host, and bear thee hence with me,
And carry thee away to Seistan,
And place thee on a bed, and mourn for thee,
With the snow-headed Zal, and all my friends.
And I will lay thee in that lovely earth,
And heap a stately mound above thy bones,
And plant a far-seen pillar over all :
And men shall not forget thee in thy grave.
And I will spare thy host : yea, let them go :
Let them all cross the Oxus back in peace.
What should I do with slaying any more ?
For would that all whom I have ever slain
Might be once more alive ; my bitterest foes,
And they who were call'd champions in their time,
And through whose death I won that fame I have ;
And I were nothing but a common man,
A poor, mean soldier, and without renown ;
So thou mightest live too, my Son, my Son !
Or rather would that I, even I myself,
Might now be lying on this bloody sand,
Near death, and by an ignorant stroke of thine,
Not thou of mine ; and I might die, not thou ;
And I, not thou, be borne to Seistan ;
And Zal might weep above my grave, not thine ;

Sohrab and Rustum.

And say—*O son, I weep thee not too sore,*
For willingly, I know, thou met'st thine end.—
But now in blood and battles was my youth,
And full of blood and battles is my age ;
And I shall never end this life of blood."
  Then, at the point of death, Sohrab replied :—
" A life of blood indeed, thou dreadful Man !
But thou shalt yet have peace ; only not now ;
Not yet : but thou shalt have it on that day,
When thou shalt sail in a high-masted Ship,
Thou and the other peers of Kai-Khosroo,
Returning home over the salt blue sea,
From laying thy dear Master in his grave."
  And Rustum gaz'd on Sohrab's face, and said :—
" Soon be that day, my Son, and deep that sea !
Till then, if Fate so wills, let me endure."
  He spoke ; and Sohrab smil'd on him, and took
The spear, and drew it from his side, and eas'd
His wound's imperious anguish : but the blood
Came welling from the open gash, and life
Flow'd with the stream : all down his cold white side
The crimson torrent pour'd, dim now, and soil'd,
Like the soil'd tissue of white violets
Left, freshly gather'd, on their native bank,
By romping children, whom their nurses call
From the hot fields at noon : his head droop'd low,
His limbs grew slack ; motionless, white, he lay—
White, with eyes clos'd ; only when heavy gasps,
Deep, heavy gasps, quivering through all his frame,
Convuls'd him back to life, he open'd them,
And fix'd them feebly on his father's face :
Till now all strength was ebb'd, and from his limbs

Sohrab and Rustum.

Unwillingly the spirit fled away,
Regretting the warm mansion which it left,
And youth and bloom, and this delightful world.
  So, on the bloody sand, Sohrab lay dead.
And the great Rustum drew his horseman's cloak
Down o'er his face, and sate by his dead son.
As those black granite pillars, once high-rear'd
By Jemshid in Persepolis, to bear
His house, now, mid their broken flights of steps,
Lie prone, enormous, down the mountain side—
So in the sand lay Rustum by his son.
  And night came down over the solemn waste,
And the two gazing hosts, and that sole pair,
And darken'd all ; and a cold fog, with night,
Crept from the Oxus.   Soon a hum arose,
As of a great assembly loos'd, and fires
Began to twinkle through the fog : for now
Both armies mov'd to camp, and took their meal :
The Persians took it on the open sands
Southward ; the Tartars by the river marge :
And Rustum and his son were left alone.
  But the majestic River floated on,
Out of the mist and hum of that low land,
Into the frosty starlight, and there mov'd,
Rejoicing, through the hush'd Chorasmian waste,
Under the solitary moon : he flow'd
Right for the Polar Star, past Orgunjè,
Brimming, and bright, and large : then sands begin
To hem his watery march, and dam his streams,
And split his currents ; that for many a league
The shorn and parcell'd Oxus strains along
Through beds of sand and matted rushy isles—

Philomela.

Oxus, forgetting the bright speed he had
In his high mountain cradle in Pamere,
A foil'd circuitous wanderer :—till at last
The long'd-for dash of waves is heard, and wide
His luminous home of waters opens, bright
And tranquil, from whose floor the new-bath'd stars
Emerge, and shine upon the Aral Sea.

PHILOMELA.

HARK ! ah, the Nightingale !
The tawny-throated !
Hark ! from that moonlit cedar what a burst
What triumph ! hark—what pain !

O Wanderer from a Grecian shore,
Still, after many years, in distant lands,
Still nourishing in thy bewilder'd brain
That wild, unquench'd, deep-sunken, old-world pain—
    Say, will it never heal ?
And can this fragrant lawn
With its cool trees, and night,
And the sweet, tranquil Thames,
And moonshine, and the dew,
To thy rack'd heart and brain
    Afford no balm ?

Dost thou to-night behold
Here, through the moonlight on this English grass,

Philomela.

The unfriendly palace in the Thracian wild?
   Dost thou again peruse
With hot cheeks and sear'd eyes
The too clear web, and thy dumb Sister's shame?
   Dost thou once more assay
Thy flight, and feel come over thee,
Poor Fugitive, the feathery change
Once more, and once more seem to make resound
With love and hate, triumph and agony,
Lone Daulis, and the high Cephissian vale?
     Listen, Eugenia—
How thick the bursts come crowding through the
     leaves!
   Again—thou hearest!
Eternal Passion!
Eternal Pain!

THEKLA'S ANSWER.

(From Schiller.)

Where I am, thou ask'st, and where I wended
   When my fleeting shadow pass'd from thee?—
Am I not concluded now, and ended?
   Have not life and love been granted me?

Ask, where now those nightingales are singing,
   Who, of late, on the soft nights of May,
Set thine ears with soul-fraught music ringing—
   Only, while their love liv'd, lasted they.

Thekla's Answer.

Find I him, from whom I had to sever?—
  Doubt it not, we met, and we are one.
There, where what is join'd, is join'd for ever,
  There, where tears are never more to run.

There thou too shalt live with us together,
  When thou too hast borne the love we bore:
There, from sin deliver'd, dwells my Father,
  Track'd by Murder's bloody sword no more.

There he feels, it was no dream deceiving
  Lur'd him starwards to uplift his eye:
God doth match his gifts to man's believing;
  Believe, and thou shalt find the Holy nigh.

All thou augurest here of lovely seeming
  There shall find fufilment in its day:
Dare, O Friend, be wandering, dare be dreaming;
  Lofty thought lies oft in childish play.

The Church of Brou.

I.

THE CASTLE.

Down the Savoy valleys sounding,
  Echoing round this castle old,
'Mid the distant mountain chalets
  Hark ! what bell for church is toll'd ?

———

In the bright October morning
  Savoy's Duke had left his bride.
From the Castle, past the drawbridge,
  Flow'd the hunters' merry tide.

Steeds are neighing, gallants glittering.
  Gay, her smiling lord to greet,
From her mullion'd chamber casement
  Smiles the Duchess Marguerite.

From Vienna by the Danube
  Here she came, a bride, in spring.
Now the autumn crisps the forest ;
  Hunters gather, bugles ring.

Hounds are pulling, prickers swearing,
  Horses fret, and boar-spears glance :
Off !—They sweep the marshy forests,
  Westward, on the side of France.

The Church of Brou.

Hark ! the game's on foot ; they scatter :—
   Down the forest ridings lone,
Furious, single horsemen gallop.
   Hark ! a shout—a crash—a groan !

Pale and breathless, came the hunters.
   On the turf dead lies the boar.
God ! the Duke lies stretch'd beside him—
   Senseless, weltering in his gore.

———

In the dull October evening,
   Down the leaf-strewn forest road,
To the Castle, past the drawbridge,
   Came the hunters with their load.

In the hall, with sconces blazing,
   Ladies waiting round her seat,
Cloth'd in smiles, beneath the dais,
   Sate the Duchess Marguerite.

Hark ! below the gates unbarring !
   Tramp of men and quick commands !
"—'Tis my lord come back from hunting."—
   And the Duchess claps her hands.

Slow and tired, came the hunters ;
   Stopp'd in darkness in the court.
"—Ho, this way, ye laggard hunters !
   To the hall ! What sport, what sport ?"—

The Church of Brou.

Slow they enter'd with their Master ;
    In the hall they laid him down.
On his coat were leaves and blood-stains :
    On his brow an angry frown.

Dead her princely youthful husband
    Lay before his youthful wife ;
Bloody, 'neath the flaring sconces :
    And the sight froze all her life.

In Vienna by the Danube
    Kings hold revel, gallants meet.
Gay of old amid the gayest
    Was the Duchess Marguerite.

In Vienna by the Danube
    Feast and dance her youth beguil'd.
Till that hour she never sorrow'd ;
    But from then she never smil'd.

'Mid the Savoy mountain valleys
    Far from town or haunt of man,
Stands a lonely Church, unfinish'd,
    Which the Duchess Maud began :

Old, that Duchess stern began it ;
    In grey age, with palsied hands,
But she died as it was building,
    And the Church unfinish'd stands ;

Stands as erst the builders left it,
    When she sunk into her grave.

The Church of Brou.

Mountain greensward paves the chancel.
   Harebells flower in the nave.

" In my Castle all is sorrow,"—
   Said the Duchess Marguerite then.
" Guide me, vassals, to the mountains !
   We will build the Church again."—

Sandall'd palmers, faring homeward,
   Austrian knights from Syria came.
" Austrian wanderers bring, O warders
   Homage to your Austrian dame."—

From the gate the warders answer'd ;
   " Gone, O knights, is she you knew.
Dead our Duke, and gone his Duchess.
   Seek her at the Church of Brou."—

Austrian knights and march-worn palmers
   Climb the winding mountain way.
Reach the valley, where the Fabric
   Rises higher day by day.

Stones are sawing, hammers ringing ;
   On the work the bright sun shines :
In the Savoy mountain meadows,
   By the stream, below the pines.

On her palfrey white the Duchess
   Sate and watch'd her working train
Flemish carvers, Lombard gilders
   German masons, smiths from Spain.

The Church of Brou.

Clad in black, on her white palfrey;
  Her old architect beside—
There they found her in the mountains,
  Morn and noon and eventide.

There she sate, and watch'd the builders,
  Till the Church was roof'd and done.
Last of all, the builders rear'd her
  In the nave a tomb of stone.

On the tomb two Forms they sculptur'd,
  Lifelike in the marble pale.
One, the Duke in helm and armour;
  One, the Duchess in her veil.

Round the tomb the carv'd stone fretwork
  Was at Easter tide put on.
Then the Duchess clos'd her labours;
  And she died at the St. John.

II.

THE CHURCH.

Upon the glistening leaden roof
  Of the new Pile, the sunlight shines.
    The stream goes leaping by.
The hills are cloth'd with pines sun-proof.
  Mid bright green fields, below the pines,
    Stands the Church on high.
What Church is this, from men aloof?
'Tis the Church of Brou.

The Church of Brou.

At sunrise, from their dewy lair
  Crossing the stream, the kine are seen
    Round the wall to stray;
The churchyard wall that clips the square
  Of shaven hill-sward trim and green
    Where last year they lay.
But all things now are order'd fair
Round the Church of Brou.

On Sundays, at the matin chime,
  The Alpine peasants, two and three,
    Climb up here to pray.
Burghers and dames, at summer's prime,
  Ride out to church from Chambery,
    Dight with mantles gay.
But else it is a lonely time
Round the Church of Brou.

On Sundays too, a priest doth come
  From the wall'd town beyond the pass,
    Down the mountain way.
And then you hear the organ's hum,
  You hear the white-rob'd priest say mass,
    And the people pray.
But else the woods and fields are dumb
Round the Church of Brou.

And after church, when mass is done,
  The people to the nave repair
    Round the Tomb to stray.
And marvel at the Forms of stone,

And praise the chisell'd broideries rare.
Then they drop away.
The Princely Pair are left alone
In the Church of Brou.

III.

THE TOMB.

So rest, for ever rest, O Princely Pair !
In your high Church, 'mid the still mountain air,
Where horn, and hound, and vassals, never come.
Only the blessed Saints are smiling dumb
From the rich painted windows of the nave
On aisle, and transept, and your marble grave :
Where thou, young Prince, shalt never more arise
From the fring'd mattress where thy Duchess lies,
On autumn mornings, when the bugle sounds,
And ride across the drawbridge with thy hounds
To hunt the boar in the crisp woods till eve.
And thou, O Princess, shalt no more receive,
Thou and thy ladies, in the hall of state,
The jaded hunters with their bloody freight,
Coming benighted to the castle gate.
So sleep, for ever sleep, O Marble Pair !
And if ye wake, let it be then, when fair
On the carv'd Western Front a flood of light
Streams from the setting sun, and colours bright
Prophets, transfigur'd Saints, and Martyrs brave,
In the vast western window of the nave ;
And on the pavement round the Tomb there glints

The Church of Brou.

A chequer-work of glowing sapphire tints,
And amethyst, and ruby ;—then unclose
Your eyelids on the stone where ye repose,
And from your broider'd pillows lift your heads,
And rise upon your cold white marble beds,
And looking down on the warm rosy tints
That chequer, at your feet, the illumin'd flints,
Say—"*What is this? we are in bliss—forgiven—*
Behold the pavement of the courts of Heaven!"—
Or let it be on autumn nights, when rain
Doth rustlingly above your heads complain
On the smooth leaden roof, and on the walls
Shedding her pensive light at intervals
The Moon through the clere-story windows shines,
And the wind washes in the mountain pines.
Then, gazing up through the dim pillars high,
The foliag'd marble forest where ye lie,
"*Hush*"—ye will say—"*it is eternity.*
This is the glimmering verge of Heaven, and these
The columns of the Heavenly Palaces."—
And in the sweeping of the wind your ear
The passage of the Angels' wings will hear,
And on the lichen-crusted leads above
The rustle of the eternal rain of Love.

The Neckan.

THE NECKAN.

In summer, on the headlands,
  The Baltic Sea along,
Sits Neckan with his harp of gold,
  And sings his plaintive song.

Green rolls beneath the headlands,
  Green rolls the Baltic Sea,
And there, below the Neckan's feet,
  His wife and children be.

He sings not of the ocean,
  Its shells and roses pale.
Of earth, of earth the Neckan sings ;
  He hath no other tale.

He sits upon the headlands,
  And sings a mournful stave
Of all he saw and felt on earth,
  Far from the green sea wave.

Sings how, a knight, he wander'd
  By castle, field, and town.—
But earthly knights have harder hearts
  Than the Sea Children own.

Sings of his earthly bridal—
  Priest, knights, and ladies gay.
" And who art thou," the priest began,
  " Sir Knight, who wedd'st to-day ?"—

The Neckan.

" I am no knight," he answer'd ;
  " From the sea waves I come."—
The knights drew sword, the ladies scream'd,
  The surplic'd priest stood dumb.

He sings how from the chapel
  He vanish'd with his bride,
And bore her down to the sea halls,
  Beneath the salt sea tide.

He sings how she sits weeping
  'Mid shells that round her lie.
" False Neckan shares my bed," she weeps ;
  " No Christian mate have I."

He sings how through the billows
  He rose to earth again,
And sought a priest to sign the cross,
  That Neckan Heaven might gain.

He sings how, on an evening,
  Beneath the birch trees cool,
He sate and play'd his harp of gold,
  Beside the river pool.

Beside the pool sate Neckan—
  Tears fill'd his cold blue eye.
On his white mule, across the bridge,
  A cassock'd priest rode by.

The Neckan.

" Why sitt'st thou there, O Neckan,
  And play'st thy harp of gold ?
Sooner shall this my staff bear leaves,
  Than thou shalt Heaven behold."—

The cassock'd priest rode onwards,
  And vanish'd with his mule.
And Neckan in the twilight grey
  Wept by the river pool.

In summer, on the headlands,
  The Baltic Sea along,
Sits Neckan with his harp of gold,
  And sings this plaintive song.

A DREAM.

Was it a dream ? We sail'd, I thought we sail'd,
Martin and I, down a green Alpine stream,
Under o'erhanging pines ; the morning sun,
On the wet umbrage of their glossy tops,
On the red pinings of their forest floor,
Drew a warm scent abroad ; behind the pines
The mountain skirts, with all their sylvan change
Of bright-leaf'd chestnuts, and moss'd walnut-trees,
And the frail scarlet-berried ash, began.
Swiss chalets glitter'd on the dewy slopes,
And from some swarded shelf high up, there came
Notes of wild pastoral music : over all

A Dream.

Rang'd, diamond-bright, the eternal wall of snow.
Upon the mossy rocks at the stream's edge,
Back'd by the pines, a plank-built cottage stood,
Bright in the sun; the climbing gourd-plant's leaves
Muffled its walls, and on the stone-strewn roof
Lay the warm golden gourds; golden, within,
Under the eaves, peer'd rows of Indian corn.
We shot beneath the cottage with the stream.
On the brown rude-carv'd balcony two Forms
Came forth—Olivia's, Marguerite! and thine.
Clad were they both in white, flowers in their breasts;
Straw hats bedeck'd their heads, with ribbons blue
Which wav'd, and on their shoulders fluttering play'd.
They saw us, they conferr'd; their bosoms heav'd,
And more than mortal impulse fill'd their eyes.
Their lips mov'd; their white arms, wav'd eagerly,
Flash'd once, like falling streams :—we rose, we gaz'd:
One moment, on the rapid's top, our boat
Hung pois'd—and then the darting River of Life,
Loud thundering, bore us by : swift, swift it foam'd;
Black under cliffs it rac'd, round headlands shone.
Soon the plank'd cottage 'mid the sun-warm'd pines
Faded, the moss, the rocks; us burning Plains
Bristled with cities, us the Sea receiv'd.

Requiescat.

REQUIESCAT.

STREW on her roses, roses,
  And never a spray of yew.
In quiet she reposes :
  Ah ! would that I did too.

Her mirth the world required :
  She bath'd it in smiles of glee.
But her heart was tired, tired,
  And now they let her be.

Her life was turning, turning,
  In mazes of heat and sound.
But for peace her soul was yearning,
  And now peace laps her round.

Her cabin'd, ample Spirit,
  It flutter'd and fail'd for breath.
To-night it doth inherit
  The vasty Hall of Death.

THE SCHOLAR GIPSY.

" There was very lately a lad in the University of Oxford, who was by his poverty forced to leave his studies there; and at last to join himself to a company of vagabond gipsies. Among these extravagant people, by the insinuating subtilty of his carriage, he quickly got so much of their love and esteem as that they discovered to him their mystery. After he had been a pretty while well exercised in the trade, there chanced to ride by a couple of scholars, who had formerly been of his acquaintance. They quickly spied out their old friend among the gipsies; and he gave them an account of the necessity which drove him to that kind of life, and told them that the people he went with were not such impostors as they were taken for, but that they had a traditional kind of learning among them, and could do wonders by the power of imagination, their fancy binding that of others: that himself had learned much of their art, and when he had compassed the whole secret, he intended, he said, to leave their company, and give the world an account of what he had learned."—GLANVIL.'s *Vanity of Dogmatizing*, 1661.

Go, for they call you, Shepherd, from the hill;
  Go, Shepherd, and untie the wattled cotes:
    No longer leave thy wistful flock unfed,
  Nor let thy bawling fellows rack their throats,
    Nor the cropp'd grasses shoot another head.
    But when the fields are still,
  And the tired men and dogs all gone to rest,
    And only the white sheep are sometimes seen
    Cross and recross the strips of moon-blanch'd
      green;
    Come, Shepherd, and again renew the quest.

The Scholar Gipsy.

Here, where the reaper was at work of late,
  In this high field's dark corner, where he leaves
    His coat, his basket, and his earthen cruise,
  And in the sun all morning binds the sheaves,
    Then here, at noon, comes back his stores to use;
      Here will I sit and wait,
  While to my ear from uplands far away
    The bleating of the folded flocks is borne;
    With distant cries of reapers in the corn—
      All the live murmur of a summer's day.

Screen'd is this nook o'er the high, half-reap'd field,
  And here till sun-down, Shepherd, will I be.
    Through the thick corn the scarlet poppies peep
  And round green roots and yellowing stalks I see
    Pale blue convolvulus in tendrils creep :
      And air-swept lindens yield
  Their scent, and rustle down their perfum'd showers
    Of bloom on the bent grass where I am laid,
    And bower me from the August sun with shade;
      And the eye travels down to Oxford's towers :

And near me on the grass lies Glanvil's book—
  Come, let me read the oft-read tale again,
    The story of that Oxford scholar poor
  Of pregnant parts and quick inventive brain,
    Who, tir'd of knocking at Preferment's door,
      One summer morn forsook
  His friends, and went to learn the Gipsy lore,
    And roam'd the world with that wild brotherhood,
    And came, as most men deem'd, to little good,
      But came to Oxford and his friends no more.

The Scholar Gipsy.

But once, years after, in the country lanes,
  Two scholars whom at college erst he knew
    Met him, and of his way of life enquir'd.
Whereat he answer'd, that the Gipsy crew,
  His mates, had arts to rule as they desir'd
    The workings of men's brains;
And they can bind them to what thoughts they will:
  " And I," he said, "the secret of their art,
  When fully learn'd, will to the world impart:
    But it needs happy moments for this skill."

This said, he left them, and return'd no more,
  But rumours hung about the country side
    That the lost Scholar long was seen to stray,
Seen by rare glimpses, pensive and tongue-tied,
  In hat of antique shape, and cloak of grey,
    The same the Gipsies wore.
Shepherds had met him on the Hurst in spring:
  At some lone alehouse in the Berkshire moors,
  On the warm ingle bench, the smock-frock'd boors
    Had found him seated at their entering.

But, mid their drink and clatter, he would fly:
  And I myself seem half to know thy looks,
    And put the shepherds, Wanderer, on thy trace;
And boys who in lone wheatfields scare the rooks
  I ask if thou hast pass'd their quiet place;
    Or in my boat I lie
Moor'd to the cool bank in the summer heats,
  Mid wide grass meadows which the sunshine fills,
  And watch the warm green-muffled Cumner hills,
    And wonder if thou haunt'st their shy retreats.

The Scholar Gipsy.

For most, I know, thou lov'st retired ground.
  Thee, at the ferry, Oxford riders blithe,
    Returning home on summer nights, have met
  Crossing the stripling Thames at Bab-lock-hithe,
    Trailing in the cool stream thy fingers wet,
     As the slow punt swings round :
  And leaning backwards in a pensive dream,
    And fostering in thy lap a heap of flowers
    Pluck'd in shy fields and distant woodland bowers,
    And thine eyes resting on the moonlit stream

And then they land, and thou art seen no more.
  Maidens who from the distant hamlets come
    To dance around the Fyfield elm in May,
  Oft through the darkening fields have seen thee
     roam,
    Or cross a stile into the public way.
     Oft thou hast given them store
  Of flowers—the frail-leaf'd, white anemone—
    Dark bluebells drench'd with dews of summer
     eves—
    And purple orchises with spotted leaves—
    But none has words she can report of thee.

And, above Godstow Bridge, when hay-time's here
  In June, and many a scythe in sunshine flames,
    Men who through those wide fields of breezy
     grass
  Where black-wing'd swallows haunt the glittering
     Thames,
    To bathe in the abandon'd lasher pass,
     Have often pass'd thee near

"

The Scholar Gipsy.

Sitting upon the river bank o'ergrown :
   Mark'd thy outlandish garb, thy figure spare,
   Thy dark vague eyes, and soft abstracted air ;
     But, when they came from bathing, thou wert
     gone.

At some lone homestead in the Cumner hills,
   Where at her open door the housewife darns,
    Thou hast been seen, or hanging on a gate
   To watch the threshers in the mossy barns.
     Children, who early range these slopes and late
      For cresses from the rills,
   Have known thee watching, all an April day,
     The springing pastures and the feeding kine ;
     And mark'd thee, when the stars come out and
     shine,
     Through the long dewy grass move slow away.

In Autumn, on the skirts of Bagley wood,
   Where most the Gipsies by the turf-edg'd way
    Pitch their smok'd tents, and every bush you see
   With scarlet patches tagg'd and shreds of grey,
    Above the forest ground call'd Thessaly—
     The blackbird picking food
   Sees thee, nor stops his meal, nor fears at all ;
    So often has he known thee past him stray
    Rapt, twirling in thy hand a wither'd spray,
     And waiting for the spark from Heaven to fall.

And once, in winter, on the causeway chill
   Where home through flooded fields foot-travellers go,
   Have I not pass'd thee on the wooden bridge
   Wrapt in thy cloak and battling with the snow,

The Scholar Gipsy.

Thy face towards Hinksey and its wintry ridge?
  And thou hast climb'd the hill
And gain'd the white brow of the Cumner range,
  Turn'd once to watch, while thick the snow-flakes
    fall,
  The line of festal light in Christ-Church hall—
    Then sought thy straw in some sequester'd
    grange.

But what—I dream! Two hundred years are flown
  Since first thy story ran through Oxford halls,
    And the grave Glanvil did the tale inscribe
  That thou wert wander'd from the studious walls
    To learn strange arts, and join a Gipsy tribe:
    And thou from earth art gone
  Long since, and in some quiet churchyard laid;
    Some country nook, where o'er thy unknown
      grave
    Tall grasses and white flowering nettles wave—
    Under a dark red-fruited yew-tree's shade.

—No, no, thou hast not felt the lapse of hours.
  For what wears out the life of mortal men?
    'Tis that from change to change their being rolls:
  'Tis that repeated shocks, again, again,
    Exhaust the energy of strongest souls,
    And numb the elastic powers.
Till having us'd our nerves with bliss and teen,
    And tir'd upon a thousand schemes our wit,
    To the just-pausing Genius we remit
    Our worn-out life, and are—what we have been.

The Scholar Gipsy.

Thou hast not liv'd, why should'st thou perish, so ?
  Thou hadst *one* aim, *one* business, *one* desire :
    Else wert thou long since number'd with the
      dead—
  Else hadst thou spent, like other men, thy fire.
    The generations of thy peers are fled,
      And we ourselves shall go ;
  But thou possessest an immortal lot,
    And we imagine thee exempt from age
    And living as thou liv'st on Glanvil's page,
      Because thou hadst—what we, alas, have not

For early didst thou leave the world, with powers
  Fresh, undiverted to the world without,
    Firm to their mark, not spent on other things ;
  Free from the sick fatigue, the languid doubt,
    Which much to have tried, in much been baffled,
      brings.
      O Life unlike to ours !
Who fluctuate idly without term or scope,
    Of whom each strives, nor knows for what he
      strives,
    And each half lives a hundred different lives ;
      Who wait like thee, but not, like thee, in hope.

Thou waitest for the spark from Heaven : and we,
  Light half-believers of our casual creeds,
    Who never deeply felt, nor clearly will'd,
  Whose insight never has borne fruit in deeds,
    Whose vague resolves never have been fulfill'd ;
      For whom each year we see

The Scholar Gipsy.

Breeds new beginnings, disappointments new;
    Who hesitate and falter life away,
    And lose to-morrow the ground won to-day—
    Ah, do not we, Wanderer, await it too?

Yes, we await it, but it still delays,
    And then we suffer; and amongst us One,
        Who most has suffer'd, takes dejectedly
    His seat upon the intellectual throne;
        And all his store of sad experience he
            Lays bare of wretched days;
    Tells us his misery's birth and growth and signs,
        And how the dying spark of hope was fed,
        And how the breast was sooth'd, and how the
            head,
        And all his hourly varied anodynes.

This for our wisest: and we others pine,
    And wish the long unhappy dream would end,
        And waive all claim to bliss, and try to bear
    With close-lipp'd Patience for our only friend,
        Sad Patience, too near neighbour to Despair:
            But none has hope like thine.
    Thou through the fields and through the woods dost
            stray,
        Roaming the country side, a truant boy,
        Nursing thy project in unclouded joy,
            And every doubt long blown by time away.

O born in days when wits were fresh and clear,
    And life ran gaily as the sparkling Thames;

The Scholar Gipsy.

Before this strange disease of modern life,
With its sick hurry, its divided aims,
  Its heads o'ertax'd, its palsied hearts, was rife—
  Fly hence, our contact fear!
Still fly, plunge deeper in the bowering wood!
  Averse, as Dido did with gesture stern
  From her false friend's approach in Hades turn,
  Wave us away, and keep thy solitude.

Still nursing the unconquerable hope,
  Still clutching the inviolable shade,
  With a free onward impulse brushing through,
By night, the silver'd branches of the glade—
  Far on the forest skirts, where none pursue
  On some mild pastoral slope
Emerge, and resting on the moonlit pales,
  Freshen thy flowers, as in former years,
  With dew, or listen with enchanted ears,
  From the dark dingles, to the nightingales.

But fly our paths, our feverish contact fly!
  For strong the infection of our mental strife,
    Which, though it gives no bliss, yet spoils for rest;
  And we should win thee from thy own fair life,
    Like us distracted, and like us unblest.
    Soon, soon thy cheer would die,
  Thy hopes grow timorous, and unfix'd thy powers,
    And thy clear aims be cross and shifting made:
    And then thy glad perennial youth would fade,
    Fade, and grow old at last and die like ours.

The Scholar Gipsy.

Then fly our greetings, fly our speech and smiles!
  —As some grave Tyrian trader, from the sea,
    Descried at sunrise an emerging prow
  Lifting the cool-hair'd creepers stealthily,
    The fringes of a southward-facing brow
      Among the Ægean isles:
  And saw the merry Grecian coaster come,
    Freighted with amber grapes, and Chian wine,
    Green bursting figs, and tunnies steep'd in brine;
    And knew the intruders on his ancient home,

The young light-hearted Masters of the waves;
  And snatch'd his rudder, and shook out more sail,
  And day and night held on indignantly
O'er the blue Midland waters with the gale,
  Betwixt the Syrtes and soft Sicily,
    To where the Atlantic raves
Outside the Western Straits, and unbent sails
  There, where down cloudy cliffs, through sheets
      of foam,
    Shy traffickers, the dark Iberians come;
    And on the beach undid his corded bales.

Stanzas.

STANZAS

IN MEMORY OF THE LATE EDWARD QUILLINAN, ESQ.

I saw him sensitive in frame,
    I knew his spirits low ;
And wish'd him health, success, and fame :
    I do not wish it now.

For these are all their own reward,
    And leave no good behind ;
They try us, oftenest make us hard,
    Less modest, pure, and kind.

Alas !   Yet to the suffering man,
    In this his mortal state,
Friends could not give what Fortune can—
    Health, ease, a heart elate.

But he is now by Fortune foil'd
    No more ; and we retain
The memory of a man unspoil'd,
    Sweet, generous, and humane ;

With all the fortunate have not—
    With gentle voice and brow.
Alive, we would have chang'd his lot :
    We would not change it now.